THE SECRETS ON

CHICORY

LANE

A NOVEL

RAYMOND BENSON

Skyhorse Publishing
A Herman Graf Book

Skyhorse Publishing books may be purchased in bulk at special discounts for sales promotion, corporate gifts, fund-raising, or educational purposes. Special editions can also be created to specifications. For details, contact the Special Sales Department, Skyhorse Publishing, 307 West 36th Street, 11th Floor, New York, NY 10018 or info@skyhorsepublishing.com.

Skyhorse® and Skyhorse Publishing® are registered trademarks of Skyhorse Publishing, Inc.®, a Delaware corporation.

Visit our website at www.skyhorsepublishing.com.

10 9 8 7 6 5 4 3 2 1

Library of Congress Cataloging-in-Publication Data is available on file.

Cover design by Erin Seaward-Hiatt
Cover photo credit: iStockphoto

Print ISBN: 978-1-5107-2294-1
Ebook ISBN: 978-1-5107-2295-8

Printed in the United States of America

For Randi

ACKNOWLEDGMENTS

The author wishes to thank the following individuals for their help: Laurie Fraser, Mike Graczyk, Herman Graf, Julie Hyzy, Kim Lim, Cynthia Manson, Jim Marks, William Simon, Pam Stack, and my most trusted critic, Randi Frank.

AUTHOR'S NOTE

Limite is an invented town in West Texas. It has been used before in some of my other works, such as *Evil Hours* and *Artifact of Evil*. Its similarity to a real place is intentional, but this is a work of fiction. All characters and events are the product of a fevered imagination.

1

One of the most frightening and challenging things a human being can do the first thing in the morning—and by that, I mean *after* you get out of bed, pee, put on something warm, and have some breakfast and coffee (that last part is essential)—is to sit down at a computer and begin to write a new novel.

I hate it. Actually, no, let me rephrase that. I hate *starting* a new book. I *love* everything else about the writing process, but I've always found it difficult to initially propel myself into that quagmire of caffeine-induced, delirious hair pulling and sleepless torment, because I know this will be my reality for the next couple of months until I get my groove on and become comfortable with the characters and storyline.

That's what I'm attempting to do when I hear the doorbell downstairs, followed by the sound of Billy opening the door. Voices—the mailman. I glance at the digital clock on my desk—is it already eleven? It's nice that my postman delivers the mail early; other people I know in Chicago complain that their carriers don't come until nearly supper time. I reckon Billy will bring it up—right now the important thing is to stare dutifully at that blank page on my screen and figure out how the hell I am going to start the next Patricia novel without becoming an "imitation of myself." That was what some genius in one of those book review magazines said about the most recent Patricia. Even after forty-two Patricia Harlow books and a handful of stand-alones, a comment like that can still bug me. I might be successful, but what the hell, I'm also human.

I'm taking the criticism to heart—I really want to start the next one with something completely different from what I've done in the past. There is already a finished book going through the editing stage at my publishing house. The manuscript I'm supposed to start today is the one that will appear after that, and it probably won't see publication until two years from now. Nevertheless, a deadline is the biggest motivator in this crazy business of mine. I know I'll get it done. I've averaged a book every ten or eleven months since I was in my thirties, and I don't have any plans to retire yet. Writers never do that. As long as we can still think, dream, and somehow lay it all out on paper, we will continue to work.

But after age sixty, it does get harder.

I glance at the now-empty coffee cup and decide to boost the caffeine dose. Procrastination is my friend. *Hmm, maybe I should have another cup of joe, shower, do my hair and nails, and exercise early. Shake up the routine.*

"Shelby?"

It's Billy, downstairs.

"I'm up here!" I call.

"Should I come up?"

"Is that the mail? Bring it up, will you? But start a fresh pot of coffee first, okay?"

Billy, my personal assistant, is thirty-eight, gay, single, and an excellent secretary. Once I became an international bestselling author, I found that I couldn't handle everything alone. Fan mail, social media updating, proofreading, and all the other stuff authors have to do that isn't actually writing, which can suck up half a day or more. I pay Billy to come in part time and do it for me, especially the social media nonsense, which regrettably is vitally important these days. He often works on updating my website; he is good at stuff like that. He also meticulously makes sure anything about me that appears on other websites is accurate and up to date, and I trust him to take care of my "brand." Billy has a small workspace on the first floor of my three-level townhouse. My office is one of three bedrooms on the top floor, which sometimes causes a lot of shouting up and down the stairs. When I'm in the zone, I prefer a solitary, lonely cocoon of silence. Sometimes I put on music, which doesn't bother me.

After a few minutes, Billy appears in the open door and knocks. "Is this Shelby Truman's office?" he asks.

"Unfortunately . . . yes."

"Your mail, madam." He brings it over and places the bundle on my desk. "Mostly bills, junk mail, and this . . . I signed for a piece of registered overnight mail from, well, look."

The return address on the top of the envelope indicates that the sender is Robert Crane Esq. of Limite, Texas. I know the name.

Eddie's attorney.

A twinge of anxiety starts deep in my chest. I'd been trying not to think about Eddie, but that's impossible this week.

The thing is, I've *always* thought about Eddie. We go way, way back, to when we were children living in Limite.

Billy stands there, waiting for me to open the letter. I look at him, and he shuffles his feet. "Oh, sorry, I guess you want to be alone. I'll go get the coffee. Should be ready in a minute."

"No, stay. Open it and let me see what Mr. Crane has to say."

He carefully uses a fingernail to open the envelope and hands me the contents—a message printed on the law firm's letterhead, official and neat. My hand trembles as I read.

"Well, *hell*," I mutter, sighing heavily.

"What?" Billy asks.

"All of the appeals have been denied."

"He's going to be executed?"

I nod. "Barring some kind of miracle stay from the Board of Pardons and Paroles or the governor of Texas, yeah." I look at the calendar on the desk. "In four days."

"Jesus, you'll be in Texas then."

"That's not all." I hand Billy the letter and he reads it, wide-eyed.

He looks up. "You gonna go?"

"I don't know." I take the letter back and reread what Mr. Crane has written.

Eddie requests that you visit him this week. He says he has something important to tell you. I have placed your name on the visitation list and the warden has already approved it. Note that this is highly irregular, but an exception has been made. Please let me know as soon as possible if you can make it. I know Eddie will be pleased to see you. Please call my office. In the meantime, I will phone you.

"Crane says he'll phone you."

"He hasn't yet."

Billy nods at the answering machine that sits on a little table near the printer, which is normally out of my sight line unless I actually *look* at it. Of course, the number "2" blinks on the LED. I roll my chair to the table and punch the Play button. Mr. Crane relates the same message that is in the letter, and leaves his phone number. Twice.

"I guess I missed those." As I roll back to my position at the desk, I sigh again. Lately I've been doing a lot of sighing. "I'm supposed to be in Limite for the park dedication ceremony on the day of his execution."

"I know."

"I suppose I could swing by Huntsville on the way."

"Do you *want* to?"

"I don't know, Billy. Why don't you get the coffee and let me think about this."

He nods at the blank Word document on the computer monitor. "I see you've got Patricia in a fine mess this time."

"Don't rub it in. I'm a little too preoccupied to think about who Patricia is going to sleep with next." As I say it, I realize it's the truth. Perhaps that's why I can't seem to get started this morning. My mind is already on Eddie. It has been for quite some time.

"I'll just get that coffee . . ." Billy steps out of the room and leaves me alone with my apprehension.

Why the hell does Eddie want to talk to me? We haven't spoken in twenty years, long before his crime. When he received the death penalty, he wouldn't let me visit and we never communicated. I resigned myself that I'd never see him again. The advocacy group tried to get me to attend the execution and protest outside the prison, me being a celebrity and all. I had decided long ago that I wouldn't attend, even if I were invited to be a witness to the execution. Giving them money and allowing them to use my name and a quotation is one thing, but I prefer not to show my face for the cameras down in Texas. My plan is to be nowhere near the southeast part of the state; however, I will soon be traveling instead to the western portion near that right angle at the bottom of the Panhandle.

I check the paper calendar again. Today is Monday. The park dedication in Limite is scheduled for Friday, as is Eddie's execution. I'd committed to a speaking engagement at a library in Schaumburg on Wednesday evening, so my original plan was to fly to Texas on Thursday. There is no direct flight to the Limite airport from Chicago O'Hare; I have to fly to Dallas and change planes. I could cancel the library event, although I don't like doing that.

You see, they are naming a park after me in my old hometown: the Shelby Truman Community Park. It was where we used to play as children—all of the kids on our block—since it was just another street over. If the place had a name then, I don't remember it. It was unique because along with standard swing sets, slides, climbing structures, and a merry-go-round, there sat, incongruously, a World War II–era airplane and a yacht. Each hulk was propped up with supports and had ladders and slides attached so kids could actually climb inside and play. The passenger section was empty of seats, but you could look out the windows. I remember sitting in the plane's cockpit and pretending I was flying. The cabin of the boat was more intimate, and the older teenagers used it as a place to make out. Again, there was no furniture or machinery. I doubt running around in those derelict ships was very safe, but that was back in the sixties. I recall more than one cut or scrape from some sneaky sharp edge.

Eventually the plane and yacht were taken out of the park, sometime when I was a young adult. It was then known as East Limite Family Park. Now the powers-that-be want to honor a hometown-kid-that-made-good and rename the grounds. Sure, I'm flattered, but I don't relish returning to Limite. Too many unpleasant memories. After all, the death of a family member—a sibling in this case—changes the dynamics of a household.

After the summer of 1966, things were never the same in my family. Mother certainly wasn't. My parents stayed in Limite when I left for college in '72, and I went back to visit as often as I could stand it. After their deaths, I figured I'd never have to see those flat desert plains and pumpjack oil wells again. High school reunions never interested me. No other relatives live there. There simply never was a good reason to return to

West Texas, but now I have an obligation to go. The price of fame and fortune.

Perhaps the real truth of why I don't like going home is the feeling of melancholy—and fear—that hovers over me whenever I am back. Dark clouds of pain and sorrow. They continue to haunt me even now. Bad things happened on Chicory Lane, the street where I grew up. I truly believe that Evil—with a capital "E"—visited my neighborhood that summer of 1966. It slithered inside at least three houses that I know of, and set about destroying lives and delivering misery. In the end, it affected so many of us. Sadly, I think it did the most damage to Eddie Newcott, the boy who lived across the street.

2

There is much to consider. Do I really want to see Eddie again? Why does he want to talk to me? What will he have to say? Does he think I *owe* it to him? There is no question that there exists a unique bond between Eddie and me. A lifelong connection. At one time, we were closer than salt and pepper shakers—and that's a pretty apt metaphor for what Eddie and I were, especially when we were kids on Chicory Lane. In the later years when he and I became . . . well, I'm not sure what to call it . . . it was something else. A madness, perhaps.

After our last encounter in the mid-nineties, we mutually parted ways and never spoke again. This was about a decade before he committed the crime. I would have responded to Eddie had he reached out during his legal ordeal, and in fact I contacted his lawyer—the same Robert Crane—myself to see if Eddie might want to talk to me. My inquiry was politely declined. Later, during the penalty phase of the trial, I once again offered to provide a character witness in the hopes that he wouldn't get death. And again, my willingness to help was dismissed, Crane told me, expressly by Eddie himself.

Eddie received the death penalty for capital murder. It was the charge the DA went for and got, because that's the only classification in Texas for which one can receive the death penalty. The defense raised some legal brouhaha, saying the crime wasn't really capital murder because it was a domestic situation, but the prosecutor and judge didn't buy it. Eddie still had a shot at an insanity appeal, but he gave up and refused to pursue one. His lawyer did it for him as a matter of course. Still, it was as if Eddie *wanted* to die.

We all knew that Eddie was guilty of murdering the woman he was living with at the time, along with their unborn child. Unfortunately, the original jury didn't believe the defense's contention that he'd done it because he was off his meds, so the verdict didn't swing in Eddie's favor. The shocking revelations about his childhood made good live television, but the twelve jurors held them against the accused. Eddie apparently resigned himself to his fate, and he deliberately provoked the jury when the verdict was announced. He actually stood, pointed at the twelve men and women, and, as the media put it, "cursed them with a Satanic spell."

That was the real reason Eddie had received the death penalty. He was an outspoken atheist. The woman he killed, Dora Walton, was a fellow atheist who lived with Eddie in his childhood home, where for years they produced and distributed a newsletter about Satanism. Naturally, his neighbors didn't like it. Even in the eighties, Eddie had already received national notoriety amid pressure against him to leave his old neighborhood, which he vehemently fought, claiming his and his mother's rights to stay in their house. Dora Walton's murder was described by the media as a Satanic ritual.

The truth is that Eddie went off his meds.

When he was arrested, the press elevated the story to international status and even gave him a nickname that caught on—"Evil Eddie." "Satanist in Gruesome Ritual." "Suspect Claims to be The Devil." "Evil Eddie Goes to Trial

TODAY." "EVIL EDDIE FOUND GUILTY!" The more salacious tabloids spelled it out with repugnance—"WOMAN SLAIN IN DEATH ORGY." "RITUAL MURDER!" "DEATH IN BLACK MASS." "WITCHCRAFT!—LIMITE'S SHOCKING SATANIC SEX CULT."

In this day and age, practicing witchcraft isn't supposed to be considered a crime if that's what a person does in private. Obviously, Eddie crossed the line into something far more serious. The way Eddie murdered his girlfriend was so shockingly heinous that the jury thought the convicted killer was the devil himself. Eddie had become an infamous celebrity smack dab in the middle of the Bible Belt. In the minds of that West Texas jury of good ol' conservative boys and girls, he *was* Evil Eddie. It was best to simply execute him.

It was a tragedy.

I stare at Crane's letter, debating whether I should call his office or not. Crane, a good man who has always done all that he can for Eddie, took on the case pro bono. Why would Eddie break his silence just days before he is scheduled to die? To apologize for not accepting my help? I don't need an apology, but I admit part of me wants one. I believe Eddie refused to contact me during the trial because he didn't want me involved in his sensational story—after all, at that time in the early 2000s, my career as a well-known romance author was on a solid, steady plateau. The media never connected Eddie and me as childhood friends who grew up on the same street, though I don't think it would have bothered me—or hurt my sales, I dare say—if the tabloids had tied us together.

There is only one thing that makes sense: Eddie simply wants to see me before he dies. Surely that's all there is to it. Christ, I think I *do* owe it to him. I have to do it. I am going to have to visit him. Otherwise, I'll regret it. I'm already a member of the

AARP; I don't want to spend the precious years I have left with the guilty feeling that I'd done him a disservice.

I make up my mind, pick up my phone, and dial Crane's office. When I tell the receptionist who I am, she quickly transfers me to the attorney.

"Hello, Ms. Truman?"

"Yes, hello, Mr. Crane, how are you?"

"Fine, and you? It's been a few years."

"Yes, it has. I'm doing well."

"So I've seen. Congratulations on your success."

The West Texas accent is very pronounced. I used to have one, too, but my many years of living in the Midwest have changed all that. However, after a few drinks, it does tend to slip out.

"Thank you. So, I got your letter. And your phone messages. Sorry, I should have responded sooner."

"That's all right."

"I've decided I will come, I think. Do you know what Eddie wants to talk to me about?"

"Not at all. Eddie is always pretty quiet. After being locked up on death row at Polunsky, he's even more withdrawn. That kind of solitary confinement is terribly . . . lonely."

This alarms me. "What kind of mental state is he in?"

"Not too good, I'm afraid. I'll be honest with you. That place will drive anyone crazy, and he's been there for years. You and I know he suffers from depression and anxiety, and it's unclear how well he complies with medication. I don't think he takes it at all. He refuses any medical or psychiatric help; he always has. Mostly he lives in another world inside his head—on purpose, I might add—but he is capable of understanding and interacting with the real one when he wants to. His request to see you is sincere; I can tell you that, Ms. Truman."

"You can call me Shelby. If I really do this, what can I expect? Will he be able to touch me?"

"No. Contact visits aren't allowed with death row inmates. You'll talk to him from behind a plexiglass partition. On a phone. You'll be able to see him, and he'll be able to see you."

"And for how long?"

"Two hours usually, but since you're traveling over 250 miles, they'll let you have four. That's the maximum time allowed, but I doubt he would talk to you that long. Like I said, he's usually quiet and withdrawn, and when I've visited him he's lucid for a while, and then he occasionally goes into a sort of surreal rant. Like what you see a homeless person doing. Babbling. You know what I mean?"

"I think so."

"He doesn't make much sense when he does that. Anyway, the visit can be whatever length *you* want. It could also be as short as five minutes, and that may be *his* choice. You never know with Eddie. Whenever I've gone to see him, he will listen and tell me what he wants me to do in a coherent, sensible way, and then he'll zone out, go into babble-speak, and abruptly end the meeting. He's a pretty sick man."

"That's terrible. How can the state allow him to be executed? It's inhuman."

"You're preaching to the choir, Ms. Truman. I'm doing everything I can in last-minute appeals. Unfortunately, there's a precedent. Texas has executed more than one inmate that was believed to be mentally ill."

"It's so wrong."

"And just so you know . . . I'm the only visitor he's had for twenty years."

"Oh my God. All right. Tell me what I need to do. I have to be in Limite, coincidentally, on Friday."

"That's the date of the execution."

"I know. And I don't want to see him the day before he dies. What about Wednesday, can I do that?"

"That would be a good day."

"All right. I'll fly to Houston tomorrow and get settled somewhere near the prison, and then I'd have all day free on Wednesday. Is that possible?"

"Let me make some calls and I'll get back to you to confirm a time. Thanks, Shelby, I think Eddie will really appreciate it."

I confirm that he has all of my information, and we hang up.

The trip to Texas is going to be longer than originally planned, so Patricia is going to have to wait until I return before embarking her on a new adventure with some hunky bad boy. I get up from the desk without bothering to save my open Word document and go downstairs with my empty coffee cup.

"I'm going," I announce.

"Really," Billy responds without looking up from his monitor. "I'm impressed."

"Why?"

"I didn't think you'd go."

"Why not?"

"I don't know." He shrugs. "Because it's painful. I know the whole story." Then he looks at me.

"Mm, you don't know the *whole* story; but you're right, it will stir up some old emotions that I'd just as soon do without."

"You mean it'll feel like ripping a scab off a wound and putting salt on it?"

"Something like that."

"Then why are you putting yourself though it?"

"Because I have to. I owe it to Eddie."

"You don't owe Eddie anything, Shelby. You know that, right?"

"Billy, he hasn't had a visitor for twenty years. He's going to die on Friday. He has no family or friends. I'm the only person from his life that he's chosen to remember. I never thought he deserved the death penalty. He's mentally ill."

"I know, but he did some pretty creepy shit."

Billy has me there. I look away and study a map of the United States that I have pinned to a corkboard.

"Sorry, Shelby," he says. "I didn't mean——"

"It's okay. Look." I gesture to the map. "Huntsville is just a bit of a drive from George Bush International. Eddie's in Livingston, over here nearby."

"What will you have to do to get into the prison?"

"I don't know. I imagine it's like going through security when you get on a plane. Mr. Crane will tell me, I guess. Now, about that coffee."

I go to the kitchen, fill my cup with fresh brew, and return upstairs. Instead of working on Patricia 43, I pull a suitcase out of the closet and bring it to my bedroom. As I use one half of my brain to figure out what I need to take on the trip, the other half dwells on a rush of mixed feelings.

Yes, Eddie did some pretty creepy shit. But it never would have happened had he not suffered what he did as a child. Eddie had been damaged, but he covered it up with his eccentric intellect and talent as an artist. He would have benefited from not having dropped out of high school, that's for sure. Instead he joined the army and went to Vietnam for a couple of years, which darkened him even more.

There's no question about what happened to Dora Walton—and the baby she was carrying in her womb. Eddie was caught red-handed. Only a psychiatrist could analyze how the trauma Eddie endured as a child contributed to his illness and ended up informing a horrific murder later in life, but one thing is for sure—Eddie could not have been in his right mind when it happened.

It occurred ten years ago, in 2005. Eddie was fifty years old. He lived with Dora Walton in the same house on Chicory Lane, across from where I'd resided with my parents. A controversial pair, neighbors ostracized them, but Eddie refused to abandon his parents' house. On Christmas Eve, Eddie threw a party and invited another couple, Wade Jones and Catherine Carter. He decorated the entire place with his disturbing artwork that depicted devilish symbols and imagery, and then lit a hundred black candles to illuminate it. When I knew him as an adult, Eddie once admitted to me that while he was truly an atheist, the Satanism thing was merely something he did to shock people. It was just "art," he said.

That night, Eddie took his art to the extreme. Wade and Catherine left the house after midnight. Eddie and Dora continued to party. Eddie drugged the wine. Dora drank it; he didn't.

After that, Evil Eddie made a statement for all the world to see.

3

I like to be at the airport early, so I had Billy drop me off two hours before my flight to Houston. O'Hare is hopping, as usual. You never know when lines will be super-long at one of the world's busiest airports. As I've grown older, I've found that my nerves are less tolerant of unexpected stress. I don't like to be rushed. I'd rather be way too early than a minute too late.

One of the best things about being a well-known author is that your *face* isn't necessarily well-known. Sure, I've been on TV talk shows and my picture has been in tons of magazines—I even made a "50 And Still Hot" list in *People* eleven years ago!—but I'm not a movie star. Very few people recognize me, and I'm perfectly fine with that. My blonde hair has whitened, but my blue eyes remain the same. I'm able to travel like anyone else, go to restaurants, hotels, the theater, whatever—and still maintain a decent degree of anonymity. Every so often a serious fan will know who I am and maybe say something complimentary about my books, and that's always nice. I've never had a bad experience with notoriety. Today is no different.

After going through security, I browse in the bookstore and, out of habit, check to see if they have any of my books. They do. I buy the new Sandra Brown and then get coffee and a snack.

With my purchases in hand, I sit at the gate an hour before we start to board, ready to relax and enjoy my food and beverage.

Relax. *Right*. Apprehension has been my master since I agreed to see Eddie. I try to begin the book I bought, but my mind wanders and I can't concentrate on the words in front of my eyes. I keep thinking about Eddie, dammit. A tidal wave of memories continues to bombard me: like when Eddie sold his crazy artwork at the mall during Christmas time in the nineties; the smell of pot and booze from the seventies; and glimpses of the sixties, which are dominated by memories that mostly occurred in a playground and a bomb shelter. Eddie at twenty-one, Eddie at thirty-nine, Eddie at eleven . . . I've come to the conclusion that it would be a good idea, if not essential, that I attempt to think of the remembrances in some kind of chronology so they make some sense. Perhaps going over everything I can recall will be a helpful exercise to prepare for the eventuality of sitting face-to-face with him.

We really can't remember much of our childhoods. It's just a fact. We recall major events, but we can't tell you what happened minute by minute. It's impossible. A person might "remember" his first trip to Disneyland when he was seven years old. The truth is that he'll remember going and that he *did* it, but he won't be able to say specifically what he had done and in what order. There will be flashes of memory, such as his fright in Space Mountain, or the wonder of the fireworks that struck him as magical, but *that's it*. A "playback" of the entire experience is usually unachievable.

Our capability of memory storage is even worse when it comes to our mundane day-to-day lives. How much do you really remember from your childhood? You might know the names of all your teachers, first grade through high school, maybe. You wouldn't be able to recall *when* you learned *what* in school, though. You'll certainly remember who your good friends were, the kids you hung out with. Some of the toys or games you played with. Perhaps you'll recall seeing a favorite movie with someone special. That's the key to memories. Events in your life have to make a personal impression in order to be stored in the archives of your mind.

That's why we often have no problem recollecting significant trauma. A sickness, an accident or, God forbid, violent incident. I can always evoke an image of me with chicken pox back when I was four or five—I'm looking into a mirror at the spots on my face and I start to cry. Fortunately, that's it; that's my single, entire memory of having chicken pox. Thank goodness we don't relive the physical pain of an ordeal—we only remember that we were *in* pain.

My recollections of growing up on Chicory Lane in Limite, Texas, are sketchy at best. My high school years—tenth through twelfth grade—I remember the clearest; after all, that's when I was almost an adult. I was much more aware, my brain operating like a receptacle for knowledge. I stayed active in high school—I was involved in the Drama Department, acted in plays, dated boys, was on the student council—so there are plenty of wonderful flashes of remembrances from those years. Memories of junior high school—seventh through ninth grade—are more elusive. It was an unhappy, awkward, and confusing time of my life, as I'm sure it is for a lot of other girls. I certainly didn't feel particularly pretty then.

And before that, there was the "prehistoric era"—the first through sixth grades of elementary school. In Limite, kids usually started first grade at age seven and left elementary school at age twelve or thirteen. These are very important years in our lives, yet we barely remember them, am I right? Only glimmers of events, a handful of snapshots, or brief video clips in our brains.

Limite—pronounced "la-meet," although the correct Spanish pronunciation would have been "la-meet-tay"—sits at the bottom of the Panhandle in West Texas, within an hour's drive of the New Mexico border, with a population of about sixty-five thousand back in the 1960s. Sort of a big small town. We had two high schools that were ferocious rivals, three indoor movie theaters, two drive-ins, a bowling alley, and lots of Friday night football. The economy was built around oil, cattle, and high school sports. The oil fields surrounded Limite for miles. Oil derricks and pumpjacks dotted the flat, desert-like landscape. The old-fashioned downtown with shops and department stores was already dying even in the sixties, and was later replaced by a new mall in the early seventies. It was an old segregated city— the African Americans lived on the south side of the tracks in near-poverty, with some exceptions, of course, including the four black students who attended my high school when I was there. There was probably a larger mix later, but "colored town," as that neighborhood was called when I was growing up, was still present in the nineties. Some folks, I'm sorry to say, called it by a far worse epithet I would not like to mention.

And then there were the churches. Dozens of them. There are even more now. All denominations, but only one Catholic church at that time, and, remarkably, one synagogue. Certainly no mosques. Not in West Texas.

One could say that Limite was a few years behind the big cities such as Dallas or Houston. When I was born in 1954, I'm sure the people of Limite felt as if they were just *entering* the decade of the fifties. The late sixties were still the early sixties. When I turned twelve years old in 1966, Limite still hadn't totally embraced the explosion of artistic, political, and cultural expression that defined the latter half of that decade. We had Top 40 radio, so we were well aware of rock and the Beatles and all that. Three networks—NBC, ABC, and CBS—were the only available channels on television.

Chicory Lane was a fairly new development on the east side of Limite. The houses on the block had been built in the fifties. Being situated in the desert, there wasn't a lot of vegetation. Chicory Lane had trees, which weren't particularly pretty. Whenever I went back to visit as an adult, I was always struck by how drab and brown the neighborhood appeared, as if it had been slowly baked by the bright, hot sun for years—and it had! Our street held thirteen houses on each side, brownish-red brick ranch houses with three bedrooms, a living room, a kitchen and dining room, and a "front room," with a picture window that faced the street and where our piano stood. We moved there in 1960, when I was five or six, from nearby Prescott, where I was born. I was the only child at the time, but I imagine my parents were planning on another one since they had bought a house with three bedrooms. Michael didn't arrive until six years later. In the meantime, Mom used the third bedroom as a sewing room until it became a nursery.

I can count the snippets of memories of my earliest years, prior to grade school, on two hands. Mere snaps of images that flit through the brain. Walking with and holding my father's hand at the rodeo. Making cookies with my mom. The kids on the block. Sally, the girl who lived up the street and who was my best friend when I was *really* little; Sally the redhead who had freckles, millions of them, which contributed to her nickname, "Freckles." It's funny; that's about the only thing I remember about her. We grew apart in junior high. Greg and Dean, two older boys who lived on the street, and their pal Joey, who resided a block over. Greg and Dean, who lived next door to each other, may as well have been joined at the hip. They were always in the neighborhood throwing balls. I didn't like them much;

they acted like bullies most of the time. There were others, but I really don't remember their names or much about them.

And Eddie Newcott lived right across the street from me.

At some time or another during those early years, we *all* played with one another in the park, which was the real center of our universe. The elementary school was next to the park, so everyone walked to classes every single day. That was a time when kids could be outside *and* safe, or so we thought. Those were the days of lunch pails, Halloween carnivals and trick-or-treating, *The Dick Van Dyke Show*, and catching horny toads, the indigenous lizards that populated the area—technically called "horned" toads, though kids always called them horny toads. Since Chicory Lane was a fairly new development right on the edge of town, we could walk two or three blocks beyond the park and be in vacant lots. The desert. It was not uncommon to see all kinds of lizards and snakes and bugs around our little world decorated with mesquite and tumbleweeds. West Texas winds are notorious—they rival Chicago's!—and the dust storms are atrocious. But there's something dreamy about the sight of a tumbleweed being carried along the ground in a wide, open space. I suppose my favorite thing about growing up in Limite was the view of a hundred-and-eighty-degree sunset, horizon to horizon. Some nights, it was breathtakingly gorgeous. The vastness of the stars—and omniscient moon—was *magnificent*.

Today all those vacant lots are developed, and the city extends for miles. Things change.

My dad worked in a bank. By the time I was in high school, he was the manager of the Fifth National Bank, holding that title until he retired. My mother was mostly a stay-at-home mom, although she took some part-time jobs as a temp secretary when I was in grade school. She was a good typist and worked on a manual machine—which is what I learned to type on. I became a competent typist, too. Good genes. Unfortunately, my mother had some serious problems and never held a job for very long. My parents, Craig and Shirley Truman.

I was the only child until my baby brother, Michael Craig Truman, was born on April 20, 1966. I was eleven years old and in sixth grade. Mom and I never spoke about why they had another child when there was such an age difference between the siblings, but I do recall Mom calling him her "little miracle." She was thirty-seven when he was born.

A month later that year, I turned twelve. The pictures of me at the time show a girl with straight, dirty-blonde hair and bangs. Blue eyes. I was of average height and weight, and I was already growing breasts. I think I started wearing a bra about the time I turned eleven. My funny-looking stage didn't last very long, thank goodness. Girls always go through a funny-looking stage—acne, weirdly proportioned limbs, awkwardly budding breasts—and afterwards they bloom.

At that frozen moment of time in May, we were a typical family; we were happy. My dad made a modest middle-class salary, and we were the epitome of baby boomer living. We went to church every Sunday. *Every* Sunday. The First Christian Church was Protestant and proud of it. I got the impression the adults there thought they were above the Baptists or Methodists. To me there was no difference. I grew up believing in God—and I suppose I still do. After all, if Evil exists, then there damn well better be some Good somewhere, right?

The Lord knows my faith has been tested over the years. The first time was when I was twelve, that summer of 1966.

My interests then were puppets, bike riding, piano playing, and storytelling. I loved to put on puppet shows. One of my most cherished toys was an elaborate puppet theater that my father built for me. I suppose that's where my talent for writing comes from; I was always making up tales. Once I got Eddie to help me carry the theater all the way to the park, where he and I put on a puppet show for anyone who wanted to watch. We drew a crowd of twenty people, which was *huge* to me at the time. Eddie could sketch and paint, so he made the scenery. Eddie was often my collaborator. Sally was my best girlfriend, but Eddie was my best *friend*. We spent a lot of time together because we were just about the same age—Eddie was just a year behind me in fifth grade. We were both eleven when Michael was born. Sometimes the kids on the block made fun of us and called us "boyfriend and girlfriend," which was embarrassing. I'm pretty sure Eddie enjoyed that misrepresentation, but I didn't. In my mind, we were more like brother and sister.

My mom didn't particularly like me spending so much time with Eddie. For one thing, he was a *boy*, and secondly, she thought his parents, Charles and Betty Newcott, were strange. His mother was nice enough, but she was sickly, and I don't think I ever saw her not wearing a ratty bathrobe and smoking a cigarette. It was Mr. Newcott who scared me. All the kids were afraid of him. A big, tough guy, he worked in the oil fields. We thought he was mean, especially to Eddie, his only child. Eddie and his mother were completely subservient to the man.

Mr. Newcott was forever threatening to "get the belt" after Eddie. Nothing Eddie did was good enough for his father. It seemed to me that Eddie was always being punished for something, usually stupid stuff. In the backyard of Eddie's home, Mr. Newcott had built a bomb shelter as big as a large single room. Families in the early sixties had built these shelters because of the so-called Red Scare. By 1966, though, no one believed a nuclear attack on American soil would happen, and the folks who had spent a bunch of money to build the shelters felt foolish. The shelter in Eddie's backyard was abandoned, and it became our secret play place, our own little safe haven—but Mr. Newcott didn't like us playing in the shelter. If he caught us in there or even *looking* like we might be thinking of going in there, he'd send me home and give Eddie a beating—I recall several occurrences.

Luckily, Mr. Newcott was usually gone during the days—sometimes several days at a time. That's when we felt the safest, and we would sneak into the bomb shelter, pretending we were living in an isolated encampment in a fantasy universe of our imaginations. When the bomb shelter wasn't possible, Eddie and I met at the park, where we could also be by ourselves away from the prying eyes of the grown-ups. Every once in a while, Eddie would also come across the street to my house where we'd play board games in the living room or watch TV together. Rarely would he step foot in my bedroom. Mom didn't think that was appropriate. And usually either she or both my parents were home when he came over.

Five houses down from mine, another interesting character lived on Chicory Lane, one who turned out to be a significant part of the story that summer. Gordon Alpine—I still think of him as simply "Mr. Alpine"—was a divorced man in his late thirties who worked at the public library, was a photographer who specialized in kids' school portraits and baby pictures, and served on the school board for one of the junior highs. Gordon Alpine also happened to be the brother of Carl Alpine, the mayor of Limite.

Mr. Alpine owned an 8 mm movie projector, and he often invited the neighborhood kids into his house to watch a bunch of cartoons and old comedy films or look through his collection of vintage toys and comic books. Mr. Alpine was always happy to show off his collection, provide a glass of lemonade or Kool-Aid and cookies, and let us play with some of his less valuable toys. Or show Charlie Chaplin or Three Stooges shorts. Mr. Alpine was a nice man. He'd always come outside and say hello whenever a group of kids was in front of his house; sometimes he'd have a handful of comic books and give them away. He was also a highlight of going to the library—he was always entertaining and funny, as well as helpful. He acted as if he wanted to be a kid again.

It turned out he had everyone fooled. We didn't know it, but Evil had paid a visit to Mr. Alpine, too. He turned out to be more frightening than Eddie's dad.

He was a monster.

4

Dashes of memories. Brief snippets of a film strip, edited and jumbled.

What happened in the months prior to the summer of 1966? In the beginning, everything seemed normal. Our family had a new member. Michael was almost two months old when school let out at the end of May. He had the loudest cry. He was a colicky baby, keeping everyone in the house up at night. Then, when you'd think he was all tuckered out and would sleep all day, he'd cry during the day, too. It was worse than nails on a blackboard, and it drove us insane.

Nevertheless, like all kids feel when school lets out, I looked forward to the whole summer in front of me. Seventh grade and junior high school seemed far in the future. When you're that young, time stretches—a three-month summer could last an eternity.

The business with Eddie and me had begun a few months earlier while I was still eleven. Before, we acknowledged each other on the street and in school, getting together with other kids for our usual outdoor play. We only started getting closer in early 1966, when my mother was pregnant. More and more, our afternoons and evenings were spent together without the other kids present. I can't recall why or how it happened; somehow Eddie and I clicked for the first time.

One thing still vivid in my mind was my young perception that Eddie Newcott was the most beautiful boy I knew. Even at ten years old (and later when he turned eleven in February that year), he was handsome like a man was handsome. Other girls at school also commented on how cute Eddie was, though they also thought he was "weird." Yes, he was a little strange. Quiet and introverted, he read comic books all the time and didn't have many friends of his own. He drew bizarre pictures in a sketchbook; you'd think he was working for a Halloween store or something, with all the scary images he created—skeletons, devils peeking out of flames, monsters, dinosaurs, and witches. Some of his more elaborate work consisted of army battlefields complete with soldiers and tanks. Eddie spared no restraint in depicting dismemberments, decapitations, and bodies riddled with bullet holes. There was a lot of red. All this would have been reason enough to discard Eddie as being truly strange, except that the drawings were *good*. He had talent. Supposedly his teacher admonished him for the subject matter of his artwork but praised his ability and encouraged him to try something else. I'm not sure if he ever did.

Eddie had very distinctive, dark, bushy eyebrows. His eyes were a deep brown and his hair was almost black, though it would turn even darker later with age. His father made him wear his hair in a buzz cut at that time, and he grew it out when he was older. He was thin and very tall for his age, with full, cushiony lips. Yes, Eddie was a good-looking boy.

I realized just how attractive he was when we walked home from school together one afternoon. Two older girls in junior high passed us, turned back, and said, "Hello, Eddie!"

"Hi," he said.

I heard them giggling as they walked on and turned to see them glance back a couple of times. *What was the big deal?* I thought. "Do you know them?" I asked.

He shrugged. "I guess."

Eddie and I continued walking, but I looked at him with a renewed respect.

"What?" he asked, catching me in the act.

"Nothing."

"You're looking at me funny."

"Those girls must think you're cute or something."

He blushed and turned away, grinning. Suddenly, I felt good about walking home with Eddie.

I didn't care that I was a year older. If other girls thought he was cute, then maybe I did, too. I'd never had a boyfriend. I didn't know much about sex at all. After all, I had just turned twelve in May. Kids these days learn about the birds and the bees at very young ages, but back in the mid-sixties, that certainly wasn't the case. I'd already gotten my period, so I understood all of *that*, but as far as I knew, sex was a mysterious thing that married grown-ups did to have babies. I wasn't too clear on the mechanics. Back in sixth grade, all the girls were taken out of class for an assembly to watch a film about periods and how our bodies would be changing in the next few years. Some of us were already doing so! However, the movie was vague on the aspects of reproduction. That didn't stop the girls from talking and trading stories and myths about boys—just as the boys did about us. We weren't *stupid.* Nevertheless, I was old enough to know what infatuation felt like—a lovely lump of feeling in the middle of the chest. The very feeling that began to grow that day as I walked back home with Eddie on the sidewalk.

From February through June of 1966, Eddie and I were inseparable. I strain to recall, unsuccessfully, a complete sequence of events. A few concrete memories, likely not in the proper order, that stand out in my mind.

I remember Eddie's cat. A pretty black cat that was free to roam both inside and outside the Newcott home. It had a boy's name, something like "Jimmy" or "Johnny." Yes, I believe it was Jimmy. My dad once commented that Jimmy would get run over one day because it tended to dart across the street at night when it was out on the prowl for unsuspecting prey, usually in our favorite park.

There were also the times we spent in the park, lazing away many afternoons while school was still on. I remember one of those days. Eddie, some of the other boys from the block, including Greg and Dean, and I were hanging out on the monkey bars. I watched as Greg and Dean, who always wore identical sports jerseys, swung back and forth. They might as well have been Tweedledum and Tweedledee. Not missing his chance to show off, Eddie mentioned that Mr. Alpine had just given him a couple of *Spider-Man* comic books, which he considered a tremendous score.

Greg stopped swinging. "Mr. Alpine is creepy," he said, adding that he refused to go by the man's house.

"Yeah," Dean concurred. Dean always agreed with Greg. Turning to look me right in the eyes, he said, "You better watch out; he's a boogey-man."

I didn't know what they were talking about. "No, he's not," I said. "He takes our school pictures." It was true—one of Mr. Alpine's jobs, aside from working at the library, was to take the portraits of the kids at school. In fact, he had recently shot an adorable photo of baby Michael. "Mr. Alpine's always been nice to me."

The two older boys laughed. "Sure, he's nice to you. I bet he's nicer to Eddie, though." Snicker, chuckle.

Eddie blushed and furrowed his brow. "What do you mean?"

"If you don't know, then never mind," Greg answered.

Then Dean said, "Don't you know he killed his kid?"

"*What?*"

"Yeah, about ten years ago. He was married and had a kid, a little boy. He lived somewhere else then."

I looked at Eddie. "Is that true?"

Eddie shook his head. "I never heard that."

Greg continued. "Yeah. Mr. Alpine's wife told the police that he killed the baby and divorced him."

"Did he go to jail?" I asked.

"Nah. He wasn't even arrested. The cops didn't believe her. You know who his brother is?"

I did know. "Mayor Alpine," I said. The mayor of Limite.

When the twins had left, I asked Eddie, "Is that true about Mr. Alpine?"

"What?"

"About his wife, his kid, and all that."

"Are you kidding? I think I knew he was married before, but I never heard that he killed his own kid. Don't pay attention to them. They're just bullies. I don't know what they're talking about. C'mon. Let's go in the airplane."

"Okay."

We wandered over to the wrecked fuselage and climbed the ladder to the cockpit. From there, we descended into the hull of the plane and sat on the dirty metal floor. I looked at my watch—my treasured Mickey Mouse wristwatch that I got for my previous birthday—and noted the time.

"I'll have to get home for dinner soon," I said. "Mom doesn't like it if she has to go outside and call for me."

"I know. My mom and I will probably end up going to the cafeteria again. She doesn't cook much except when my dad is home."

"Is he gone again?"

"He's working in the field. You want to come over after dinner? We can go down to the bomb shelter if you want."

The idea of being alone with Eddie in his backyard sanctuary shook up the butterflies in my stomach. "Better not," I said. "We might get in trouble."

"My mom doesn't care. She won't even know. She doesn't pay any attention to me or what I'm doing. And Dad's not home."

I changed the subject. "Are y'all going anywhere on vacation?"

Eddie looked at me as if I was nuts. "Vacation? The last vacation we went on was to see my grandparents in Arkansas. That was three years ago. I was eight. All I remember was the long, hot drive in the car, and then I was bored to death for a week. Horrible."

"I don't guess we're going anywhere this year, since there's a new baby in the house."

"Hey, I saw at the movie theater that they're bringing back *Help!* You want to go see it?"

"I saw it last year." Eddie was into the Beatles. I liked them all right, but he thought they were the second coming.

"I want to see that James Bond double feature that's coming, too," he said. "Maybe your parents will drive us if you want to go with me."

"I don't know if they'll let me see those movies. Aren't they for grown-ups?"

"Nah. I saw *Thunderball,* and it was great."

That was one thing Eddie did a lot of—see movies. If he didn't have anyone to go with, Eddie's mother would drive him downtown to one of the theaters on a Saturday and he'd spend all day repeatedly watching whatever was playing. Sometimes I think he just didn't want to be home on the days I wasn't available. He liked playing records, too. Not only did he have all of the Beatles' albums, but he also listened to early rock groups like the Rolling Stones, Herman's Hermits, the Beach Boys, and so on. Sometimes that's what we did together when we were at my house or his. He'd bring over a stack of 45s, and we'd play them.

Out of the corner of my eye, I noticed human figures in the window of the cockpit. Two boys from school—I don't remember their names now—were spying on us. "Hey, look, it's the lovebirds," one of them said. "What are y'all *doing* hiding in the airplane? *Huh?*"

"Shut up," Eddie said. "We're just talking."

The other one sang, "Eddie likes Shelby, Eddie likes Shelby, Shelby likes Eddie, Shelby likes Eddie . . ."

"Shut up!" Eddie repeated, standing up, ready to punch one of them in the face. They ran off laughing. That was my cue to get home, so I stood up, too.

"Where you going?"

"It's getting close to supper time. I better leave."

"You're not going to let them bother you, are you?"

"No, they're stupid." I started climbing the steps to the cockpit. "Besides, what they said isn't true. We're not boyfriend and girlfriend." As I reached the top, I heard Eddie mutter, "We're not?" I didn't say anything else as we walked back to Chicory Lane, silent.

At the dinner table that same evening, I asked my parents about Mr. Alpine. I needed to satisfy my curiosity.

"He's one of our neighbors, dear," Mom answered. "We hired him to take Michael's portrait, remember?"

"He takes our school pictures, too," I added.

"Uh huh. And doesn't he work at the library?"

"Yes."

"He's Mayor Alpine's brother," Dad said.

"I know that."

"He's also on the school board at Giddings." That was the junior high school I would start attending in the fall.

"But do you *know* him?"

Mom wrinkled her brow as if she wondered why I would ask such a thing. "We say hello when we see him."

"He comes into the bank," Dad added. "Very personable guy. He's helping to organize the Fourth of July parade. I think he does it every year."

She looked at me. "Why do you ask, dear?"

I shrugged. "I think he's nice. He's always giving stuff to everyone, comic books and candy. And he's got a movie projector and shows us cartoons and old movies."

"Really?" said Dad.

"He's got a lot of neat stuff. You know that robot from that movie we saw on TV?"

Dad looked at me sideways. "Robby the Robot? *Forbidden Planet?*"

"Yeah. Well, Mr. Alpine has a Robby the Robot toy that's this big." I used my fingers to indicate six inches off the table top. "He winds it, and it walks and lights up."

"You've been in his house?" Mom asked.

"Everybody has. To see his toy collection, watch movies . . ."

Mom paused. She seemed concerned. "You probably shouldn't do that, Shelby. If he asks you to come in again, just politely say you're not supposed to go in anyone's house without us knowing about it."

"He's a nice man," I said again, working my way up to the *real* question. "Did you know he was married once?"

My dad cleared his throat and said, "Uh, yes, that's true. That was before we moved here. He was a young man then, and he didn't live on our street."

"Did they have any kids?"

Dad and Mom glanced at each other. Dad continued, "They did. I don't know the whole story, but the baby died in its crib. A tragedy."

"Honey," Mom said, "sometimes babies die for no reason when they're really small. They call it a 'crib death.' That's what happened."

At the time, this news shocked me. Now, of course, I know about SIDS—sudden infant death syndrome—but back then no one had a term for it. The cause of death was a mystery; doctors didn't start fully studying SIDS until a decade later, and it wasn't part of the public consciousness until the eighties or nineties.

Dad turned to Mom. "He lives alone now, but did he ever remarry?"

"No. Barbara at the beauty shop dated him last year, and they went out for several months. I don't know what happened. And, gosh, wasn't he engaged a few years ago? You know, to that teacher at the high school."

Dad furrowed his brow. "I remember . . . was it Linda Perkins?"

"That's her. She was Linda Lewis then. Again, I'm not sure what happened. The wedding was called off. She ended up marrying Dr. Perkins."

"Well, it sounds like he's a confirmed bachelor now."

"What's wrong with that?" I interjected.

"Nothing," Dad said.

"Never mind, Shelby, just eat your dinner," Mom said.

Dad added, "I guess it takes some people longer to find the right person."

"What church does he go to?" Mom asked.

"The Methodist? I know he goes every Sunday. I think he volunteers for a lot of their charity events."

"What if I go in his house with my friends?" I asked.

"As long as there's a group of you, I guess that's all right," Mom answered. "Just not alone, okay?"

"I won't."

Back in the sixties, it was considered strange if you were still single and already in your thirties or forties, even if you were divorced. This was a strong sentiment, especially in the Bible Belt. I suppose that was the case with closeted gay people. They lived their lives as "confirmed bachelors," and whatever the term would be for the female equivalent—"old maid"? I don't think my parents thought Mr. Alpine was gay; after all, he *had* been married and had apparently dated. He certainly didn't come off as effeminate, although I suppose he was "theatrical"— that was the best word to describe him. He used words like "my dear" and "darling" when talking to us kids. And when he took our school pictures, he'd say to the next kid in line, "Step up there, handsome!" *Click.* "Have a seat, princess!" *Click.* "Give us a smile, cowboy!" *Click.* "Look right at the camera, miss movie star!" *Click.* He had an attitude that made us all laugh.

After that discussion, I didn't visit Mr. Alpine as much as I had before school let out—I had gone at least a couple of times with Eddie, and several other times when there was a group of kids in tow. There would only be one other time when I found myself alone in Mr. Alpine's house, but that occurred a little later—I'll get to that episode shortly.

In those early days of summer, I would persuade Eddie to ride our bicycles to the library. The building was downtown, a good three miles or more. Whenever we rode our bikes, it felt like an adventure. Around the halfway mark, we would stop at Barney's Drugs, which boasted an old-fashioned soda fountain and a variety of comic books that Eddie would buy. We would get an ice cream and a Coke, and it would start to feel like we were on a real date. The image of us sitting at the counter, sweaty and pigging out on the sweets, is very clear in my head.

I always loved the library. I'd spend hours there, not only looking at the books, but also studying the newspapers from the big cities. *The New York Times* was fascinating because there was so much to offer—Broadway theater, tons of movies I'd never heard of, and all the fashion inserts. My dream was to one day leave West Texas and go to a big city. I ended up in Chicago, so I guess I fulfilled that wish.

Mr. Alpine worked at the information desk, so Eddie and I would go over to say hello. As a man in his thirties, he was, to us, very much an adult. He was of medium height, a little chubby, and he wore glasses. His hair was short, with a greasy shine to it, some kind of hair gunk. Maybe that's why he hadn't remarried. He wasn't "handsome" in the traditional sense, but in my opinion he wasn't bad looking. He seemed to me at the time to be an attractive man, fun to be around, and very smart.

Mr. Alpine smiled and greeted us warmly. "Well, well, is it Hansel and Gretel, or Romeo and Juliet, or Spencer Tracy and Katharine Hepburn?" I didn't know who that last pair was, but the way he said it made us laugh. "I know," he continued, "it's Sir Lancelot and Guinevere. Those names suit you more. And what, pray tell, are you darlings up to this afternoon?"

"Just visiting the library," Eddie answered. "Got any good books?"

Mr. Alpine laughed. "Nah. There are no good books here." He turned to me and asked, "Shelby, my dear, I haven't seen you lately. How's that sweet baby brother of yours?"

"Michael's fine. He cries a lot."

"Ah, well, babies do that, don't they? He was an angel when I took his picture."

"He was being good that day, I guess."

Mr. Alpine cocked his head and winked at me. "So why don't you ever come visit me? I never see you! You're breaking my *heart*!"

I didn't care what my parents or anyone else thought; I thought he was funny and charming. "Maybe I will, with Eddie."

"Great. I'm off work tomorrow. I'll just be working on plans for the parade. Why don't you both come by?"

There was something I was supposed to do the next day. Swimming lessons? Piano lessons? I didn't remember exactly, so I made up an excuse.

Mr. Alpine switched his attention to Eddie. "Well, then, Eddie, my good friend, why don't you come over? I have some new comics for you."

I sensed Eddie hesitate, but then he said, "All right."

"Good. We'll have some fun. Maybe I'll beat you at Battleship this time." He turned to me and said, "Eddie's the Battleship king."

That was news to me, but I didn't really mind.

"Oh," he added, "speaking of the parade, I'm organizing a float with a bunch of school kids on it. Would you two like to be on it? Want to be in the Fourth of July parade?"

It sounded like fun, and we happily agreed. I left Eddie to chat with Mr. Alpine, venturing off to look at the new books in the children's room. When Eddie finally joined me at the shelves, I said, "Mr. Alpine almost treats you like his son."

At first, Eddie didn't respond. Then he made a little sarcastic laugh. "He'd be a better dad than my real one. Mr. Alpine is pretty cool."

I agreed with Eddie. That was back then.

Among everything else that happened that one carefree summer day, lost in the sea of forgotten memories, I do recollect one thing: Eddie and I planned to get together the next day.

We were going to play in the bomb shelter.

5

That afternoon in the fallout shelter represented a significant moment in my childhood. I can't replay the entire episode in my head, just brief glimpses of what happened, vague emotions, snippets of conversations. It was the first sexual experience I ever had with the opposite gender—at twelve years old. Sometimes I'd ask myself if what we did was "normal" for curious kids. Wasn't there an expression for it? Kids playing doctor? That's all it was. Show me yours, and I'll show you mine.

But no—as an adult, I became more educated on the subject of sexual development in children, and I now realize that this was inappropriate behavior for our age group. "Playing doctor" normally occurs between the ages of five and seven, and there is usually no sexual gratification component to it. It's simple, natural curiosity. What Eddie and I did at our age was not innocent activity. The fact that it was mutual doesn't make much difference.

I met Eddie at the park after lunch, and we went back to his house. Eddie's father was away, and his mother was in the living room, watching television and smoking cigarettes. Eddie led me to the backyard by way of the wooden gate on one side of the house. Everyone on the block had fences. The bomb shelter door was located on one side of the yard near the house. It appeared extremely large and heavy to me. Made of metal, it sat about a foot off the ground as if it had grown out of the grass, one end slightly higher than the other. I don't remember it being locked. Eddie simply went over, grasped the handle, and pulled it open. It squeaked. A wooden staircase led down into the darkness. I'd been inside before with a group of other kids, and Mr. Newcott had yelled at us. The place was supposedly off-limits to Eddie and his friends, and poor Eddie got a beating because of it. From then on, we only dared to venture into its depths when Eddie's dad was away.

"Are you sure this is all right?" I asked, looking around. I was more concerned about doing something grown-ups would disapprove of rather than worried about going into the shelter alone with Eddie. I *wanted* to go in there with him. I trusted him. Nevertheless, I was nervous—but excited at the same time.

"It'll be fine. Come on."

I gingerly descended, guided by the daylight streaming through the open door. Eddie followed and closed the door above us. He flipped a switch near the top of the stairs and the lights came on.

The space was large and rectangular shaped, I'm guessing twenty by thirty feet in size. Two cots, covered in small mattresses, sheets, and blankets, sat on opposite sides of the room. A third cot was placed perpendicular to those. Shelves on the wall behind the cot were stocked with dusty old canned goods and nonperishables, likely dating back to the late fifties or early sixties. Big jugs of water that Mr. Newcott must have filled himself sat on the floor beneath the shelves. I spotted flashlights, batteries, candles, and boxes of matches. Behind the stairs was a toilet hidden by a privacy screen, or a door—I can't remember. Maybe it was a partition that you could slide open. The commode actually flushed! I thought it was amazing that they could build a bathroom underground.

I also had other things on my mind. *Oh my gosh,* I thought. *I am alone with Eddie.* It was definitely a thrill, but to tell the truth, I felt a little claustrophobic. The uneasiness was alleviated when Eddie took my hand and led me to one of the cots. We sat and inexplicably started giggling. We were being *naughty*—and it was *fun*.

"No one comes down here anymore, so I don't understand why we're not supposed to play in it," Eddie said. "I come here all the time when my dad is gone. It's my 'secret cave.' Oh, and guess what: I have the best hiding place in here." He stood and gestured for me to follow him back to where the toilet was. Getting on his knees, he crawled behind it. Eddie traced his fingers around the edge of a concrete slab in the floor and somehow got it to move. Grabbing hold of the edges, he lifted it, revealing a perfectly square cubbyhole in the ground, lined in concrete, maybe twelve inches deep.

"I call it 'Davy Jones's Locker,'" he explained. "I'm pretty sure it was made to store valuables—you know, money and jewels and stuff." At that moment, the hole contained *his* valuables—comic books, magazines, a knife, some small toys, and I don't know what else. I asked about the knife. He just shrugged and said it used to belong to his grandfather. It was more of a sentimental keepsake rather than an item he might use as a weapon.

He made a big deal out of the comics and magazines, some of which were issues of *Playboy*. I recall being surprised. I'd seen *Playboy* in the rack at 7-Eleven, so I knew what the covers looked like, and I knew each issue had photos of naked women in it. But I'd never seen the inside of one or any alleged nude pictures. So, we went back to the cot and looked at them together. I thought we were doing something really wrong, but I didn't care. It was thrilling. I was with a boy whom I liked and thought was cute, and we were alone, and we felt safe. And I was fascinated by the magazines. When Eddie opened up the centerfolds to show me what they were all about, I couldn't believe it. I was shocked but also, I must admit, a little turned on. It's possible I didn't fully comprehend those feelings at the time, or perhaps I had already experienced pleasuring myself by that age, even before that day in the bomb shelter.

I don't recollect how it started. We were talking about the women in the magazine, and why they would pose that way. Eddie said it was to "turn on men." I was curious as to how that actually worked. He told me about erections, or, as he called them, "hard-ons." I'd certainly never seen anything like that. At previous babysitting jobs, I'd changed baby boys' diapers so I knew what a penis looked like, but not one that was aroused. I don't believe I'd ever seen my father's at all.

"Do you have one of those now?" I asked, wide-eyed, my jaw to the floor.

"What?"

"What you said. A . . . hard-on."

"Yes."

"Really?"

"Do you want to see it?"

My heart pounded in my chest. I answered, "Yes," and he showed me.

I'm pretty sure I was speechless. Here, the memory goes out of focus. Maybe I watched him for a while. I don't quite recall everything, but at some point, a few minutes later, I was showing him what *I* had between my legs. He stared and touched himself. And that was it. I don't remember buttoning up and leaving the shelter, but we must have done so quickly because I *do* recall getting that feeling of claustrophobia again. The cool dampness of being underground had gotten to me. How would I have ever lasted if I had to live for days in a bomb shelter in the event of a real-life crisis?

That night, in my own bed, I couldn't sleep. I thought about what had happened. I couldn't get the image of Eddie out of my head. Was he unusually big for an eleven-year-old, or was it simply the fact that I'd never seen an erection before? Had I experienced an orgasm that afternoon in the bomb shelter? Probably not, but it was close. One thing was for sure: I learned that day how pleasurable sexual activity could be.

Whether or not Eddie intentionally initiated the event is unknown, but it was clear that he knew more about what he was doing than I did. I mean, he was looking at *Playboy* magazines in private, and he had no problem with me knowing about it, or gazing at the pictures together with me. He was obviously already into sex. At eleven years old, in 1966, Eddie knew terms and expressions I'd never heard before. When I was older, I recognized that Eddie had a confidence with his sexuality, more so than what was normal for an eleven-year-old. Where had he learned it from?

As for me, I admit to being precocious. Boys *did* interest me when I was twelve. And Eddie was mysterious, cute, and cool. But before that day, I had never, ever experienced with a boy what Eddie and I had done, and I couldn't believe I was willing to do so. I went right along with the program and enjoyed it. It's a memory for which I have mixed emotions.

We met again in the bomb shelter just a day or two later. We experimented with kissing. It was the first time I had kissed like the adults you see on TV and the movies, with the tongue and all. I thought it was fantastic. Just to have a boy's arms around me felt wonderful. Jimmy the cat, who was down there with us, wanted attention but we weren't giving him any!

We had make-out sessions in the bomb shelter two, maybe three, more times. Once, Eddie wanted to show me his erection again, and I said that I didn't want to see it.

"I thought we were going to do what we did last time," he said.

"No, let's just kiss."

We continued, but I could tell he wasn't very happy.

In the month of June, 1966, Eddie Newcott and I officially became boyfriend and girlfriend. We kissed a lot. The other kids made fun of us, so we did our best to avoid everyone. My mother expressed concern, but there wasn't much she could do about it. Eddie lived right across the street, and if we couldn't visit each other at our respective homes, then we'd meet at the park. We made out in the derelict yacht. We kissed in the airplane cockpit.

The hiding place in the floor of the bomb shelter also became the medium for a game. We would be somewhere, the park perhaps, when Eddie would say, "Davy Jones's Locker." That meant it would be up to me to go to his backyard *by myself*, when he wasn't around, and sneak into the bomb shelter. I learned how to lift that concrete slab in the floor and search the hiding place. Several times, Eddie left me notes or presents. A package of M&M's. Notes that were the eleven-year-old equivalent of love letters, written on Big Chief ruled tablet paper and printed in block letters—a writing style that Eddie kept throughout his life. "For my prinsess across the street," one note read. There were drawings of lips, meant to signify kisses. I wish I'd kept those early communications from Eddie, but at the time I was afraid to do so. My mother or father might find them, and I feared they wouldn't understand.

For a week, we pretended to be secret agents, using the hiding place to leave clues for each other to solve a hide-and-seek puzzle. I made one up and he made up another; I had to solve his and vice versa. I remember having to find a *Spider-Man* comic book hidden in the airplane in the park. Everyone was spy-crazy in 1966. Television and movies were full of spy shows like *The Man from U.N.C.L.E.* or *I Spy* or *The Avengers*, and there were movies with James Bond or Matt Helm or Derek Flint. He was the dashing Sean Connery type and I was the gorgeous Diana Rigg clone. He'd say to me, "Davy Jones's Locker," and I knew immediately where I needed to go to get the instructions for my next mission, instructions like: "Meet me at the park at noon"; "Your prize is inside the empty vase outside the house;" "Call me at 7:00 sharp." It was silly, but it was fun. For an eleven- and twelve-year-old, playing spies was exotic and exciting.

We were at the park on one such day, gliding back and forth on the swings and discussing various topics. Since Eddie saw a lot of movies, he would tell me about them and practically act out all the parts. It was very entertaining. He was a talented actor but didn't seem to have the desire to pursue the craft at that time. Later, however, the persona he adopted as an adult was a magnificent performance of artifice, and one that few people saw through.

In the middle of swinging conversation, Eddie suddenly said, "Davy Jones's Locker."

I groaned aloud and told him I didn't want to play that game anymore.

"Well, you'll miss out, then," he said, which did the trick to tempt me.

Conveniently, Eddie had to leave with his mother some-where—a dentist appointment or something like that. Mr. Newcott wasn't home. As soon as they left in the family car, I went across the street and into their backyard. Without hesitation, I opened the fallout shelter door, turned on the lights, and climbed down—a familiar route. Everything looked the same; the cots were made up neatly with sheets and blankets. Long-expired canned goods and other essentials lined the shelves. I crossed the floor to the other side, went behind the partition, and got on my hands and knees behind the toilet. It was always difficult to get a grip on the concrete slab at first; there was a knack to doing it, and it took me several tries before I managed to pry it open.

Along with Eddie's usual supply of magazines and toys, there was an envelope with my name on it. Inside, I found a note printed in his easily recognizable hand, along with a drawing of a prince fighting a dragon. An inscription read, "I WILL BE YOUR NIGHT—Eddie." Okay, he wasn't the best speller; I knew he meant *knight*. The note touched me deeply. It's among the few mementos I kept—and still own—from that period of our relationship.

Later, I got another note:

JUNE 21, 1966

DEAR SHELBY—

THANK YOU FOR LIVING ACROS THE STREET. YOU ARE THE BEST THING IN MY LIFE. I DONT NO WHAT I WOOD DO WITH OUT YOU. I LOVE YOU.

EDDIE

Despite the spelling and grammatical errors, it was sweet. He really did know how to charm a girl.

Over the remaining course of our young romance, Eddie and I never did anything like that first peek-a-boo session in the bomb shelter again.

At least, not until we were in our twenties.

6

The airline crew member makes the announcement that it's time to board the plane. I'd been so lost in my thoughts that I forgot to go to the ladies room, as I usually do before flights. It's too late now; the call has come for first class passengers to step up to the gate. Once I claim my seat and get settled, I use the lavatory, return to my seat, and strap myself in. We take off on time. I gaze dreamily out the window as the memories of June 1966 return.

Our house on Chicory Lane. I can visualize certain things about it—the squatty brown exterior with a picture window that was the mouth of an imaginary face, for example. The single-car garage door that acted as a right eye, and two of my bedroom windows that served as the left one. My father was the one who pointed this out to me when I was little. I was sitting in the front seat of the car—a no-no today, but in the early sixties kids climbed all over the inside of a car while it was on the road—as we pulled up into our driveway. It was dark outside. The light was on in our front room, and we could see Mom standing at the window, peering out at us. Dad said, "Shelby, doesn't it look like Mom is inside the mouth of a big face? Look! You see it?" I squinted to look, and after a second or two, my brain put the puzzle pieces together and I got it. It was indeed a face. I'll always remember that.

Strangely, my recollections of the inside of the house are more elusive. I can recall the path through the house to my room from the front door. The front room contained the piano, where I used to spend a lot of time; I was never very good at piano, though, and obviously I never pursued it. To this day, I don't have a clue what my parents' bedroom looked like. My own was, in my mind, a generic American girl's bedroom with all the standard accessories—twin bed with stuffed animals, a simple painted oak desk and chair, a bookcase, and a closet. When I first visited home after going away to college, I was struck by how small it was. For the longest time, we only owned a black-and-white television. When the other kids talked about how their families had gotten color TVs, I was jealous. When we finally got one, it was after the tragic events of 1966. By then, it was too late. It wasn't pleasant sitting in that living room in front of our color TV, attempting to be a normal family again.

All the houses on the block were more or less the same.

I had a habit of leaving the front door unlocked in the daytime so I could go in and out without a key. In those days, kids didn't carry house keys like they do now. I don't think I even owned one. Sometimes, my mother would admonish me. "We can't have any Tom, Dick, or Harry walking in our house," she'd say. The fact that our neighborhood was, allegedly, very safe didn't make locking the door a huge priority for me. Mom kept saying she'd get a key made that I could use, but I guess she never did.

As a matter of fact, the kids in our neighborhood did have something of an unofficial open-door policy. If you were good friends with someone, and his or her door was unlocked, you could go inside. There were times when I'd come out of my bedroom, walk down the hall, enter the living room—and there was Eddie, sitting and waiting for me. Several days that June, during the weeks Eddie and I were fooling around, he just let himself in and turned on the television. It was fine, a regular occurrence at our house. We'd sit and watch a show together while my mother tended to baby Michael in the nursery, the bedroom next to mine. I wouldn't have been allowed to have Eddie over if we were alone. Mom stayed in the bedrooms most of the time, and Eddie and I were often by ourselves in the living room. We had to put up with her periodically coming through on her way to the kitchen and back. We managed to sneak in a few kisses. Whenever Michael did his colicky child act, Mom would calm him down and retreat to her own room to lie down. As soon as she did, he'd cry again. So, I often got up to perform the duty. The crying annoyed Eddie. He always complained that we couldn't hear the TV because of Michael.

"Let's go to the bomb shelter," he'd suggest.

One day, my mind was made up. I don't know why or how I finally came to the decision to tell him I didn't want to go to the bomb shelter anymore. It happened too long ago for me to totally recall what was going on in my head at the time. I had enjoyed the encounters in our secret place, but soon he seemed to want to do more taboo stuff than just kissing, and I felt uncomfortable. Eddie thought I didn't like him anymore. That wasn't true. I liked him tremendously; I just didn't want to do what we had done that very first time in the bomb shelter. Maybe I was afraid of being caught. Perhaps I had feelings of guilt. I still enjoyed being with him, and I allowed him to kiss me, but the truth is I was freaked out by the shelter—it was creepy. I didn't like the claustrophobic feeling I got when I spent more than a half hour in its basement. Claustrophobia is something I've experienced my whole life, I'm afraid; I have never liked confined spaces. An airplane trip is tolerable for several hours, but if it's ten hours or more in the air, I get anxious and restless. I hate excursions to the Far East!

Nevertheless, during this period, Eddie and I continued to be very close. We told each other everything—all our secrets and wishes and dreams. Eddie wanted to be a great artist, one who drew comics. I thought I wanted to act on stage—and I did, a little—but mostly I wanted to write plays. I suppose I have already accomplished my childhood goals. Eddie eventually did do some work in comics in his twenties and thirties, but not much after that.

Eddie's cat Jimmy died around this time. He was found one morning lying in Eddie's front yard. I didn't see it for myself, but I heard about it. Eddie was very upset. He displayed a vulnerability I hadn't seen before, and claimed his father had killed Jimmy because he hated the cat and wanted to punish Eddie for something ridiculous. For days afterward, all Eddie would do was curse his father and repeat how much he hated him. I felt bad for Eddie, but I was sorrier for the cat. Jimmy, though a bit wild, had been a good pet. I was finally starting to agree with Eddie that Mr. Newcott was a terrible person.

For the rest of June, Eddie and I spent a lot of time in the park. I never went back to the bomb shelter with him; we also didn't go into his house. He'd come over to mine, but he couldn't stand hearing Michael cry and would leave soon after. At the end of June, my mother finally came to me and said, "You're too young to be kissing boys." I clearly remember those distinct words and how shocked I was to hear them. How did she know? She'd never seen us. It was the first time Mom had ever said anything about me spending so much time with Eddie. She had cautiously allowed us to "play together," but she kept asking me if I knew any girls to call. What happened to Sally? I explained that Eddie was my best friend; he was like a brother to me.

"I'm not kissing boys," I responded.

"Don't lie to me, young lady, or you'll be spending the summer grounded."

I didn't argue with her, but I kept seeing Eddie. There was really no way to stop us getting together in the park without keeping me at home, and that wasn't going to happen. And besides, she really couldn't complain about me—I did my share of helping around the house with the baby and all. I had my chores, and I always did them. I fed Michael and changed his diapers and played with him. Still, most of the time he just cried. I suppose Mom took him to the pediatrician to find out if there was anything else wrong, but it was just one of those things. Some babies have a hard time being colicky, and Michael would have to outgrow it. We did everything we could—holding him, burping him more often, rubbing his back and tummy, and taking him for car rides and walks in the stroller, but they were of no use. At least Michael liked his rattle. It was a blue-and-white barbell-shaped toy about six inches long. When Michael shook it, his eyes grew wide as if amazed that he could cause the thing to make such a noise. The rattle quickly became a first-response cure for attacks of colic. "Quick! Where's his rattle? Oh, here it is, under the blanket." Though it didn't work all the time to alleviate his discomfort, the rattle became an additional appendage to his little hand.

Eddie continued to visit Gordon Alpine. He tried to talk me into going to Mr. Alpine's house with him, and I did, once. Mr. Alpine gave us both ice cream and showed us his collection of board games. After hearing about his past from my parents, I looked around his living room for evidence that he'd been married. There were no family photos that I could see, except for one of him standing with his brother, the mayor of Limite. There was definitely nothing displayed to commemorate the memory of a deceased child. Maybe he had something hidden away in another part of the house, I thought. At any rate, I never detected a problem with our peculiar neighbor. To us, he was as nice as a neighbor could be.

I can pinpoint when the trouble started—on a day approaching the Fourth of July. Eddie was over to visit. He talked about getting hold of fireworks and shooting them in the park. In those days, there were no laws against fireworks in Limite, and people went all-out on the Fourth. Fireworks vendors set up their stands on the outskirts of town and made a killing. I was looking forward to spending time with Eddie on the holiday, too.

While we were watching TV, Michael started crying. My mother was in the laundry room, or, as she called it, the "utility room," which was just off to the side from the kitchen. I got up and went to the nursery to see what I could do, as Eddie tailed along. He watched as I did the walk-around-the-room-and-bounce maneuver. All three of us—Mom, Dad, and I—had found that this method sometimes worked in quieting Michael, and we called it "the bounce." It was a fast but gentle up-and-down motion that simulated a vibrator. The bounce was successful after a few minutes, so I put the baby back in his crib. We returned to the living room, only to hear my mother calling me to help her with something in the garage. I left Eddie in front of the TV. "Listen for Michael, will you?" I said. I went out the kitchen door into our attached garage, where we kept the family car and other stuff like my bicycle, camping equipment, and miscellaneous junk. In the middle of our work, we heard Michael *screaming*. We rushed through the living room—Eddie wasn't there—and into the nursery.

Eddie stood in the middle of the room holding Michael, attempting to do the bounce. He was performing the maneuver way too hard. Mom freaked out. "Stop it!" she yelled and snatched Michael from Eddie's arms. "What were you doing?"

"Nothing! He started crying, and Shelby was in the garage. I thought I'd do what Shelby did to try and stop it."

"You could have hurt him!"

"I'm sorry, I didn't mean—"

"Eddie, I think you should go on home. I need Shelby to do some chores. Go on. We'll see you another time."

He looked at me, hoping, I think, that I would protest. I didn't. The sight of Eddie with Michael had surprised me, too. "I'll see you later, Eddie," I said.

After he'd left, Mom turned to me. "I don't want you playing with him anymore. He's not welcome in this house again. I don't like him."

"Mom!" I protested, trying to convince her that Eddie hadn't meant any harm. She wouldn't budge.

"And you're going to start locking that front door whether you're inside or out. I'll get you a key tomorrow."

She snapped at me again, and I started crying. I spent the rest of the day very upset. She never got me a key, and I continued to leave the door unlocked. My mother seemed to be going through something; in retrospect, I think her hormones had gone haywire from having a child at a later age. In general, I'm made to believe that relationships between mothers and daughters can often be stormy. Ours was particularly so. At the time Michael was born, I was getting to be the age in which I couldn't help challenging my mother. She was the parent I was around the most, so it seemed that I received the brunt of anything that displeased her. It got worse as the years went on, and I'm afraid that I'm guilty of not doing more to repair what came between us.

I told Eddie that my mother wouldn't let me see him anymore when we met the next day at the park—at least like how we'd been doing. I cried, and he got angry. He said that my mother had no business keeping us apart. He claimed he hated her, and I didn't like that. I told him I was just as mad and heart-broken about the ultimatum as he was, but I didn't hate my mom. "Maybe we *are* too young to be boyfriend and girlfriend," I said, "but we can still be friends." That made him go berserk. I'd never seen him get so agitated before. He complained that nothing good ever happened to him, and finally he said goodbye.

"I'm going to Mr. Alpine's house," he said. "*He* appreci-ates me!" He left me inside the hull of the old yacht feeling wretched. I thought I was going to die. The pain in my chest was unbearable. First heartbreak—it's a killer. There was also the self-reproach for having to hurt Eddie, who obviously took it even harder than me. Mr. Alpine would be a comfort to Eddie, I thought to myself. Visiting him would get my former boy-friend's mind off of me. How do you like that? I was more con-cerned with how badly Eddie had taken our "breakup" than how I personally felt about it. Still, it was painful. I tried to tell myself that we'd still see each other. We went to the same school and he lived right across the street! And there was always the park. It was impossible to avoid each other. Wasn't that a good thing?

As the Fourth of July approached, I didn't see Eddie at the park or on the block. I ventured outside once to look for him, but one of the kids said he had seen Eddie going into Mr. Alpine's house. Fine, I thought, if he's going to hide, then so be it. He would get over it eventually. By July 3, though, I was beginning to get a little anxious. I figured it wouldn't hurt just to *see* him and find out how he was doing. Show that we were still friends.

It was a Sunday, and again I went searching for Eddie. For-getting that I was alone, I went over to Mr. Alpine's house and rang the doorbell to see if Eddie might be there. The library was closed for the holiday weekend and Mr. Alpine was home. He was surprised to see me.

"Well, if it isn't my darling Shelby!" he announced with a flourish. It made me laugh. "What brings such a fascinating creature such as you to my doorstep?"

My face felt hot and I became shy. "Is . . . is Eddie here?"

"No, ma'am, young Master Newcott isn't here at the moment. But would you like to come inside for a glass of ice-cold lemonade and a cookie?"

You know, it was hot. West Texas is murder in the summer months. A glass of cold lemonade sounded *real* good. To heck with my parents, I thought. "Sure," I said. He held the screen door open for me and I entered a real devil's lair—I just didn't know it at the time. We went through the parlor hallway and into his den, where his television, comics, and some pieces of his toy collection were kept. Strangely, I noticed a number of unframed portraits of babies scattered on a table—then I quickly remembered that he photographed infants as well as the kids at school. There were also a few framed photos of babies on the wall. Among them, I found the portrait he'd taken of my brother Michael. He noticed that I was staring at them.

"Ah, some of my lovely subjects," he said. "I like to display my favorites. Aren't they beautiful? Not too fond of dirty diapers, but I love the babies!" He laughed.

"That's my brother," I said, pointing.

"So it is! Yeah, I think that's one of my best ones, don't you?"

"Sure, I guess so." At the time, something felt instinctively weird about his displaying of baby pictures in his own home. But I shook it off. There wasn't anything particularly wrong with that, since he was a part-time photographer. Looking back, I realize how naive I was. Photos of other people's children, hanging in his living room?

A portable movie screen was set up on one end of the room, and the projector sat on a small table in the middle. I went over to the box of small film canisters to see what he had—several reels of 8 mm celluloid, labeled with numbers. Mr. Alpine came over and quickly picked them up.

"I was watching some home movies of my family. My cartoons and comedies are over there." He moved to a shelf containing other boxes of reels and put that box back. I may be mistakenly recollecting his actions, but I distinctly remember thinking that he wanted to hide the numbered reels from me.

"How are your mom and dad?" he asked.

"They're fine." I kept thinking about the child that died, but I didn't dare mention it. Instead, I asked, "Do your . . . where do your parents live?"

"Oh, they live in El Paso."

"Is that where you grew up?"

"Sure did. Me and my brother Carl. Lemonade's in here."

I followed him through the den and into the adjoining kitchen. He opened the fridge, retrieved a bottle, and poured two glasses. He clinked my glass and said, "Cheers. May all your dreams become reality, my princess."

It tasted fresh, cold, and wonderful.

"Would you like to watch a movie?" he asked. "I'll make some popcorn."

Suddenly, I could hear my mother's voice in my head, telling me not to go to Mr. Alpine's house alone. "No, thank you," I said, and made some excuse to leave.

He performed a little bow. "Well, you crush me, fair maiden, but I will allow you to fulfill your obligations."

I laughed again; I liked this guy.

"Oh! You should see the antique dolls I got from Germany. I bet you'd like those."

"I'm too old to play with dolls."

"Of course you are, my dear, but you're also old enough to appreciate their beauty and the artistic talent that went into creating them. They're hand-painted."

"Where are they?"

"In my bedroom. Come and see."

Alarm bells went off in my head. At the time, I'd simply felt uncomfortable about going into his bedroom; it was only later, when I was older, that I realized my defense instincts had kicked in.

"No thanks, I need to go. Thank you for the lemonade, Mr. Alpine!" And I was out the door.

I never returned to his house again.

I didn't find Eddie the rest of the day and chalked it up to the possibility that he was avoiding me. It made me feel bad, but perhaps this was what he had to do to cope with the breakup.

The Fourth of July holiday began with a great breakfast my mother made. My dad was off work for a few days, and we had planned to take a trip to New Mexico to see Carlsbad Caverns. Fireworks began around ten in the morning, and the crying started early. Michael didn't like the noise. I remember going out to a vacant lot with my father in the afternoon to shoot some Black Cats—actually Dad did most of the work while I watched and held my ears.

That night, a bunch of people shot fancy fireworks in the park. They weren't organized in any way, and it was probably dangerous as hell, but in those days no one thought anything about it. Michael was finally asleep, so Mom, Dad, and I went outside to our backyard to watch the display. We could see the airspace over the park from there—we had the best view. I remember Mom being antsy; she didn't want to spend too much time outside since Michael was asleep inside. Dad assured her, saying that there were plenty of quiet moments between the explosions in the sky to hear the baby cry if necessary.

However, Mom was still worried. Early on, she asked me to go inside and check on my brother. I really didn't want to miss any of the fireworks, but I dutifully obeyed. Michael was safely in his crib, fully awake. He wasn't crying, but he was wiggling and being fussy, as if he was about to go into his screaming fit. I placed the rattle in his hand and he shook it furiously. Then I heard shouting outside in the front, on the street. I went to the front door and opened it. Some of the neighborhood boys were running toward the park, yelling at each other. I squinted to see if I could spot Eddie across the street in front of his house, but it was dark out and I wasn't sure. I did, however, see the figure of Mr. Alpine. He was on the sidewalk, strolling toward the park.

He turned his head and saw me in the doorway. He waved. I waved back at him. I distinctly remember that image to this day.

The fireworks were still going on, so I closed the door—and, God help me, I know I didn't lock it—and returned to the back-yard.

We continued to watch the spectacular show in the sky, but Mom was still restless. Five to ten minutes later, she couldn't take it anymore and went back inside to check on my brother. A blood-curdling scream shook the house. Dad and I looked at each other and ran in. My mother's back was against the wall of the nursery, her hands over her mouth, and her eyes wide with terror. She pointed to the crib.

It was empty.

7

My memories of the days that followed that fateful July fourth are hazy at best. It was a horrible time for my family. Mostly, I remember the pain. My mother was inconsolable. She had to be drugged to keep from becoming hysterical. My father hated that he was powerless to help her. I felt completely lost, caught in a whirlwind of grieving grownups and suspicious police officers. My own guilt of leaving the front door unlocked is something that has never left me. I spent most of the 1980s in therapy for it.

Someone had entered the house and snatched my baby brother from his crib while we were in the backyard watching fireworks. Whoever it was had not only taken the baby, but also the blue blanket in which he'd been swaddled and the plastic blue-and-white barbell rattle. Nothing else was missing.

The fact that I was responsible for the unlocked front door caused a great deal of consternation on everyone's parts. My mother blamed *me*, not the perpetrator. In her agony, she needed a scapegoat, and I'm afraid I was it. From then on, I'm sorry to say, something broke in the already rocky relationship between my mother and me. Maybe I'm the only one who felt it, but I doubt it. Mom was destroyed by the event. It started her downward spiral into the depression that eventually killed her.

The police interviewed everyone on our block. Nobody had seen anything, but of course anyone who was outside had been focused on the fireworks. It was either Greg or Dean who told the cops that he'd seen Mr. Alpine on the sidewalk near our house at some point after the fireworks had begun. I also reported that I'd seen him and that he'd waved to me. The officers talked to Mr. Alpine himself, but he, like everyone else, claimed to be walking toward the park to watch the fireworks. His own testimony, the cops informed my parents, was that he saw nothing unusual on the street. Alpine named several neighborhood kids he'd seen either on the street or in the park, including Greg, Dean, Joey, and Eddie. None of this was helpful, especially because it was dark at the time and the folks outside weren't paying attention to other people. As far as the physical evidence went, there was none. The police didn't have the types of sophisticated forensic procedures back then as they do now, and Limite was a small town. I believe all they looked for were fingerprints, but there was nothing conclusive. Looking back, there may have been some scrutiny placed on my mother for a day or two. When my father figured out that the cops suspected *her*, he yelled at them; the absurdity of that notion was almost too much for him to bear. Eventually, the cops dropped that idea when it was established that my mother never left the house except to watch the fireworks in the backyard with my father and me.

I believe it was July 6 when two detectives came over once again to question my mother, as my father and I sat alongside her in the living room. One of them was tall and friendly. He gave me a piece of gum. His partner was an older and heavier man who seemed to be in charge. He called all the shots rather gruffly and unpleasantly and didn't seem very empathetic to what our family was going through.

During the questioning, I distinctly remember the moment when my mother abruptly bolted upright and said to one of the men, "Eddie. Did you talk to that boy across the street? Eddie Newcott?"

"Yes, Mrs. Truman, we did. He was in the park like everyone else," answered the tall officer with the gum.

"Did anyone else see him? Did you get—what do you call it—collaboration?"

"You mean corroboration, but . . ."

"It wasn't *him*!" I started to protest, but she cut me off and told the detective how we had caught Eddie in the nursery a few days ago, holding the baby and shaking him.

"He wasn't shaking Michael," I said. "He was trying to do the bounce to stop him from crying."

"No!" Mom spat. She was growing more agitated and irrational by the second. "He was deliberately trying to harm Michael! He was *molesting* my baby! That boy is *strange*. There's something wrong with him. There's something wrong with that whole family over there. You need to arrest him!"

"Honey," Dad said, putting his arm around her. "Please, you're upset. I don't think Eddie Newcott would ever do anything like that."

I didn't believe it for a second. He would never do anything to hurt my little brother. My mother was simply not right in her head. She was still in shock, distraught, and drugged. When the detectives left, I started crying and told my mother between sobs that she was wrong. I pleaded with my father not to let the police arrest Eddie; that's what I thought they were going to do next.

"They're just going to talk to him again, honey," Dad said. "Don't worry. Maybe he saw something. He could be an important witness."

As it turned out, there was plenty to worry about. The next day, the police showed up across the street and took Eddie to the station, accompanied by his father and mother. He was there nearly fourteen hours, and I learned much later how traumatic the interrogation was for him. I remember sitting in our front room, watching Eddie's house for the entire day. The police had taken Eddie in a cruiser, followed by the Newcotts in their car, first thing that morning. They only returned to the house after dark. I saw their car pull into the driveway. Eddie bolted out of the back seat and ran into the house. I heard Mr. Newcott shout at him, "Eddie!" Mrs. Newcott, hunched over, appeared resigned and beaten. Mr. Newcott put his arm around her. They walked inside and shut the door.

The very next morning, police sirens screamed on our street. Dad, who was taking days off from work, was home. The three of us stepped into the front yard—I was still in my pajamas—and saw three police cruisers parked in front of Mr. Alpine's house down the street. It looked as if the entire Limite police force had descended on the Alpine home. "I'm going to find out what's going on," Dad said and walked toward the mayhem. The cops sent him away. He returned to the house and called one of the detectives that had questioned us the other night. No luck.

We didn't hear anything until the day after *that*. The two officers returned and sat down with my parents in the kitchen. That was when I learned their names: Detective Jim Baxter was the tall man who had been nice to me; Detective Blake Donner, the heavier man, had ignored me. Detective Baxter told me that they needed to talk to my parents privately for a few minutes, and asked if I would mind waiting in my room. He gave me another stick of gum, which I stuck in the pocket of the skirt I was wearing. "Sure," I answered, but instead of going to my bedroom, I stood in the hallway and eavesdropped on some of the things that were said. Apparently, the police had received a tip that Gordon Alpine had abducted Michael. They obtained a warrant to search his house and found Michael's barbell rattle hidden in a dresser drawer in Mr. Alpine's bedroom. I heard the rustling of a paper sack as the detective took out the rattle from a bag for my mother to identify it. She cried out in horror, answering the man's question. Though I strained hard, I didn't catch everything, and I'm sure I didn't understand a lot of what was being said at the time. Words I'd never heard before. Something about photographic equipment. I heard the words, "he was suspected before," no doubt referring to the death of his child a decade earlier. And, of course, the word "mayor" came up a few times. After a while, Detective Baxter called for me to come into the kitchen. Detective Donner barked at me, asking what I knew about kids visiting Mr. Alpine. I answered the best I could—that he often invited the neighborhood children into his house to watch cartoons, play with vintage toys, and drink lemonade.

"And that's all that happened?" Donner asked in that serious tone grown-ups have when they want you to tell the truth . . . or else.

"That's all that happened," I answered, because it *was* the truth.

"Did Mr. Alpine ever touch you inappropriately, or did you ever see him touch any of the other kids?"

The idea was absurd to me. I shook my head and said Mr. Alpine wouldn't do that. Detective Baxter wrote something down in a notebook and asked me to go back to my room.

"Wait, there is something else," I said.

"What's that?" Baxter asked.

"Mr. Alpine has a picture of Michael on his wall."

The two detectives looked at each other. Donner gave a slight nod, as if he was confirming something.

My father said, "What? His picture?"

"Yes, sir," Donner answered. "Mr. Alpine took your son's portrait, is that correct?"

"Yes, he did."

"There are several photos of babies displayed on his living room wall. There was one conspicuous empty space; a photo frame had been removed. The hook was still there."

"And?"

"The photo of your son was in the dresser drawer with the rattle."

"Oh my God!" my mother shrieked.

Mr. Alpine had been arrested and taken to the police station the previous day. Everyone in the neighborhood was shocked and surprised. The mayor was conspicuously silent. My mother wanted to kill the man. But the big question above everything else was—where was Michael? Other than the presence of the rattle and the portrait, there was no baby. The police dug up Mr. Alpine's backyard and tore his house apart, but they found no tiny corpse. The detectives were confident that the prisoner would eventually talk. Surely a soft man like Mr. Alpine who worked in a library would rather confess to where he'd hid Michael than be moved from the city jail to a bigger prison to await trial. There was speculation that Alpine had most likely wrapped the baby in a garbage bag and had thrown him into a dumpster, or perhaps buried him in a vacant lot or in the oil fields.

Over the next few days, my parents wouldn't let me go out into the street to see any of the other kids. I heard later that the gossip was rampant. The story that Mr. Alpine had killed a child once before was circulating like wildfire. Now he'd abducted and murdered another one. Why? He was a madman, a monster, an animal. Greg—or was it Dean?—changed his story and said he *had* seen Mr. Alpine go into our house. After Mr. Alpine was arrested, he called the police and told them of his new realization. He said that hearing about the man being arrested was a jar to his memory.

The mayor finally spoke out on the six p.m. local news. At first my parents didn't want me watching it, but I insisted. I can't recall much of what Carl Alpine said about his brother, only that he would make sure our ex-neighbor received the best legal representation. No protestations of innocence.

Though I wanted to know more about the investigation, I wasn't allowed to read the newspaper. Years later, when I was an adult, I went to the Limite Public Library and looked up the papers on file for that week. In the edition that came out the day after Mr. Alpine was arrested, there was an "I told you so" interview with Mr. Alpine's ex-wife, to whom he had been married from April 1958 to March 1959. She was still convinced that he had also killed *their* baby, also two months old at the time. The incident occurred in October 1958. "He wasn't much of a husband," she said. "We had marital problems. He didn't love me. I didn't love him. He resented the baby. That's why he killed my darling little boy. The police and medical examiner were wrong. It wasn't one of those unexplained infant crib deaths. I know. And Gordon was never charged. I left him right after that." Something odd struck me about the dates, so I did the math. If the baby was two months old in October, then he had been born in August. Gordon Alpine married his wife in April, which meant she was already pregnant at the time. A forced marriage?

The papers featured a few articles about the investigation, but they left a lot of stuff out—things I learned much later. The most striking headline was published on July 9, when the chief of police announced that they had obtained a confession from Mr. Alpine. The mayor was quoted as being "disappointed and ashamed."

But Gordon Alpine never had a chance to tell his side of the story in a courtroom. Before dawn on July 10, before being moved to the county jail, the man hung himself in his cell. The police had not taken adequate precautions to prevent it. After all, those kinds of things never happened in Limite. How were they to know the guy was a suicide risk?

His suicide pushed my mother over the edge. We would never know what happened to Michael's little body. Mr. Alpine may have confessed to abducting and killing Michael, but he had been notoriously silent on where the body was hidden. His secrets died with him. The detectives promised they would keep searching, that they would never give up, and that they would eventually find my brother's corpse.

They never did.

I didn't see Eddie again for days. Word on the street from my friends was that the cops had given Eddie a fairly rough time. The police interviewed him that second time at the Newcott house, but apparently Eddie grew upset and became belligerent, so the cops took him to the station with his parents in tow. I heard that Eddie had cried and was defiant all day even as the cops put him through the wringer. It was so cruel—he was only eleven, for Christ's sake. When Mr. Newcott's lawyer finally showed up—at eight o'clock at night—the cops freed Eddie with no charges whatsoever. My father and I both felt it had been an unfair thing to do to my best friend. My mother never said anything about it.

When I finally saw him in the park, days later when my mother released me from my forced seclusion at home, he glared at me and growled, "Your mother told the police I hurt your little brother."

"I'm sorry. I tried to tell them you wouldn't do that."

"Why did she have to lie? *Why?* I *loved* you, Shelby!" Tears came to his eyes and he walked away. Looking back, I know that his words were those of an upset young boy who was infatuated with the girl across the street. He didn't know what love was. Not yet, and neither did I. But at the time, what he said cut me to the core. I thought I loved *him*, too, in my own adolescent way. We were so young, I know, and it sounds silly now, but we both believed it then.

The rest of the summer was truly the worst two months of my life. I was grieving not only for my baby brother but also for the loss of my closeness with Eddie. It was inevitable that I would still see him, simply because we lived across the street from each other. Every now and then in July I'd catch a glimpse of him outside his house. He'd look back at me and I'd gaze at him. Occasionally, we gave each other a little wave. Then he'd turn and go inside or hop on his bike and take off. I stopped seeing him at all toward the end of the month, and it wasn't until school started in September that I found out he wasn't living in the house anymore. He had gone to "live with other family members." I never knew where.

Eddie mysteriously vanished for an entire year.

8

Seventh grade totally sucked, of course. That was true of junior high in general. Something had died in my heart. The atmosphere in our home was subdued, to say the least. Mom didn't like it when I watched television—the laugh tracks made her cringe—and she'd make me turn it off or turn the volume down so low I could barely hear it. She stayed in her bedroom a lot. I don't know what she did while I was at school and Dad was at work. The alcohol and pills didn't start until later, so I imagine she sat in front of the television and watched soap operas. She ceased doing any temp work. She built a wall around herself and stayed inside it for the rest of her short life. I knew that she was going through something terrible, that I was witnessing someone deal with grief. It was best to give her space. She became extremely withdrawn, preferring to be alone, and she would snap at us if we tried to get her to do something she didn't want to. Dad continued to be his complacent, friendly self, but my mother's dark mood affected him. They were a damaged couple, and at the time I was too young to contemplate what they were going through.

We took it day by day. Although we went to church every Sunday, my own faith was shattered, for I couldn't understand how God could let something like that happen to my brother. My mother and I had a terrible fight sometime during the fall of that year. The conversation had begun badly, with the two of us arguing about something—a typical teenage girl/mother drama, except that it was heightened by Mom's condition. When she said something about Michael's abduction being "God's will," it made me very angry. I challenged her, saying that I didn't believe God would do things like that. The crime wasn't part of a divine plan; it had just *happened*. Brave words for a twelve-year-old girl to say, and I almost can't believe I had the strength to say them. She grew furious. Then I poured salt onto the wound by proclaiming, "It certainly wasn't God who came calling at our house that night, it was Evil!" My mother slapped me. Yelling, she ordered me to my room. I was stunned, stinging from the slap. She shouted at me again, and that time I turned and ran from her. I'm afraid I don't recall how things cooled down, but I know I was in my room for a long time. From then on, any mention of Michael was accomplished only by walking on eggshells.

We got through the school year and the first anniversary of my brother's abduction. That fourth of July was particularly difficult. Mom stayed in her bedroom, wore earplugs to block out the sound of fireworks, and covered her eyes with a face mask. She was quite medicated. Dad and I watched the spectacle from our backyard, as usual, in an almost meditative silence. I kept thinking that Michael would have wanted us to continue to enjoy the holiday. That sounds silly, since he was a two-month-old baby, but I liked to imagine he was growing up in Heaven, with a mind of his own.

Eddie returned to the house across the street at the end of August 1967. Right before school started, I saw him outside the house with his father, walking from the car to their front door. He turned, and we locked eyes. He seemed thinner, but otherwise, from that distance, he looked basically the same. Taller, perhaps. Yes, definitely taller.

I waved.

He didn't, but continued to stare at me until his father said something to him. Eddie then jerked his head away and went into the house. Despite the distance between our houses, I could usually intuit Eddie's mood whenever I saw him across the road. This time, I was unable to read his gaze. A hateful one? An unhappy one? Was he glad to see me?

And then nothing happened. I hardly saw him. He didn't contact me. I didn't dare call him. That was the extent of our communication for the next six years. I believe the correct term is that we "grew apart." Sometimes I wonder what would have happened if my mother hadn't banned me from seeing him when she did. Would we have stayed close, even through the ordeal of the previous summer? I don't know.

I didn't find out where he had been during the past year until much later. Eddie's life had gone in a different direction from mine as we worked and played and studied our way through junior high and high school. He was truly existing in a very different universe from mine. Eddie was still one grade behind me; he must have kept up with his education wherever he had been when he was away. I'd see him in the school hallway and we'd maybe nod or say, "Hi," but I don't believe we ever stopped to talk to each other. It was a case of awkward avoidance but also of maintaining politeness.

My junior high school experience was perhaps atypical from my peers in that everyone knew I had lost my brother. I had a mystique attached to me, and I wasn't sure if that was good or bad. It must have changed my personality, for I soon found myself with a completely new set of friends—kids I'd never associated with before, including new students from other elementary schools who funneled into my junior high. Not much else stands out in my filing cabinet of memories from that period. Junior high was something to get through. Oh, right, and I had braces, too, which didn't help my self-image as an oddball.

At least by the time I reached high school, the events of 1966 seemed to be in the distant past. The braces were gone. I "blossomed," as they say, and moved on by becoming involved in extracurricular activities. I took drama and acted in plays, read a lot, and for the very first time started writing short stories. Though my English teachers encouraged me, at the time my goal was to become an actress. I didn't consider becoming an author until much later.

The only things to do outside of school in Limite were attending the varsity football games, going to movies, maybe bowling or miniature golfing, or simply cruising the town. Most kids had their own cars. My dad bought me my first junker when I turned sixteen and had obtained a license. A popular place to hang out in those days was the Oil Derrick, a nightclub that was divided into two sections—an eighteen-and-over side and another half that accommodated younger teens. Since the drinking age then was eighteen, it was fairly easy to cross the boundary. With the cruising came the dating and the experimentation in the front or back seats of someone's automobile. There was nothing else in town to distract us.

I still frequented the public library, too. My interest in reading—even outside of school work, which few students attempted—never lessened. Whenever I went there, I always thought about Mr. Alpine. I'd look at the information desk where he used to work and ponder how great it was that a monster like that was no longer alive. A man who murdered one, probably two, innocent and defenseless infants. A man who had everyone fooled with his church work, his volunteer activities, and his I'm-good-with-kids act. *Rot in hell*, I'd think.

There was a boyfriend named Andy for the latter half of my junior year and most of that summer. I suppose we were pretty serious for high school kids. We experimented with sex but didn't go all the way; that just wasn't done in 1970 or '71, especially in our small town. I can't remember why we broke up. We were both seniors and wanted to date other people, I guess.

I didn't smoke in high school; I've never smoked tobacco. I first tried marijuana when I was in eleventh grade, though. Everyone experimented with it at least once, I believe, at least the more adventurous kids did. I did it only a handful of times when I was out with fellow cast members from a production or at a party. I'm sure Eddie was into it, and maybe other drugs, too. Because of the more relaxed restrictions then, it was also much easier for sixteen- and seventeen-year-olds to get alcohol. Sure, I had some wild nights, especially during my senior year. I wasn't tied to a single boyfriend, and I had a crew of best friends—Marilyn and Janine. We called ourselves "The Unholy Three," after an old movie starring Lon Chaney. It was on *Strange Theater* one Friday night when we were having a sleepover—that was Limite's local TV station version of a weekly old horror film broadcast, complete with a newsman dressed up as Dracula and acting as a host.

Don't get me wrong—I wasn't a bad girl. I was actually a pretty good student; I received high grades and was in the Honor Society. Teachers liked me. Although I wasn't one of the super-popular kids that got voted Most Beautiful or Wittiest or Most Patriotic, I did all right in high school. It was the best time I'd had in my life thus far, considering that the preceding years in junior high had been so awful.

On the contrary, Eddie became an outcast. He was one of the stoner kids who grew his hair long when the dress code rules were finally eased in '71. He could often be seen hanging out with the guys most people deemed losers, occupying the smoking area behind the school. At that time, the students who smoked were not ostracized like they would be today— they were just relegated to a designated spot, which ultimately became littered with nasty cigarette butts. It was a janitor's duty to clean it up every week. At any rate, Eddie did everything he could to project a bad boy persona. He even rode a motorcycle and wore a black leather jacket. Then, when he turned sixteen in 1971 and was about to enter eleventh grade, Eddie abruptly dropped out of high school and joined the army. Word on the street was that he faked his birth year since he looked older than he really was. He volunteered to go to Vietnam and was in a ground combat unit; I'm pretty sure most of the fighting units were brought home in '72. The war was declared over for the US in 1973. That's when Eddie must have returned to Limite. I'll never understand why he joined the army. Probably to get away from his father. But I know for a fact that the experience pushed him further into darkness, and he came home a changed young man.

I graduated from high school in 1972 and, that summer, moved to Austin for college. I was eighteen. Finally, I was away from Limite and no longer had to live in the oppressive atmosphere that still informed my home. Eddie was far from my thoughts by then; he was still overseas. I completely missed his homecoming.

Austin between 1972 and 1976, my undergraduate years, was a fabulous place to be. The stimuli on campus were powerful and life-changing, and I truly *found* myself, just as most young people do when they go to college. New friends—longer lasting ones—and new lovers. One serious boyfriend my sophomore and junior years—and a bad breakup. More awareness of social issues and the youth counterculture. I got heavily into rock music and movies. Theater was my passion, and I majored in acting— although I was writing fiction more often in my spare time. I'd written a first novel by the time I was twenty. It was terrible, and I'm not sure I still own a copy. Back then everything was written on typewriters.

College was a time for more experimentation. I tried different recreational drugs, drank more alcohol, and had casual sex with boys. Signs of the times. Everything was about Peace and Love. The Vietnam War was a major concern on campus. It wasn't really over until '75. Then suddenly it was my senior year.

May of 1976—I turned twenty-two and graduated with a Bachelor of Fine Arts degree. I decided to attend graduate school and was accepted at Northwestern University in Evanston, Illinois. So I picked up and moved cross-country once again and found myself battling the Chicago winters for the first time. It was quite a contrast to Texas, but something about the city and people stuck with me, got under my skin. I fell in love with it. As it turned out, I never left.

The plane I am on begins to make its descent into the Houston area. Short flight, only a couple of hours. The time passed quickly, as I'd been lost in my thoughts. As we land, my mind focuses on the next major interlude in which my life intersected with Eddie's. Who would have thought that during the Christmas break of 1976, when I was home visiting my parents, I would randomly bump into him and begin a torrid, passionate love affair?

9

Navigating Houston International Airport is easy, although it's a big place. I catch the sight and smell of a favorite Mexican chain restaurant in the food court, and for a moment I'm tempted to stop and have a meal. But there's no time, and it's too early for dinner. I'd previously decided to rent a car to drive up to Livingston and stay in a hotel in town. It's roughly an hour-and-a-half drive—not bad. Eddie's lawyer recommended a couple of popular places to stay. I had Billy make my reservation at the newer Best Western. No doubt the Livingston and Huntsville hotel business accommodates a good deal of prison visitor traffic.

Hertz fulfills my needs—I go with a cute yellow four-door Ford Focus. A GPS is invaluable, of course, so that's a little extra cost. I could use my cell phone, but I want to save the charge.

As I pull out of the car rental lot, my stomach gets the quivers again. *I'm driving to a death row prison facility.* That is a first for me, to be sure.

Being early summer, the weather is beautiful and hot. To Houstonians, it is probably mild. For me, from Chicago, it's pretty toasty. I've been to Houston in the summer, and it can be dreadful, much worse than Austin or Limite ever were due to its proximity to the Gulf. The route is more or less a straight shot up Interstate 69, so the trip allows me to ponder the next chapter of the story of Shelby and Eddie. I'm beginning to wonder if a novel "inspired by" these events might be worth pursuing once it's all over and Eddie is gone. I'd have to change the names and fictionalize it. That type of book isn't in my comfort zone, I'm afraid. I assembly-line produce romance adventures, and they usually provide a good-time fantasy for my readers, who are mostly female. They prefer happy endings.

More than five years had passed since I'd last seen Eddie. I was twenty-two and had just finished my first semester of graduate school at Northwestern. After a couple of years' absence, I returned to the house on Chicory Lane for Christmas. My mother wasn't doing well. She had a "nervous condition," and in 1976 no one really knew what that meant or how to treat it. My dad, a trooper, did his best to take care of her, but she was not the woman she used to be. Since the summer of '66, Mom couldn't escape a dark and descending spiral. She had started taking tranquilizers when I was in high school and had become addicted. It grew worse when I went away. The truth is, she went a little mad. It broke my heart to see her that way, which may have been a reason why I didn't visit home as often as I could have during my college years. I'm afraid my mother and I were at loggerheads, and it was never pleasant to be around her. I usually preferred to remain in Austin during the summers, going back to Limite only for Christmas. There were a couple of years I didn't go home at all. My poor father, who was just as wounded as she was, had to put up with a lot. Yet he had managed to move on, as I had. He and I would never forget, but we wouldn't let what had happened ruin our lives. Unfortunately, it *had* destroyed my mother's.

The plan was to stay for a month over that holiday season of '76, as I didn't have to be back at Northwestern until the end of January. Mom looked like she had aged ten years, but my presence boosted her energy and morale. Dad told me he hadn't seen her so happy in a long time. I was afraid the visit would be depressing and interminable, but I had promised my father that I'd spend some serious time with Mom.

The neighborhood looked the same. A different set of kids were playing outside on the block. The Newcotts' house across the street hadn't changed a bit. Every time I stole a glance to look over there, it was quiet, dark, and vacant.

"Do the Newcotts still live across the street?" I asked Dad while we were in the car on a trip to the supermarket. It was my first day back.

He nodded. "Mrs. Newcott and Eddie do. You know Mr. Newcott died?"

"No! When?" It was the first I'd heard of it. The news jolted me.

"Gosh, nearly two years ago. Not long after Eddie got back from overseas. Eddie was in Vietnam a couple of years, you knew that?"

"Uh huh."

"Did you know he went AWOL right before he was set to come home?"

"No."

"That's what I understand. He left the base one morning and disappeared into the jungle. His battalion shipped out without him."

"Wow, really?" I couldn't imagine what that meant for Eddie. "So what happened?"

"Eventually he just showed up at the base one day. He'd been gone a long time. That's really all I know about it. He was discharged and came home toward the end of '73. Then Charlie Newcott had that accident."

"When was this?"

"The accident?"

"Yeah."

"Uh, the beginning of '74. You were in Austin."

"I know. So what happened? What's the story?"

"Not much to tell. Charlie fell off an oil well and broke his neck."

"No!"

"Yep. Eddie was there, too; he saw it happen. Eddie started working for his father's oil well supply company after he got back."

"So it's just Eddie and his mother over there?"

"Yep."

I had mixed feelings about Mr. Newcott's accident. I'd never liked the man, and Eddie used to hate him. I wondered how Eddie felt about losing his father.

"How come y'all never told me about this?"

Dad shrugged. "I didn't think to do so. And your mother wouldn't have. Her feelings for the Newcotts really soured after what happened to your little brother. And you didn't come home, you know."

"I'm here now. I'm sorry, it's just hard for me to be around her, Dad. She doesn't . . . oh, you know what I mean."

"She doesn't what?"

"I was going to say she doesn't love me anymore, but I know that's not true."

"Of course it's not."

"But she holds it against me, Dad. She still blames me for what happened."

"That's not true, Shelby. Your mother—the only person she blames is herself. That's what is eating her alive."

"What can we do?"

He sighed and shook his head. "Be nice to her. That's the only thing we can do now, because we've tried everything else. The doctors—I don't know if they help her or hurt her . . ."

"Don't you think she takes too many pills?"

"She makes it worse by mixing them with alcohol. I don't know, honey, I've tried to get her to go easy on that stuff, but she does what she wants. In many ways, she's a very strong-willed woman, despite her weaknesses."

It was the first in a long time that my father and I had mentioned Michael's abduction. We did our grocery shopping and returned home in silence.

That evening, after dinner, I walked alone to the park. Though the layout was the same, it wasn't completely how I remembered it. For one thing, the airplane and yacht had long been removed for being "unsafe." The playground equipment was more modern. Since it was winter, the trees were leafless and the grass was brown. The place was desolate and cold. It didn't feel the same. I turned around and made my way back to the house.

It would have been an unmemorable holiday had I not decided, four days before Christmas, that I was going mad being alone with my parents. I announced that I wanted to visit some old haunts and could I please have the car. Dad didn't mind; in fact, he encouraged me to get out of the house. I went to the Oil Derrick, which was still in business. It no longer had a separate seventeen-or-younger room—it was now all eighteen-or-over. The drinking age had not yet changed in '76, so I suppose the Limite elder statesmen decided that having an underage establishment connected to what was basically a pick-up bar was inappropriate. At least, that's what the joint had become.

The possibility of running into someone from high school was fairly high. Half the people who grow up in Limite usually stay there as adults. They go to the local community college and straight to a locally based career, and they plant roots. Some folks are just better suited for small towns. And as it was the holidays approaching Christmas, I figured *someone* I knew would be there.

It must have been around nine o'clock when I walked in through the door. A blast of music and cigarette smoke hit me in the face. People had always smoked in the Oil Derrick, but it had become worse than when I was seventeen. Never liked it. I suppose we just lived with it back then; it was part of the night-life everywhere. Today, I wouldn't be able to step inside a place like that without choking.

I distinctly remember the song I walked in on, that duet Elton John did with Kiki Dee, "Don't Go Breaking My Heart." I almost started laughing at the irony. After all, what the hell was I looking for in a bar in Limite, Texas? Certainly not romance. I was never into one-night stands, despite the few I'd had in college. Dancing with a stranger wasn't on my to-do list, either.

Maybe I just wanted a stiff drink. The dark cloud hanging over our house called for it.

I ordered something—I think it was a screwdriver—and sat on a stool at the bar. The place was a gas for people-watching, although few couples were on the dance floor. No one looked familiar, but they were all the same *type*. The men wore car-bon-copy blue jeans and western shirts. The women all had on identical *Charlie's Angels* wardrobes. And the clientele was all white, of course. Whoa. After living in Austin and Evanston, Limite was Nowheresville. I felt like a fish out of water, to be sure. Leaving my hometown and going off to college had made me grow as a person, both in knowledge and emotional matu-rity. It opened my mind to so much more than what Limite had to offer. I like to say I learned how to think abstractly once I left home. I studied art and theater and literature and film—and everything else that excited and interested me. I'm not proud to admit it, but it was no wonder I unwittingly felt superior to everyone in the Oil Derrick that night. I just thought they were *hicks*; I, on the other hand, was smarter, more attractive, and more liberal-thinking. Perhaps I was a little full of myself.

Within the space of two minutes, a young man—college age—approached me and asked if he could buy me a drink. I was sitting there with a full one. "No, thanks," I said, and turned away to give him the message. *Go away.*

Three minutes later, another man approached me. He was older, more the thirty-something type. Probably divorced, or perhaps even still married, and he was actually quite good-looking.

"Never seen you here before. Hi, I'm Jack." He held out his hand. I didn't take it.

"Hi Jack, I'm Shelby."

He smiled and awkwardly lowered his hand. "Do, uh, you come here a lot?"

"Nope."

"I didn't think so. I'd know it if I saw you before. Where do you mostly roost?"

"I beg your pardon?"

"Where do you usually go? There's not that many good clubs on this side of town."

"I'm not from here, I'm visiting my folks. I live in Chicago."

"Oh, I see." He started to sit down on the stool next to me, but I held up my hand—"Please, I'm expecting someone."

"You are?"

"Yeah. Sorry. It was nice to meet you."

"Sure, okay. Sorry. It was nice to meet you, too." He nodded sheepishly, smiled, and backed away. Maybe I was too harsh, but I didn't want to talk to any men that night. My visit to the Oil Derrick was really for anthropological purposes. And to get a drink. A full five minutes passed, and I was halfway done with my screwdriver. It was a weak drink, so I figured I'd stay just long enough to have a second one; after that it would be back to the castle.

Then another young man walked up to me from the shadows and spoke. "Shelby?"

The fact that he knew my name got my attention real fast. I turned and looked at him. Time stopped for a second or two, and then a lightning bolt hit me.

Unbelievable. He was the last person I expected to see.

Eddie Newcott.

10

He had changed quite a bit. Actually, his face looked pretty much the same as it was the last time I saw him at school in '71—only he looked older than twenty-one. Harder, darker. He wore his coal-black hair long to his shoulders, and his face was framed with full, shiny facial hair. And those dark brown eyes— they were so soulful and pained and gorgeous. I swear he looked like Jesus.

And his physique—my God, he had bulked out. The military must have done a transformation number on him. He had put on pounds, but in all the right places. His shoulders were broader, and I could see the muscles bulge in his arms and pectoral areas. Plus, he had on tight blue jeans that were like a second skin, with special emphasis on his crotch. He wore a black shirt and black shoes.

Holy mackerel, I now believe Eddie Newcott became the model for the guy embracing Patricia Harlow on the covers of the romance novels I would later write—subconsciously, in my head.

He was an Adonis.

"Eddie? Eddie Newcott?"

His eyes twinkled warmly when he smiled. "It *is* you!"

"Oh my gosh, Eddie, I can't believe this. Gosh, how are you?" I was flustered and surprised and completely giddy from the alcohol and the sight of the beautiful man standing in front of me.

"I'm good. How about you?"

"Good, good."

It was discomforting. I was tongue-tied, until he suggested that we sit down in a booth and have a drink together. I said okay, lifted my nearly empty glass, and indicated I'd have another screwdriver. He got something hard for himself, probably a Scotch whiskey. On the way over to our seats, I caught that guy, Jack, checking us out. He must have been ticked off that it was Eddie I'd been "expecting."

We sat across from each other, talking loudly to be heard over the mid-seventies soundtrack that was blasting over the sound system. I suggested moving to another part of the night-club where it wasn't so loud. We found a new booth, where we had to sit closer together, at a right angle to each other.

Of course, I can't remember everything we said or even how we skipped past the awkwardness into having a very nice conversation. I told him about graduating with a BFA in acting, and that I'd just finished my first semester of graduate school in Evanston. It was probably one of the first times I said aloud that I was thinking of switching my creative focus from drama to literature. There were the excuses about my bad first novel, but I said that I wanted to try again. Other than that, my life wasn't anything remarkable. My parents were still living in the same house, my father still worked for the bank, blah blah blah. I didn't mention that my mother was not herself.

Then it was his turn. Eddie told me that he had hated school and that he and his father hadn't gotten along. "I dropped out. Simple as that. I did it to piss off my dad," he said.

"How old were you?"

"Sixteen."

"Oh, right. I remember."

"I was a pretty angry kid. I needed to take out a lot of frustration, so I joined the army."

"I heard that. Gosh, you never seemed like the soldier type growing up."

He laughed. "I used to draw bloody battle scenes, remember that?"

That made me laugh, too. "Yes."

"I also did it to get away from my father. A friend of mine got me an ID that said I was eighteen. So I went to Vietnam."

His eyes darkened when he said the name of the country. Eddie proceeded to tell me how he was put right in the thick of it at the end of '71, after boot camp. The whole thing was madness, in my opinion. Especially now, in retrospect, I think it was a huge blunder.

I asked the inevitable question. "Did you see, uh, action?"

Eddie nodded. "Quite a bit."

My voice dropped. "Did you kill anyone?" He swallowed and his eyes darted past me, before he shrugged. "I guess that means you did?"

He nodded. "It drove me a little nuts toward the end."

"I heard . . . my dad told me you'd gone AWOL?"

Eddie told me the whole story. It was summer of '72. His unit was about to be brought back to the US—but he stayed. He had met a Vietnamese girl named Mai and had gone to live with her at her home in the country, some eighty miles from Saigon. He purposely didn't tell anyone where he was going. "I wanted to hide from the world," he said. "It was a crazy thing to do."

"So what happened?"

"I was thinking of marrying her and bringing her back to the US. We were together about a year, and then I guess I came to my senses. It was a real mess over there, and we didn't do much to clean it up. If you ask me, it was hell on earth. Finally, I just got out and came home. Dishonorable discharge, but what the hell."

After a pause, I asked, "What was she like?"

He shrugged. "Small. Friendly. Cute. I met her in a bar in Saigon. She couldn't speak English at all; she knew just a few essential words in order to communicate with GIs. It never would have worked, though. Things were different between us once we were living with her family."

"How so?"

"I don't know. Let's change the subject, okay?"

"Sure."

Upon his return in the fall of '73, Eddie had started working for his father's drilling company. He hated it but there weren't many opportunities for young GIs home from the war. He still had to get his GED.

There was definitely a harder edge to Eddie. When we had been close in the sixties, he boasted a rather sarcastic sense of humor and a cynical personality. Now I could feel that this aspect of his demeanor was even more pronounced. The thing was, I agreed with him. I empathized with him and completely understood why he was being so derisive. I hadn't noticed at the time, but afterward I realized he downed his whiskey pretty quickly and ordered another one before I was half-done with my drink. He was definitely self-medicating. There was a lot of pain inside him, and, God help me, I felt for him. I wanted to help somehow.

He then rolled his eyes and added, "And then Dad went and fell off an oil well."

"Gosh, tell me about that. What happened?"

"It was a couple of months after I had come home and started working for Dad. I was with him at a drilling site. There was something wrong on the crown block—that's the very top of a derrick, a little platform where you can stand and work with the block and tackle. Anyway, we were up there, and he lost his footing somehow. Splat. Broke his neck. He was dead on the spot."

"That's terrible."

"No, it isn't. You remember my father, don't you?" I nodded. "He was a bastard. He was a no-good son of a bitch, pardon my language. Even when I was in high school, the guy beat on me and my mom. That's one reason why I worked on my body while I was in the army. After I came back, he didn't mess with me. I wasn't sorry at all about my dad falling off that oil well. Good riddance, if you ask me."

I didn't know how to respond to that.

"Since then, I've just been living with my mom in the same house across from yours. I quit my dad's business and started drawing comics. I'm, uh, I'm a little better than I was back in elementary school."

"I believe it."

"I'd really like to show you some of my work."

"Do you make any money from it?"

"A little. I sent some stuff to a handful of comic publishers but I haven't heard anything back. On the other hand, I've sold some pieces at a flea market I go to. Right when I got back from Vietnam, I was in California for a couple of weeks. I went to a convention for people who buy and collect comics. It was on Harbor Island, near San Diego. I sold some stuff there and talked to a lot of publishers." He laughed. "You'll get a kick out of the comic book I created. It's called *Devil Man*, and it's about a demon with superpowers who comes to earth and causes all kinds of hell. He's a bad guy that you love to hate. I've got three issues drawn already."

The description made me laugh, too. "You always used to draw creepy things like monsters and bugs!"

I'm pretty sure there were refills on the drinks by then.

"How are you supporting yourself and your mother if you don't have a job?" I asked.

"Oh, Dad had some pretty good insurance. We're okay. The house is paid for."

We continued to talk through the night. He asked about Chicago, since he'd never been there. I was dying to know more about Vietnam, but he seemed to want to avoid that subject, except for the few stories he told me about some of the friends he had made over there.

Then, after a few moments of silence, he said, "You know, Shelby, you had a pretty good high school experience. I could see that you did."

"Thanks. I'm sorry you didn't."

"Didn't junior high suck?"

I laughed. "It did." Then I remembered. "Hey, where were you that one year you were gone? You went away that . . . that summer."

"Oh. Yeah. I, uh, went to live with some relatives in Wichita Falls. My parents thought it would be good for me."

I wondered, *why?* Then I recalled what had occurred prior to his leaving. Michael had been abducted, and Eddie had been extensively interrogated by the police. "Eddie. We never got to talk after what happened. I mean, really talk."

"I know."

"That was a painful time. For all of us."

"It was. That goddamned Mr. Alpine."

"I tried to tell them you had nothing to do with it. My mother . . . she wasn't right in the head. She still isn't."

"I understand that now. It's all right. I lived through it."

"Were the police rough on you?"

Eddie shrugged. "I don't remember too much about it. I was real scared, I know that. I was pretty traumatized by the ordeal. There was a good cop/bad cop thing going on. The bad cop was a real asshole. He scared the shit out of me. And my fucking dad made it even worse. He acted like I brought all that trouble onto the family even though I didn't do anything. He *blamed* me, just because I was . . . me. That's the reason I went away. I did sixth grade in Wichita Falls. It was pretty awful. But maybe it was better than being at home with my dad during that time period. Anyway, at least Mr. Alpine got what he deserved."

"We never found out what happened to Michael's body. Mr. Alpine died without revealing his secrets."

"I know. The coward shouldn't have hanged himself. He got what he deserved—death—but it should have been by the book. There should have been a trial. You're right."

I sighed. "I still don't understand it. It doesn't make sense."

Then Eddie looked at me with those intense brown eyes. I swear, they were mesmerizing, as if he could look deep into your very soul. He said, "Evil lives where you least expect it," and I got chills. Just the way he spoke the words sent a shiver down my spine.

We continued to talk, and time passed. We even danced, I think, one dance. Eventually I said I needed to get back to my folks. We mutually ended what turned out to be a meaningful and enjoyable catching up. He asked for the phone number at my house and wondered if I'd like to get together again with him while I was home for the holidays.

I said yes.

11

My mother was absolutely horrified that I had a date with Eddie Newcott. She went on and on about how the neighbors across the street were "strange" and "snooty"—as she always had. When I asked what she meant, Mom said that they always gave her dirty looks. Did she consider that perhaps the Newcotts held it against her that Eddie had been roughly interrogated by the police for an entire day in 1966? I didn't say that, though.

Yes, the Newcotts had been strange from the beginning. Charles Newcott was a cruel, alcoholic, wife-and-son-beating bastard. I agreed with Eddie on that one—good riddance. As for Eddie's mother, I believe she had been so abused by her husband that she had become a mere shell of a woman. According to Eddie, she was an alcoholic, too, and I imagine she suffered from depression, just like my own mother. In many ways, both our mothers were similarly damaged.

All my father had to say about my date was that he hoped I knew what I was doing and that we should have a nice time.

Eddie and I got together on December 23 to go to a movie— *Network*, that film about a fictional television network starring Faye Dunaway and Peter Finch. For the rest of the evening, Eddie and I kept laughing and reciting the famous quote, "I'm mad as hell and I'm not going to take it anymore." It was a good show. Afterward we went back to the Oil Derrick, which was hopping as usual. We sat at the same table we were at the other night. Lord, I don't remember what we talked about, but we were there until midnight. Eddie opened up to me. He spoke about how his father had hurt him and his mother ever since he was a toddler. It was shocking. In the mid-seventies, domestic abuse was rarely talked about in the media. It was one of America's ugly, dark secrets. Women didn't want to press charges for fear of losing their livelihood in the form of a working husband. Kids were just plain scared to tell on their parents. At least in the past forty years, the public has become somewhat more aware of the problem, and measures are now in place to combat it, although there could be a lot of improvement in that regard.

At some point, the conversation drifted to the memories of our childhoods on Chicory Lane. We talked about hunting horny toads in the vacant lots and riding our bikes downtown to the library. The names of some of the neighborhood kids— Dean and Greg and Sally and others—came up, and Eddie filled me in on what he knew about them. It wasn't much. None of them lived on the block any more. Both Dean and Greg still lived in Limite—Dean was married. He didn't know what happened to Sally.

We were both a little intoxicated by the time we got in his car—a beat-up Chevy Nova. Eddie said he still had a motorcycle and usually preferred using it, but for the date he borrowed his mother's car. We made it safely to Chicory Lane and he parked in his driveway.

"You want to see my artwork?" he asked.

I thought, *Sure, why not?* It wasn't as if I had far to go to get home. I said okay, and he led me into the house. I hadn't been in there since '66, but it still looked the way I remembered it. Betty Newcott wasn't the greatest housekeeper. The furniture was old and run-down. There was clutter everywhere, mostly stacks of newspapers and magazines. A light had been left on for him in the living room.

He held a finger to his lips and said, "Mom's asleep. Let's go out back."

"Out back?"

"Yeah, my studio's in the bomb shelter!"

The bomb shelter. "Really?"

"Yeah, you remember the bomb shelter, don't you? Come see what I've done to it."

If I hadn't had three screwdrivers, I might have made an excuse and said I'd come back during daylight hours. But I felt giddy and reckless. I followed him through the back door and into their yard. The shelter door looked the same as I recollected, except there was now a big padlock on the handle. Eddie pulled a key chain out of his pocket, found the right key, and opened the door. He went in first, turned on the lights, and called for me to descend into the ground.

It was a very different space. Eddie had decorated the walls with his art, which was the first thing that struck me as I gazed at the room. Most of it consisted of black-and-white sketches, but there were several full-color paintings. A drafting table and chair stood in front of the partition that separated the living quarters from the bathroom. A work-in-progress sat on the table, depicting a devil crucified on a cross. A *devil* crucified on a cross. It was very disturbing.

In fact, *all* of the artwork was creepy and scary. It was the stuff of nightmares—demons, monsters, near-naked women, scenes of pain and suffering, and abstract collages that were violently powerful. I would have been completely turned off had it not been for the fact that the work was so good. Eddie's style and technique was original and highly accomplished. I knew a little about art from my years at UT—drama majors were required to take an Art Appreciation course, and I personally enjoyed visiting the Art Institute in Chicago where I saw famous paintings I'd only seen before in books.

"My God, Eddie, these are—wow," I said. "I mean, it's pretty creepy stuff, but you're so *good*."

"Thanks."

"You were always into drawing this kind of stuff, weren't you?"

"You know I was."

I stepped closer to a color painting that portrayed demons throwing babies into a pit of fire—with pitchforks, no less. Despite the sickening subject matter, the detail was so intricate and well-executed that I was amazed.

"You are one sick bastard," I said,

That made him laugh. "Yeah, I am. Blame it all on my childhood. I let out all my pain and suffering through my work. Just like van Gogh."

"Vincent van Gogh didn't paint monsters throwing children into hell."

"Yeah, but I bet he felt like doing so at times. He's the guy who cut off his ear and gave it to his girlfriend, you know. He was mad as hell and couldn't take it anymore!"

The rest of the shelter was decked out as living quarters. The three cots were gone, but a double bed occupied one side of the space, along with a night table and lava lamp. A television sat on a small table on the opposite side of the room, with a record player and sound system next to it. There were maybe a hundred albums and cassettes on a shelf.

"You *live* down here?"

"Not all the time. I still have my bedroom in the house. But I think I sleep here more often. I'm usually up late working, so I just crash here." He showed me that he had installed a refrigerator and a heating/AC unit. I also noticed a roach clip and the butts of a few marijuana joints in an ashtray next to the lava lamp. He noticed me looking, so he turned it on.

"It takes a while to get going," he explained. Then he put on a record. "You like Pink Floyd?"

"I guess so."

"You *guess* so? What's wrong with you?"

"I like them all right. They're not my favorite."

"Who is?"

"I don't know. I like David Bowie. Linda Ronstadt."

He furrowed his brow. "Those two don't go together."

"So what?"

He just laughed. I continued to examine his artwork. "Don't the paint fumes get to you down here?"

"Nah, it's well ventilated. And I have a fan." He opened the fridge. "Want a beer?"

"No, thanks, I've had enough for one night." He pulled out a can for himself and popped it open.

"Hey," I said, "wasn't there a secret hiding place in the floor?"

"You remember that, huh?"

"Behind the toilet. What did you call it?"

"Davy Jones's Locker."

"Right. I sure have a lot of memories of this place."

He looked at me. His stare was intense. "Yeah, me too."

Did he remember everything we had done in here? Probably. If I did, then he did. I wasn't about to bring it up, though.

"Hey, do you smoke pot?" he asked.

I laughed. "Uh, I *have*."

Eddie immediately went to a drawer in a filing cabinet and pulled out a baggie full of the stuff. "Let's get high, then."

"Mm, not tonight, thanks. I'd really better get back across the street."

"Why? Aren't you old enough that your parents don't wait up for you?" He had already started rolling the joint.

"Well, sure, I just . . . I don't know . . ." Maybe I was feeling some of the claustrophobia I recalled feeling from those days in the sixties when we were in the shelter. But the music, the lava lamp, and my insane attraction for Eddie changed my mind.

He lit the joint, took a hit, and handed it to me. I don't know why I did it, but I grasped the thing between my fingers and inhaled. Looking back, I realized I was a bit bowled over by Eddie's good looks and charisma. He had a way of seducing you with those dark eyes of his. I've read a lot about Rasputin and the hold he had over Alexandra, the last tsar's wife in Russia. Lots of men throughout history were purported to have the ability to mesmerize women. I believe Eddie had that power.

All I recall about the rest of the night was that we ended up in that double bed, basking in the glow of the lava lamp. Whether it was because of the drugs, the alcohol, or the excitement of being in a forbidden place—one that, in my memories, was the site of many erotic experiences—I had one of the best sexual experiences of my life. My God, Eddie knew what he was doing. He took me to plateaus and peaks I never knew existed. His body was muscular and hard and strong. I felt myself surrender to him without compunction. He was sweet, too, inquiring first about contraception—whether or not he should wear a condom. I told him no, I was on the pill, and he seemed very happy about that. We must have made love three or four times that night, and it was incredibly intense. I do recollect closing my eyes so I couldn't see all that demonic art around us; however, there was also something otherworldly about being in the shelter with this beautiful man. It made the encounter that much more electrifying.

Afterward, we fell asleep and didn't wake until morning. I caught hell from my parents when I finally did the walk of shame back across the street.

12

I'm getting close to Livingston, and I suddenly feel tired. It's still early afternoon—I think I could use a cup of coffee—so I pull off at the next exit, where, lucky me, there's a Starbucks. I go inside and find the place full of women, some with kids. Prison families. Have to be. The wives need a little pick-me-up before a visit to Polunsky. Are any of them there to see death row inmates? The odds are low; the entire facility is huge and houses nearly three thousand inmates, out of which only two or three hundred are on death row. Many of the women most likely have husbands or fathers in the general population.

That's a world I can't imagine.

Armed with caffeine, I return to my rental car and continue the journey. My thoughts go back to that morning after I'd first slept with Eddie. Both of my parents were upset, but it was my mother who really gave me hell. I think my dad went along with her because *she* was so upset. "How could you have done that with *him*?" she bellowed, as if Eddie was a convicted felon. Well, at least he wasn't a felon *then*.

I told her I was an adult, and we got into a fight. Looking back, I realize I was only twenty-two, and I certainly didn't know *everything* like we all think we do at that age. And I had just disrespected my parents by coming home for the Christmas holidays and spending the night with the boy across the street. Had I used my best judgment in sleeping with Eddie? Who knows; probably not. However, at the time, I was truly dazzled by him. He hadn't even been trying to seduce me, really—it just happened. And we both wanted it. We were young and stupid. Not as young as when we fooled around in his bomb shelter in the sixties, but still, we were in our very early twenties, a time of life when one's sensory receptors are wide open, ready to experience new feelings and emotions. We were rookies at being adults.

Maybe I was rebelling a little against my mother, too. While I understood perfectly why she was depressed and irritable all the time, I believed she could do something about it. Now I know that's not necessarily true. If only she hadn't become hooked on tranquilizers, she might have overcome her grief over losing Michael. Instead she misused the prescriptions, and the doctors were happy to keep writing them. The words *mental illness* were not ones that we often used back then. And I'm sorry to say I resented it at the time. Living with her was very difficult and unpleasant. I always felt she held Michael's abduction against me because I left the front door unlocked. She never once said, "I forgive you." When I was in therapy in the eighties, my doctor said I probably should have *asked* her for forgiveness, but I never did. I'll have to live with that one, too.

At any rate, what happened, happened.

For the rest of Christmas break, I made it worse—Eddie and I embroiled ourselves in a torrid affair. We had only two weeks left in January to be together, after which I would have to go back to Evanston. So we made it count. Boy, did we.

Mother was mortified, and Dad was at a loss. Even Eddie's mother questioned her son about it. We weren't subtle at all.

I'd go across the street, and we'd practically live in the bomb shelter almost every one of those fourteen days. Sometimes I'd spend the night. I tried to be with my parents at mealtimes and for a little while in the evenings before they went to bed. Then it was over to Eddie's for hedonistic indulgence. We drank wine together, we smoked pot together, we made love together. The stereo blasted Eddie's eclectic taste in music the whole while. I remember there was a lot of Pink Floyd and harder stuff like Black Sabbath. The two weeks were a binge of sex, drugs, and rock and roll—no question about it. And I wasn't ashamed, either.

Probably because I was in love, or I thought I was.

Whatever magic Eddie possessed, he put a spell on me that December and January of 1976–77. I truly was in another world, lost in a whirlpool of sensual delights. In many ways, it was my first experience of real passion. Much of it is a blur now. When the time finally came for me to return to Illinois, I was heartbroken. I went over to say goodbye—I'd spent the previous night in my old bedroom—and we made love one more time before I left for the airport. We promised to call and write, and I assured him I would return to visit sooner than usual. He vowed to come to Chicago.

I won't ever forget the heartache I felt for the first few weeks of the spring semester. It was pretty bad. Eddie and I talked a lot on the phone. I lived alone in an apartment, so there were no problems dealing with put-out roommates. He rarely wrote to me though, maybe only two times, his words written in the same printed block letters he always used. I asked him over the phone why he didn't write me more often, and he replied that he was more expressive with his art, so if I preferred he could draw something for me and send it.

Somewhere tucked away in an envelope in one of the filing cabinets in my office are seven original sketches—one in color—by Eddie Newcott. That includes the early one from the sixties depicting a prince fighting a dragon, in which Eddie wanted to be my "night." I've been told I could sell them for a lot of money. There are sickos out there who would pay for them—collectors of Charles Manson and John Wayne Gacy memorabilia and the like. Eddie, with the media's "Evil Eddie" persona attached to him, had already attracted the yellow journalists and ephemera seekers. He had received two proposals of marriage since being sentenced to die. No doubt I could sell those drawings and do very well. But I won't. Not yet, anyway.

At any rate, he never came to Chicago, but I went home for spring break the last week of March, 1977. Eddie and I had been anticipating our reunion for nearly three months by speaking on the phone every other evening and cooing like fools in each other's ears. It's a wonder I did all right in school. My mind was floating most of the time, but I managed to pull off A's and B's. Diving into my classes helped to keep me from obsessing about Eddie *every* waking minute!

Dad picked me up at the airport, as usual. During the ride home, he asked if I would be seeing Eddie.

"Of course," I replied.

"Well, for your mother's sake, I hope you'll spend some time at home with us."

"I will! I wouldn't abandon you guys."

But of course I did. I was terrible to my parents. I had only a week away from school, and I spent more of my time with Eddie than with them. We didn't stay in the bomb shelter as much as the last time, though, and instead went out on the town, as it were, at night. Once, he took me to dinner and a movie. We ate at the Red Shack, a nice steak restaurant that Limite was always known for. It was a lovely evening, although Eddie insisted that we move to a different table when a family with children sat near us. A child in a high chair started crying, and Eddie tensed up.

"What's the matter?"

"I don't like babies," he said.

I think I muttered that I didn't care for it when they made a scene in public either, but then I remembered how, back when we were kids, Eddie couldn't take it when baby Michael cried. He must have carried that dread with him into adulthood.

After dinner, we went to see *Rocky*, which had won the Oscar that very week and was playing in town. I had already seen it, but Eddie hadn't. We went to a Denny's afterward for some comfort food and—big mistake—coffee. The two of us ended up in the bomb shelter, staying up all night. However, already when we were at Denny's, I noticed that Eddie was his less talkative self. He seemed darker and withdrawn.

"What's wrong?" I asked.

He looked at me as if I had no reason to inquire. "Nothing's wrong."

"You liked the movie?"

"Oh, it's not that. I mean, the boxing was cool. Yeah, I liked it. I was just thinking"—he laughed a little—"about my dad, of all people."

"Why?"

"He *loved* boxing. He practiced on me and my mom every day."

His statement jolted me out of my mood at the moment. Eddie noticed my reaction and said, "Sorry. That was a joke."

"Eddie, geez . . ."

"Except, what the hell, it's pretty true. Maybe not *every* day, but it happened a lot."

"I'm sorry, Eddie." I was, but I didn't want to talk about it back then. That element of Eddie's life bothered me. There *was* a dark side to Eddie, and I could sense that it sometimes wanted to reveal itself when he was with me. I believe he purposefully fought to hold it in check. But every once in a while,

Eddie would say something truly off the wall, a non sequitur that had to do with God or Satan or his awful father or his sick mother. And his *artwork*—that was what really gave it away. His work had become even more disturbing and strange, though still oddly beautiful. It seemed he enjoyed playing the role of the "tortured artist." And I'm afraid that's what attracted me to him. Indeed, the bad boy thing appealed to me—something rough around the edges that I simply found exciting.

We went to the Oil Derrick a couple of other nights. I remember asking Eddie how come I never saw anyone I knew from high school there. He explained that it was because they had all gotten married and that they had no need to go to a singles bar anymore. At least, that was what usually happened to the kids who stayed in Limite. Only some, like me, had left and gone to college. Eddie said we were the "smart ones."

"So why don't you leave, Eddie?" I asked him. "Why do you stay? You could go to a bigger city where you might have better opportunities to sell your artwork."

He was silent for a while as he thought about how to respond. Then he answered, "As strange as it sounds, Shelby, I'm uncomfortable when I'm out of town. I can't stand Limite, but I don't like it when I'm not here, either. There's something about this place, that street where we live, that house, the bomb shelter . . . it's my world. Besides, my mother needs me."

"Does she?"

"Sure. After all she suffered being married to Charles Newcott? Are you kidding? She became a doormat, and now I have to take care of her."

Suddenly, I had a bird's-eye view of us, sitting there in the nightclub, in love and oblivious to the disaster that our relationship would become. "Eddie, I'm never going to come back to Limite to live."

He wrinkled his brow. "I don't expect you to."

"Then what are we doing?"

"What do you mean?"

"You and me. If you're never going to leave Limite, and I don't want to come back here, are we wasting our time with each other?"

Eddie flinched a little. "Do you think we're wasting our time?"

"No, I'm just saying, I mean, I wonder—do we have a future together? Do we *want* a future together?"

He took both of my hands in his and looked at me. "I would kill for you, Shelby," he said, with those intense brown eyes drilling through me.

"Jesus, Eddie, I don't want you to do that." I tried to laugh it off. "Seriously, Eddie, does that mean you'd leave for me?"

"Of course it does. I'd do anything for you. It's the same as when we were twelve and eleven. Everything I did then was for you."

"Don't be silly."

"It was. Whatever I did back then, it was for you. You were everything to me. You still are. More."

I don't remember how the evening ended; I think we must have danced. Maybe that night I went home to sleep in my own bed for a change.

The thing was, it seemed to me that I had truly left Limite behind, and aside from my parents and Eddie, I had no real ties there anymore. Already, I felt as if I had progressed from a small-town hick girl to a more urban and sophisticated young woman. I had grown more cultured and, dare I say, snooty. Limite was yesterday's news in my life, and I was a fish out of water there. Home was now Evanston, Illinois, though at the time I couldn't have imagined that I would end up staying in Chicago for the rest of my life. All I knew was that I didn't belong in Texas anymore.

For the rest of the spring semester, Eddie and I continued our long-distance relationship through phone calls, letters from me, and sketches from him. I know I received more drawings than what I still own. Perhaps I only kept the really good ones, though I don't recall ever throwing them out. Even though I stayed in Illinois, I've moved four times since those years in grad school. Stuff gets weeded out with every move.

As soon as school was out in May, I skedaddled back to Limite to see my parents. And Eddie, of course. In fact, I planned to stay in Limite the entire summer, or maybe talk Eddie into coming up to Illinois with me. Whatever happened, I wanted to be with him for those three months, not doing anything else.

It didn't turn out that way.

13

I check in to the Best Western and find myself in a comfortable no-frills room on the second floor. The only nonsmoking room available has two queen beds in it. Fine—I throw my suitcase on one and plan to use the other for myself. It's nearly dinnertime, but before going out to explore the "metropolis" that is Livingston to find a place to eat, I phone Eddie's lawyer. He had told me to call him when I arrived. Mr. Crane is in town all week long from Limite and staying at a different hotel.

"I'm here," I say when he answers.

"Welcome to Texas. How was the flight?"

"Fine. No problems. Rented a car and drove to Livingston. I'm in the Best Western."

"Good choice."

I tell him I'll soon be off to dinner, and he recommends a few joints, none of which sound very appealing. Tex-Mex is something I can't get in Chicago, though, so there is that. He apologizes—he has an appointment with a client's family and can't have dinner with me, but I hadn't expected to eat with him so I tell him it's all right.

"So, everything is arranged. You're on the visitor list, the warden's approved, and you're set to go," he says.

"And what's the plan?"

"I will meet you there in the registration area just inside the main entrance at ten o'clock. You remember the dress code I told you about?"

"Don't wear white because that's the color of the inmates' clothing. Don't wear anything that shows cleavage. No shorts, no short skirts—I wouldn't dare these days—no hats, no sandals or shoes that show my toes, and no T-shirts with slogans protesting the death penalty."

"Right."

"I plan to wear a pantsuit. It's blue."

"Bring plenty of change, if you have it; otherwise they have bill-changing machines in the reception area. You can't take bills in to see Eddie. Not that you'd be able to hand any to him through the glass."

"So why have change?"

"For the vending machines inside. It's good protocol to buy something for the inmate—a drink or package of snacks or whatever. Just remember that you can't touch the product that comes out of the machine. An officer handles it and delivers it to the inmate, so you can both sit there and have a nosh while you talk. If you want."

"Will Eddie expect it?"

"I always get him a Snickers. He likes that."

"All right."

"Bring your ID, and you should probably have your plane ticket with you to prove you traveled over 250 miles. It's already in the notes for your visit, but just in case."

Whew. The rules are overwhelming. What do they think? A sixty-one-year-old woman is going to stage a breakout?

Crane tells me to allow thirty minutes to drive to the prison from my hotel, go through the front gate, park, and enter the main building.

"Okay. I'll see you there."

He must detect the anxiety in my voice because he asks, "Are you all right, Shelby?"

With a sigh, I answer, "Sure. It's going to be harder than I originally thought. I'm afraid it'll be depressing."

"Well, I'm sorry, but it will be. I imagine you'll feel pretty wretched when you leave. Polunsky does that to people. It's a very depressing place. It's hell on earth. That's just the way it is. It's a prison. Prisons aren't nice."

"Gotcha. I'll put on my heart-guard and wear blinders."

He chuckles. "You'll be okay. People visit death row every day. It can be emotional, for sure, but no one's ever committed suicide in the visitation room."

I think that's an insensitive statement to make, but I don't mention it.

After hanging up, I leave the room and ask the young Hispanic woman at the front desk how to get to La Colonia, the Mexican restaurant I want to try. It isn't far, a ten-minute drive. The place looks pretty low-rent, but it's authentic. I order a fajita plate with rice, charro beans, *pico de gallo*, and guacamole with flour tortillas. And it's darned good. I just hope it won't upset my stomach; my insides are already topsy-turvy to begin with. However, the two margaritas help calm my nerves. Over dinner, my thoughts return to that summer of 1977, when my long-distance relationship with Eddie came to an abrupt end. The alcohol serves as a travel guide of sorts into my memories.

When I came home to Limite that May, the first thing I noticed was that my mother looked terrible. Maybe I hadn't paid much attention the last time I was there, but it seemed as if she had aged ten years since I'd last seen her. She'd lost weight. Dark circles surrounded her eyes. When I hugged her, it felt as if I could easily crush her fragile frame with little effort. Dad looked pretty much the same, although it was obvious he was having a difficult time dealing with her. He took me aside and told me the news.

"She doesn't do much anymore," he said. "She stays home, won't go out, and doesn't see her friends. I'm worried about her."

"What does the doctor say?"

"That she's depressed. She takes these . . . pills. Frankly, I think they do her more harm than good. They make her like a zombie most days."

At the time, I simply trusted that her doctor knew what he was doing; I didn't bother looking into what drugs she was taking. I would later find out that she was on a cocktail of Elavil, a tricyclic antidepressant, and Valium, a benzodiazepine, otherwise known as a tranquilizer. No wonder she got hooked and fell into a whirlpool of mental illness.

This time, I was determined to spend more time with her while I was home, but I also wanted to see Eddie as soon as possible. I phoned his house, spoke to his mother, and learned that he wasn't home at the moment. She'd tell him that I called.

I spent a couple of hours with my parents over dinner. It was difficult to have a decent conversation with my mother; she didn't have a whole lot to say. She had managed to cook a nice meal—with my help. Dad and I did most of the talking. At any rate, Eddie called around nine p.m. and I went across the street. Opening the gate at the side of his house, I crossed the yard to the bomb shelter door and knocked. There was no answer, so I opened it myself.

"Eddie?"

"Down here!"

The whiff of marijuana smoke hit me in the face. I remember disapproving. I hadn't really indulged at school for the past few months. The partying of my first semester at grad school had tapered down during the second half. Courses had been more difficult, and my mind was on Eddie, among other things. I wasn't prepared to get blitzed with him again. Nevertheless, I went down the steps into the dimly lit, compressed space. The lava lamp was going strong, the smoke filled the room like a blanket, and the television was on. After coughing a bit, I said, "Geez, Eddie, how can you breathe in here?"

"It's ventilated, just like always." He embraced me, and we held each other for a moment. I guess I'd never really noticed how smoky the shelter got whenever we partook before. My eyes burned and I coughed some more as he tried to kiss me. His hands were all over me. I pushed him away, perhaps a little too roughly.

"What's wrong?" he asked.

"It's too smoky in here, Eddie. Can we go outside? It's nice out. Let's take a walk around the block, or go to the park."

He shrugged. "Okay." He turned off the TV and we left the shelter. The sun had just set, and the moon was bright and the stars were out. "The cops don't like people in the park after dark," he said.

"When did that start?"

"I don't know. I think it's always been that way."

"When we were kids we were in the park at night."

"I know. That was a long time ago."

We walked toward the park anyway. At one point, he stopped, put his arms around me, and gave me a long, sensual kiss. "Happy birthday," he said. "You're a year older than me again."

"Thanks."

"There's a present waiting for you back at the bomb shelter. And it's not another drawing."

I laughed. "That doesn't matter, I'm just happy to see you again."

He held my hand and asked how I was doing. I told him that my mother wasn't well, and he explained that his mother wasn't doing great either. She was drinking more than usual. "How come both our mothers are in bad shape?" I asked. "Isn't that strange?"

"I don't know. My father did it to my mother. What's your mom's prob—oh. I remember."

"She was never the same after Michael's abduction."

"Yeah. Sorry about that."

"It's not *your* fault."

"No. Fucking Mr. Alpine."

"Let's not talk about that, all right?"

"Sure."

We reached the park and sat in the swings under the moonlight. Something felt different, but I couldn't put my finger on it. For one thing, Eddie was stoned and I wasn't. There was that.

"Too bad the yacht is gone," he said. "We could've hid in there and done it."

The thought of making love in that old yacht wasn't appealing. "Eddie. Is that all you're thinking about?"

"Well, hell, Shelby, I haven't seen you in a couple of months. What's going on? Don't you want to?"

"Sure, but . . . I don't know, I didn't want to jump into bed as soon as I saw you." Maybe I said it a little too sternly. He made a grunting noise and became quiet. I could tell he was sinking into a mood. "I'm sorry," I said. "I think I'm upset about my mother. And I don't really want to get stoned right now. Maybe I'm disappointed that you were high when I came over."

"I'll tell you something, Shelby. I'm high a lot. It's the only way I can cope."

"Cope? Cope with what?"

"My mother. My art. My life."

"What are you talking about? You don't have it so bad."

He gave a little laugh. "Try making a living selling comics. *Devil Man* does okay, for an independent comic book. Did I tell you I got a distributor?"

"No. Really?"

"Yeah, it's sold nationwide now in comic stores. That is, it's sold in the stores that actually stock it. Not many do, 'cause I'm not with Marvel or DC. *They* weren't interested in my work. They want to own everything they publish." Back in the seventies, independent comics were rare. It wasn't like it is now, with plenty of graphic novel and comics publishers to choose from.

"At least it's published," I said. "Hey, you're talented. You'll get more work as an artist."

"Hasn't happened yet."

"Eddie, you're in *Limite*. You need to get out of here. Go to a big city. Go to LA or New York."

"I don't like big cities."

"Well, you're not going to get work *here*."

"I know, I know."

We went on like this, until our conversation turned into an argument. He finally got frustrated, bolted out of the swing, and started walking back to our neighborhood.

"Eddie, stop! Where are you going?"

"How about I see you tomorrow, Shelby?" he called without looking back at me. I ran after him, caught up, and grabbed his arm. He jerked it away from me. "Go home to your crazy mother, Shelby."

"Eddie!"

He moved on. I stood there, stunned that he would say such a thing.

Something was definitely wrong.

14

The next day I tried calling Eddie, but his mother said she hadn't seen him. "Is he in the bomb shelter?" I asked. He wasn't— she had just gone outside to check after making breakfast. His motorcycle was gone. She had no idea where he was.

Fine. If he was going to be that way, there was nothing I could do about it. I went about my business at home. Dad was at work, so I stayed at the house with Mom. She remained in bed all morning and didn't come out of the bedroom. The cabin fever got to me after a while, so I decided to walk across the street to check out the shelter for myself. Maybe Eddie had left a note or some other clue as to where he was. When I arrived, I saw that the padlock was missing. Eddie usually brought it with him into the shelter, so I opened the steel door and went downstairs. The padlock lay in its spot beneath the stairs. The lights were on and the lava lamp was still bubbling. The smoke had cleared but the room still reeked of pot. Eddie's bed was unmade and the place was a mess. His artwork, spread over his drafting table, was covered in a large black ink splotch, as if he had spilled the bottle over it. An accident, or had it been done on purpose?

I'd always known Eddie was troubled. Growing up with a father who had beat him must have screwed him up in a major way. His fascination with demonic imagery and violence wasn't what you'd call normal. If I'd known then what I knew now, I might have run the other way and never become involved in a relationship with him. But at the time, at the age of twenty-two, I was still in something of a rebellious stage of my life, experimenting with the stimuli that made me tick. In other words, I was discovering myself. I wanted to be open to darker elements in the world. After all, I had grown up in a fairly sheltered environment in a small town. My eyes were first opened in Austin during undergraduate school, and even further in Chicagoland.

There was no question that Eddie had a powerful sexual hold on me. He was so damned attractive, so charismatic, and he did things to me in bed that no one else had ever managed to do before or since. That's the truth. A lot of my romance novels deal with heroines who fall for the bad boy, and all that comes from my experience with Eddie.

At least during the beginning of that summer, Eddie still occupied my heart, and I wanted to correct whatever had occurred the night before. Maybe my maternal instincts—ha ha—wished to cure him of the darkness that enveloped him. Perhaps I simply wanted him to love me, which I believed he did. Whatever the motivation was, I was determined to keep the relationship alive.

I made Eddie's bed and started to straighten up the room. I picked up his dirty clothes, which were piled in a corner, and put them in the laundry hamper he kept near the stairs. The toilet behind the partition was pretty disgusting, so what did I do?—I cleaned it. Call me crazy. That's when I noticed the concrete slab in the floor—Davy Jones's Locker—that had been Eddie's secret hiding place. I wondered if he still kept treasures in there, and I considered if I should try lifting the lid to see.

"What are you doing?"

His voice startled me, and I yelped. "Jesus, Eddie! You scared the shit out of me!"

He stood behind me and laughed. "Sorry. What are you doing?"

"I just cleaned your filthy toilet! It was gross, Eddie. What if I needed to use it? I wasn't about to sit on that thing." I got up off my knees and moved past him around the partition. "So, have you noticed what I did? How do you like the way your room looks?"

He looked around and nodded with approval. "Very nice. I think I'll keep you."

"You didn't act like it last night."

"I'm sorry. I was drunk. I was stoned. I wasn't in a good frame of mind."

"Why?"

"I don't know. I get that way a lot these days. Come sit down, I have a birthday present for you." He took my hand and led me to the bed, asking me to sit. He went to a bookshelf and retrieved a small box that was wrapped in blue paper and a ribbon; I hadn't noticed it before.

"Geez, what's this?"

"Open it and find out."

I was surprised to find a pair of beautiful black pearl earrings in gold-plated settings. "Oh, Eddie, I love them!" I took them to the only mirror in the shelter and put them on. "Wow, they're gorgeous. Thank you!"

"You're welcome." He put his arms around me and kissed me. The previous night felt like it had never happened. Things were as they were. He checked again and asked if I was still on the pill. I told him I was. We fell into bed and spent the rest of the day there in decadent, blissful ecstasy. Looking back, I find it ironic how I didn't know at the time that I would never have children. That nightmare would come later.

The memories are hazy, of course, but I'm sure at least a couple of weeks went by in this fashion. Things were pretty good between Eddie and me, as I recall, although he was drinking and getting stoned a lot more than before. I indulged only a handful of times during this period; I found I actually appreciated reality over the haze of euphoria. Eddie was very persuasive, though. It was very easy to follow his lead, do what he wanted, and go with the flow. I figured the summer would be a rather selfish and lackadaisical break from graduate school—I would do nothing but enjoy myself and wallow in the pleasures of the flesh.

By the middle of June, things started to turn sour. I'm not sure exactly what happened. Eddie stopped making me laugh. He grew morose and moody, retreating into the dark recesses of himself, which he kept secret from me and the rest of the world. When I asked what was bothering him, he answered with the usual, "Nothing," but I could tell otherwise. The demons he drew on paper were haunting him. The ghost of his father? I had no idea. While being with me certainly was the most important thing in his life, he was terribly unhappy. As I grew older, I started to wonder if some people just have a melancholic nature, and they're not happy unless they're *un*happy, if that makes any sense. Now I wonder if it might have been an early sign of the illness that hit him full-on in the eighties.

One night we went to one of the shadier nightclubs that was on the highway leading out of town. It was populated mostly by cowboys, oil field roughnecks, and women I would call less than chaste. An older crowd. I believe Eddie and I were the youngest patrons in the joint. The thing was, a lot of people *knew* Eddie, at least the bartender and some of the women did. There were two older ladies who actually flirted with him in front of me. The men stared at us, particularly at him—Eddie had long hair and was unlike any of them. Eddie ordered beers for us, and we sat at a table near the jukebox that was blasting out a Fleetwood

Mac song from *Rumours*, which was *the* album you heard every-where that summer.

"Do you come here often?" I asked him.

"Sometimes."

"Why? It's not your—it's not *our* kind of place, is it?"

He shrugged. "I don't know. It's seedy and full of white trash. It suits me fine."

"I don't much like it. You know those women?"

"Sure."

"How?"

"Are you jealous?"

"No, but they acted like they know you pretty well."

"We'll leave after we finish our beers, if you like."

"All right."

It wasn't easy to talk with the music pounding next to us, so we sat quietly in the smoke-filled bar and chugged the beers. But just as we were about finished and ready to leave, a man sauntered over to our table. He wore a baseball cap and greasy overalls and appeared to be in his forties or fifties.

"Ain't you Charlie Newcott's kid?" he shouted over the music, looking at Eddie.

"What?" Eddie asked.

"You're Charlie Newcott's kid, ain't you. I recognize you. You were there at the rig when he fell."

Eddie didn't say anything.

"I was there, too," the man said. "I worked with Charlie for twenty years." He said it with a decidedly threatening tone. It made me uncomfortable.

"Congratulations," Eddie said.

"He was a friend of mine."

"Good for you."

The man leaned close so that he was face-to-face with Eddie. I could smell the man's liquor-fueled breath from where I sat. "You know what I think?" the man asked with a snarl.

"You can think?" Eddie spat.

"You punk. I think that was no accident when Charlie fell. You were up there with him at the top of the rig." When Eddie didn't respond, the man kept going. "Charlie would never slip. He was a pro. You killed him, didn't you? You fucking pushed your father off the platform."

Eddie shoved the man away and stood. "Come on, Shelby, let's get out of here," he said, holding out his hand to me. I gladly took it and got up.

But the man wouldn't have it. He actually grabbed Eddie's shirt with a clenched fist. "Admit it, you hippie shit. You murdered your old man. We all know you did."

"Get your goddamned hand off of me."

"All of us that worked there that day, we knew. The cops may have believed your story that he lost his footing, but we know better."

It happened suddenly, and it scared the crap out of me. Eddie had somehow taken hold of his empty beer bottle in one hand and brought it down hard on the man's head. The bottle shattered and the man let go of Eddie's shirt as he stumbled backward, stunned. Time halted for a moment as everyone in the bar focused their attention on us. Eddie stood there with half the broken bottle in his fist, ready to jam it into the man's face if he came closer.

The man shook his head like a wet dog and felt his scalp. Blood was oozing down his forehead. "You little shit!" he shouted as he leaped for Eddie. I screamed. Eddie swung the sharp edge of the bottle across the man's face, slicing it in three distinct red stripes. This time the man screamed and covered his face with his bloody hands.

The man's buddies came forward—four men who looked like they could tear Eddie apart. Eddie stood his ground, holding the jagged-edged bottle. One man bravely rushed Eddie, only to be jabbed in the chest with the weapon. I must have been shouting, "Eddie, stop! Eddie!" I'm pretty sure I heard the bartender yell, "I'm calling the cops!"

"Let's go," Eddie said as he took my arm with his free hand and backed us out of the joint. He never dropped the broken bottle or turned his back on his adversaries. When we were out the door, he shouted, "Run!" and we did. The men burst out the door after us. We got in his mother's car, shut the doors, and locked them. He fumbled for the keys.

"Get out here, you shit!"

"Come out and fight like a man!"

"Eddie, let's go!" I cried.

They reached the car and tried to open the door on the driver's side. A rock hit the windshield and caused a spiderweb crack. I screamed again.

Finally the engine turned over. The tires screeched on the gravel parking lot as Eddie backed out of the space, almost hitting one of the men behind us. They were still shouting as he tore out of the lot and onto the highway.

"*Jesus*, Eddie!" I was near hysterics. I had never in my life been that close to violence. I'm sure tears were streaming down my face.

"It's all right," he said. "We're safe. No one got hurt."

"No one got hurt? Are you crazy? You nearly cut that man's face off!"

"He deserved it."

"What was that he said? He accused you of killing your father!"

"He's an asshole."

"Eddie, what was that all about?"

"*Shut up!*"

The force of his words startled me. I did shut up. But Eddie drove recklessly and broke the speed limit. As soon as we entered the city limits, a police cruiser pulled out of its hiding place. The cop turned on his red-and-blue lights and hit the siren. Eddie cursed, slowed the car, and pulled over. I didn't say a word, but I was thinking, *Serves you right.*

Eddie had been doing eighty miles per hour in a forty-five mph zone. Eddie handed over his driver's license and registration. The cop went back to his car while we sat in silence. Finally, Eddie said, "Sorry, Shelby. I kind of lost it back there."

I just nodded; I was still very upset. I'd also never been in a car that was pulled over by a policeman before. I was pretty scared.

A traffic ticket might have been the end of it, but unfortunately the policeman must have received word about the fight at the bar while he had returned to his cruiser. The man came back to our car with his pistol drawn.

"Step out of the car, please," he ordered. Eddie complied. I got out, too, but the policeman barked, "You stay in the car, miss," so I got back in. The man commanded Eddie to put his hands on the side of the vehicle and to spread his legs. The cop frisked him and then quickly put handcuffs on him. "You're under arrest for assault. Come with me." He roughly pulled Eddie toward the cruiser. I panicked and got out of the car again.

"Wait! What about me?" I called.

The policeman answered, "Stay there. I'll be right back."

"Take the car home, Shelby!" Eddie shouted. "The keys are still in the ignition."

By then, the cop had pushed Eddie into the cruiser's back seat and slammed the door. The policeman returned to me and asked, "Were you a witness to the fight at the bar?"

"Yes, sir."

"Then you may need to make a statement. Your friend hurt two men, one pretty badly. He may lose an eye." He asked for my ID and wrote everything down. "Follow us to the Limite police station, would you, please? We'll ask you some questions there."

The rest of that night is a haze. I remember going to the station and telling my side of the story while Eddie was kept in another room. The man at the bar, whose name I can't recall, was in the hospital. The other guy—the one Eddie jabbed with the sharp edge of the bottle—had been treated for a minor injury and released. Both men were pressing charges. I told it exactly how I saw it—the man had approached Eddie in a threatening manner and essentially accused him of being a murderer. When we tried to leave peacefully, the man grabbed Eddie's shirt with the intention of hurting him. Eddie was only defending himself.

After I gave my statement, they let me go. I drove the New-cott family car back to Chicory Lane and parked it in their drive-way. The house was dark, so I figured Mrs. Newcott was asleep. Nevertheless, I rang the doorbell. Twice, three times. Finally, the door opened and a haggard-looking woman stood behind the screen door. I barely recognized her as Eddie's mom, and I realized I hadn't seen her at all in the few weeks since I'd been back. Like my own mother, she appeared as if she had aged several years.

"Mrs. Newcott, Eddie's in trouble," I said, breathlessly. "He's been arrested."

"What?"

I told her the story, and she simply shook her head. "I'll deal with it in the morning," she muttered, and then she shut the door. Christ! I was flabbergasted. The woman didn't care; or maybe she was just too out of it to give a damn. Whatever—I stood there for a minute attempting to figure out what I should do. In the end, I did nothing. I turned, walked across the street, and entered our home. The place was dead quiet, a single lamp in the living room left on for me. Mom and Dad were asleep. Silently, I made my way to my bedroom, undressed, and climbed into bed.

I'm not sure if I slept or not.

15

Eddie was released on bail the next day. He called when he got home, so I went across the street to see him. He was in the fallout shelter, lying on his bed, staring at the ceiling. Music I wasn't familiar with was blaring—heavy rock and the dark, metal stuff, probably Black Sabbath. Eddie had been listening to a lot of Black Sabbath; he identified with the band's Satanic imagery and themes. It wasn't my cup of tea.

His mother had hired a lawyer and posted a five-thousand-dollar bail to get her son out of jail. "She's not talking to me now," he said.

"Eddie, why did you have to hit the man with a bottle? Couldn't we have just walked out of the bar?"

"You heard what he said," he answered. "Besides, I don't think he would have let us walk out without following us and doing something in the parking lot."

"Do you really go there often?"

"Not that often. There are a few kicker bars just outside the city limits that have a seediness that appeals to me."

"Why?"

"I don't expect you to understand." With that, he lit a joint, inhaled deeply, and handed it to me.

"No, thanks."

"Suit yourself." He continued to take drags.

I didn't know what else to say, and I didn't want to stay. I got up. "Well, I need to help my mom with something today. I'll see you later."

As I returned to our house, thoughts churned in my head. Eddie was not the same person I had fallen in love with. What had changed him in such a short time? It had only been a few months since Christmas.

His lawyer contacted me after a few days, requesting a deposition, so I gave him one. It must have helped, for two weeks later at a preliminary hearing, the case was thrown out. No criminal charges would be filed against Eddie, but that didn't mean the man wouldn't file a civil suit. Luckily for Eddie, it didn't happen. The man must have sucked it up to a few stitches and let it go.

One night, I went over to the bomb shelter with some trepidation. It was very early July, I remember, before the Fourth. The month of June had been a trying one for Eddie and me, and our relationship was strained. I cared about him a great deal, but when we saw each other it felt as if he was pushing me away. He was keeping secrets from me; I could tell. It was the way he acted; I can't explain it. Most women have an innate ability to spot a liar. Not that I thought Eddie was *lying* to me, it's just that there were things he wasn't telling me. That afternoon, I had called and told him I wanted a "serious discussion." He said, "Uh oh." We agreed to meet at the bomb shelter at nine o'clock.

When I opened the squeaky steel door, I was hit with a thousand decibels of what I guess was Black Sabbath. I climbed down the steps into the smoky man cave, beheld the ever-bubbling lava lamp, and found Eddie lying drunk as a skunk on his bed.

"Hiiii, Shelby," he said.

"Oh, Eddie." I was disappointed. "It's stuff like this that made me want to talk to you."

He actually waved me away. "It's okay, Shelby. Go. Leave me. You shouldn't be with a fuckup like me."

"*Eddie.*"

He attempted to sit up, faltered, and managed to do so. I'd never seen him this smashed. There were two half-empty bottles of tequila and Southern Comfort on the little table that we usually ate on. That was a pretty deadly mixture. He had probably had a shot of one, and then a shot of the other. Repeat until blotto.

"You knew I was coming over," I said.

"Oh yeah, I knew. That's why you're seeing me as I really am." He spread his arms. "Take a look, Shelby. This is the real Eddie Newcott. The one that can't be with you, Shelby. I'm bad for you, and you know it."

"Stop it, Eddie, that's not true." It was what I said at the time. I couldn't stand seeing him in such depths of self-hatred. I remember feeling more angry than sorry for him, but it hadn't been my intention that day to break up. Deep down, I knew that Eddie was an incredibly sensitive person. He *was* an open wound. And I was close enough to see the lesions.

And yet he still had secrets that he kept away from me.

"Eddie, what are you hiding? What are you not telling me?" I asked.

He started laughing. *Laughing.* "My God, Shelby, are you kidding me? There's a *ton* of shit I'm not telling you. And that's exactly why you gotta go." He stood with trembling, wobbly legs. "You need to forget me. I'm no good, Shelby, I've already done terrible things, and I will do more. I'm evil inside. I've been made evil by my father and—by my father and what he did to me."

For a second, I thought he was going to finish his sentence differently: ". . . by my father and——." But I don't know what it was. Still, I was skeptical. "What are you talking about, Eddie? What terrible things have you done? What you did out at that bar—you were right, that guy maybe deserved to be taught a lesson—so that's not a terrible thing. So, what? What else are you talking about?"

"I really *did* kill my father!"

"I——" I was struck dumb. There was a stretch of silence before I responded with a simple "What?"

He became very animated and agitated, pacing back and forth unsteadily in the small space. I had to move back against the bookcase to give him room. "Shelby, my father beat me and humiliated me and hated me. When I was young I saw how he beat and humiliated and hated my mom."

I was shocked by the things he was saying. "Why did you come home and live in the same house after your discharge from the army?"

"I had no choice. I had no money. It was going to be for a short time, but it didn't work out that way."

"So you killed him?"

He nodded, speaking very fast. "Uh huh, that's what I did, I really did. I got a job at his company because he, well, hell, he forced me to. You don't understand, I wasn't a son to my father; I was just a *thing* he wanted to control. So, one day out in the field, something happened with the block and tackle. You get to it way up on the top of the derrick. Dad told me to follow him up there so he could show me how to fix it. It was a scary climb on rungs that were part of the derrick grill, you know what I mean? It was a windy day, too! We got up to the top, the crown block, the little platform up there. Even there he yelled at me for taking too long to make the climb. He called me a sissy—even after I'd been in the goddamned army. The ground was a fucking long way down. I knew then that I had my chance to get rid of that bastard. He squatted and started working with the cables, you know? I was handing him tools and there was a moment that he leaned over and was off-balance, you know what I mean? And . . . I just pushed him. That's all I did. Just a little push. And off he went. I knew he wouldn't survive the fall. It was a fucking long way down."

He plopped down on the bed and sat there with his face in his hands.

I couldn't believe what I'd just heard. And yet, even though the news was so shocking, in some way, it didn't seem like *news*. I wasn't all that broken up about it. Charles Newcott had been a horrible human being. I'm not even sure I could call him a person.

"Eddie, are you telling me the truth?"

He looked up, one hand still on his face, one eye peeking through his fingers. The image reminded me of one of the more memorable sinners in Michelangelo's Sistine Chapel painting of Judgment Day, which depicted the soul's utter realization of the terrible deeds he had done.

Eddie nodded.

I swallowed and said, "Eddie, you should know that I fully understand why you did it. It was wrong, but I do understand."

The hand dropped, and he looked at me suddenly with a very strange smile on his face. Like he was a little devil about to pull a prank on an unsuspecting victim. "You won't tell on me?"

"Eddie . . ."

He waved me away again. "Go, Shelby. Forget about me. Forget I told you that. Go on with your life, Shelby. I'm no good. I can't corrupt you anymore."

My heart shattered. That's the only way I could describe it. I'd experienced minor romantic mishaps up to that point, but Eddie was the most serious relationship I'd ever had in my young adult life. It was my first real heartbreak—after our very first "breakup" as children—and it hurt. It really did.

"Do you mean that?" I asked.

"Yeah. Go. Go back to Illinois. Forget about me. Please." He hung his head.

We were silent for a moment. Then I said, "Goodbye, Eddie," turned, and left the bomb shelter.

I wouldn't see Eddie again until seventeen years later. We would be very different people by then.

16

Back at the Best Western, I tell myself it's going to be an early night. At least I'm hoping it will be. I'm one of those people who can never sleep well when traveling, and I dislike not having my own pillow. Nevertheless, I open my tablet and connect to the Internet in order to check my email and the like. The television is tuned to a mindless talent competition show—sometimes music can be nice in the background. If only the judges would shut up.

After taking care of business, I go to Google on a whim and type "Edward Newcott Evil Eddie" in the search box. Dozens of links appear. Evil Eddie had attracted attention, infamous on a national basis. I didn't know the extent of his fame overseas, but I see URLs for a London and a Paris news outlet. Most of the recent articles are about the trial and the upcoming execution. Eddie is painted to be a demon, a creature that deserves to die by lethal injection.

I am very torn. Recalling the night he told me he'd killed his father prompts me to reexamine *everything*. I want to be prepared for my face-to-face with Eddie tomorrow. Even if he is so far gone mentally that we're barely able to speak to each other, I am determined to fully come to terms with how I feel about him and the things he's done. What he did to Dora Walton and her baby is unthinkable. No question about it. I shouldn't have anything more to do with Eddie because of that, but I can't help but believe he was sick in the head. The Eddie I know couldn't have done that horrible deed.

Could he?

After all, he'd killed before. He'd admitted to me—and only me—that he caused the death of his abusive father.

How the hell do I feel about any of it? I don't know. God help me, but I am torn.

The TV becomes an ambient drone as my mind drifts back to that summer of 1977. The pain of Eddie telling me he didn't want me in his life anymore drove me back to Evanston earlier than I'd originally planned. I abruptly announced to my parents that I was going back to Illinois, even though it wasn't yet the middle of July. They were upset, but I said I'd get a part-time job, which would help with expenses. I did, too—I got a job as a secretary through a temp agency. I worked in the Chicago Loop in a building not far from Union Station, so I was able to take the train to and from Evanston. One of the few things I did well at the time was type. I knew a little about the WANG word processor and easily got a position in a firm that sold investor relations products. I never understood what they were, but I dutifully typed letters and answered phones. It wasn't bad money, either—eight dollars an hour, which was fabulous in 1977. Too bad I had to disappoint the firm in August when I announced I had to leave and go back to school.

I didn't hear from Eddie for a long time. It took me at least until spring of 1978 to truly get over him, but even then he was never far from my mind. I dated some, even became intimate with one guy named Brad, but he was definitely in the rebound category. That ended a month or two after it began. I did my best to concentrate on my studies. The previous semester, I had changed my graduate field of study to literature and had started writing more. It was nothing spectacular, just material that I was sure would be the next great American novel. Turned out it was crap, but it was a good learning experience. Novel number two went into the drawer, never to see the light of day. Nevertheless, the work I did in class was pretty good, if I do say so myself, and I made high marks. My professors thought I showed talent, which was very encouraging. I graduated with an MA in literature in May of 1978.

There was a teacher's aide in my advanced rhetoric class named Derek. Derek Golding. He was also in graduate school, had taken longer to get through it, and was in his fourth, and last, year. He was due to receive his MA at the end of the semester. Good-looking, smart, and much different from Eddie. For one thing, he wore glasses and was thin, nonathletic, and a bit of a nerd. But I liked him. He had a wicked sense of humor, and he made me laugh. Toward the end of the school session, he asked me out on a date. Back then, there was no stigma of teacher's aides—or even full professors—dating students. Happened all the time. We went out to dinner and had a great evening. We started dating, and as soon as school was out we were sleeping together.

The romance was going well when I suddenly received a call from my father.

My mother had died suddenly.

I can't describe how horrible I felt. The guilt was tremendous. All the past years I'd spent basically shoving away the reality of my sick, tormented mother caught up with me, and I broke down in a serious way. Derek did his best to console me. He offered to come back to Limite with me for the funeral, but I told him it was too soon for him to be that involved with my family. It was.

My father told me that Mom had taken an overdose of sleeping pills. Whether or not it had been intentional, the police refused to say. "Accidental" was the official report, but I think I knew better. My mother departed this world voluntarily, and as miserable as I'd seen her be, I could almost understand it. Still, I felt betrayed, guilty, and angry. Mostly, I was very sad.

Dad was crushed. Just in the few months I'd been away, he had aged a decade. His hair was completely gray, when a year earlier it had been a little salt and pepper. He handled it well, though, kept a stiff upper lip, and seemed to be more concerned about how *I* took it. The funeral in Limite was attended by all my parents' church friends—a small but supportive crowd.

I didn't see Eddie, nor did I attempt to contact him. He didn't send a sympathy card. I wasn't even sure he knew my mother had died. *His* mother surely must have known, and wouldn't it have made sense that she'd tell him? Whatever.

My father hoped I would stay in Limite for the rest of the summer, but I had another secretarial temp job that I wanted to get back to. I'm not sure I could have remained sane in that town with the ghost of my mother hovering over me, disappointed that I had left the front door unlocked and caused baby Michael's abduction, as well as mortified by my dating the boy she had wrongly accused of the crime. It was better to be back in Illinois. Besides, that's where Derek was, and I needed someone like him at the moment. He may have been a nerd, but he was sensitive and kind; and he loved me.

We got married in February 1979, when I was twenty-four. By then, we had moved into an apartment in Lincoln Park, Chicago, one of the nicer neighborhoods in an exciting but difficult city. I fell in love with it despite the oppressive winters, the traffic, the crime, and the crowding. It had art, theater, and music; film and literature; culture and food; and all the things that made a big city worth the trouble.

The big problem was that Derek and I were both writers. Big mistake. The competitiveness was mutual. His first book—a nonfiction political tome about Nixon's administration—was a bestseller. I was still struggling to write that first—no, third—novel and finding my voice, as well as holding down a nine-to-five job as a secretary.

The other issue we came up against was children. Derek wanted children; I was ambivalent. It wasn't that I *didn't* want children, I just didn't feel ready. I felt as if I had things I needed to accomplish first. Nevertheless, I gave in, and we tried. And tried. When nothing happened, both of us were tested and it turned out I couldn't have babies. I was fucking infertile. It took over a year to find out that the reason was because I had an ovarian cyst the size of a watermelon. I'm exaggerating, but that's what it felt like to me when I was diagnosed. I underwent surgery in 1981 at the age of twenty-six, which left me with a seventeen-centimeter scar on the outside of my body, a severed fallopian tube, and more scarring on the inside. Part of my ovary had to be removed; it was a big deal. Afterward, my hormones went berserk. The doctors told me that if I ever did conceive, it was likely that I'd have an ectopic pregnancy, and that didn't sound like a whole lot of fun. So I made it a point not to have a child. I went on birth control again, which helped with the hormonal imbalance, but it wrecked my marriage.

In the spring of 1982, Derek and I separated after three years and two months of matrimony. The divorce became final in 1983, just around the time I turned twenty-eight.

Thank goodness my first *good* novel—the initial Patricia Harlow romance—had been accepted by Harlequin and was due to be published later that year. It was what kept my spirits up. Otherwise I might have considered myself a failure—both in love and in work. The breakup was messy and painful, and Derek wasn't very understanding. We don't speak or communicate now. The last I heard, he was living in Seattle, happily married—to his *third* wife—with grandchildren. Good for him.

I suppose that experience soured me on relationships. It was a while before I boarded the dating roller coaster once again, but I did so with a completely different attitude. Somewhere along the way I had decided that my goal was simply to find companionship, enjoy it while it was there, and move on when it was over. To tell the truth, it was very liberating. There was no longer pressure to become the ideal American housewife and mother. I could just be me, fall in love with whomever I wanted and for however long I wanted, and concentrate on my work.

That may sound selfish and egotistical, but I'm here to say that I've been very happy with that situation. The only people I've had to please were my agent, my editor, my readers, and myself. And that was enough. I've lived with three different dogs since the early eighties—much better companions than men, I must say—and *still* enjoyed the company of the opposite sex on my own terms. I suppose my political and social attitudes kept moving further left during the late seventies and early eighties. Even though I wrote trashy romance novels, I became a fiercely independent feminist. So sue me.

The Forgotten Promise generated decent reviews and surprisingly good sales. Harlequin wanted more, so I gave it to them. I'm proud to say I've had a novel published every year since 1983, and then some—the odd stand-alone or anthology contribution. I quit my day job and became a full-time author in '84, and I haven't looked back. I moved to different places in Chicago twice and have lived in my current residence—also in Lincoln Park—since 1998. A townhouse, all to myself. Heaven on earth.

My career really took off in 1986 when Hollywood made a movie of *The Forgotten Promise*. It turned out to be a sleeper hit, and more people started buying my books. I'd like to think it was all about talent, but the practical side of me acknowledges that success in the publishing world is primarily dependent on luck—just as it is in any of the arts. I felt truly blessed when my luck held out again four years later. In 1990, they made a film of my 1989 novel, *The Moon Pirate*, which also happened to be my first *New York Times* number one. With one of Hollywood's most popular heartthrobs cast as the love interest, it attracted a lot of female moviegoers. For some Tinsel Town reason I'll never understand, the actress who played Patricia in the first movie wasn't cast in the second one, so there was an inconsistency that I believe hurt what could have been a franchise. Another film based on one of my novels was produced in 1997, which didn't do very well. I didn't mind. Dealing with Hollywood was very stressful and complicated. The money was quite good, thank you very much, but I was happy just to be my own boss and be a romance book factory. There have been a few nibbles from Hollywood since then, but I didn't allow myself to be bitten. I've made a very good living with the books alone. With the fame, of course, came a certain loss of privacy. For a while, in the early nineties, I often appeared on television—talk shows, game shows, and the like. I was thirty-six when my picture was on the cover of *Entertainment Weekly*. Not bad for a small-town girl from West Texas.

During the late eighties, I finally saw a psychologist to work out some of the issues I still had with my mother. I felt very guilty about a lot of things, not least with leaving the front door unlocked some twenty years earlier. The way I treated my mother those last years of her life was despicable. Despite the glorious success I was having as an author, my conscience was hammering at me. I had to do something about it, so I chose to pour my heart out to a shrink. The woman I saw tried hard to work with me, but I have to admit her failure was my fault—I just wasn't very receptive. After a couple of years of therapy, I stopped. Since then, I've mostly come to terms, more or less, with my guilt, but there are times when the self-reproach comes crashing back. I live with it and concentrate on my work.

As with most things, a trend is eventually replaced with new ones, and that's what started happening in 1993 to 1994. For one thing, I wasn't in the public eye as much. The TV appearances slowed down, and there were fewer requests for interviews, though luckily book sales remained steady. Thus, as I approached my forties, I regained most of my privacy. I could walk the streets, eat in restaurants, and ride the train without being recognized. The few times it happened were never unpleasant.

Again—I was blessed. By whom, I didn't know, because by that time I wasn't as religious as I'd been as a girl. Somewhere along the way—probably during my tumultuous marriage—I lost the faith. It wasn't that I stopped believing in God, it's just that I ceased paying attention to Him. I don't believe Eddie had any influence on me in that regard. He had always been an atheist, even as a little boy. He hated it when his parents made him go to church with them, and in reality they didn't attend often, only visiting on the big holidays like Christmas and Easter. On the other hand, *I* had to go every Sunday. Between the day I was born and the summer I left Limite for college, I spent nearly every Sunday morning of my life at church. By the time I moved to Austin, I'd had enough of it.

My spirituality underwent a restructuring. I believe I'm a good person, and I try to live by the tenets I learned from Christianity. I just don't bother much with the organized part of it. I respect people who do, as long as it's not waved in my face. Like several other authors in our country, I was once attacked by a fanatical religious group about the sex and promiscuity in my books. Oh, please. It's just entertainment. Sure, sex sells. Sex written for women by a woman is also perfectly healthy.

The problem, I've come to realize, is that today I still do not understand the presence of Evil, capital "E" again. It lived on our block in the form of Mr. Alpine. It resided across the street in Charles Newcott. That's a lot of Evil for one neighborhood.

My family—and especially my mother—was in turn corrupted by the Evil inside Mr. Alpine. Poor Eddie—the boy across the street—was damaged by the one inside his dad. Where did that Evil come from? If there really is a God, does that mean there really is a Satan? Eddie tried to convince me when I was twelve that there was no God, only the devil.

But enough of the philosophizing. Back to the year 1994, the period when my career was settling down to a comfortable routine without too much media attention.

That's when I crossed paths with Eddie again.

17

News of Eddie was elusive during those years between 1977, the last time I saw him, and 1994. My father filled me in on some of the well-known bits, such as Eddie going to prison for twenty months. In 1984, Eddie got into another fight at some bar outside of Limite and nearly killed a guy. For that incident, charges *were* pressed.

Around the time I got divorced and published my first novel, Dad moved out of the house on Chicory Lane. Since I rarely came home, he didn't think there was any reason to stay. Why should one person have all that space when a nice family might want it? He bought an apartment in a newer part of the city but still not far from the bank. I didn't blame him. It was a tainted house.

For that matter, so was Eddie's. Was it a coincidence that the two houses, directly across the street from each other, contained broken families? Two different tragedies, united in pain. But Eddie continued to stay on Chicory Lane. He belonged in an artistic community in a bigger city, but he didn't budge. What became abundantly clear was that Eddie was a small-town boy at heart, and he had a very strong emotional tie to Limite and the Newcott home. The bomb shelter, his man cave, was precious to him. He must have thought he would be happy there for the rest of his life.

But as it turned out, he wasn't happy at all. Instead, Eddie went over to the dark side. That's the only way I can describe it. The darker qualities he had been displaying toward the end of our relationship manifested themselves into something more sinister.

This is what I learned, or ultimately found out. *Devil Man* became a minor hit in the underground comics scene, so Eddie continued to work on his art. He probably wasn't making a lot of money from it, so I suppose he simply lived off his mother's social security and his father's insurance. A grown man living with his mom. You'd think that would be enough to tell you that Eddie lacked certain social skills, but the truth is far worse.

He developed a mental illness, and he became a Satanist.

Mind you, I'm no psychiatrist, but I'm not sure those two things were exclusive. Perhaps they were. I don't mean to say that anyone who worships Satan is mentally ill—of course not. And not all souls who suffer from mental illness become Satanists. But from what I knew about Eddie's life, and from what I heard and discovered about his behavior during this period, I do believe the two traits were linked. I found out about the Satanism fairly quickly because it was obvious. The mental illness—well, that took a while to figure out.

While continuing to publish issues of *Devil Man*, Eddie began writing and illustrating an atheistic newsletter called *Godless Times*, which had a shockingly large number of subscribers, several thousand. His audience consisted of a surprising number of intellectuals, teachers, and even ministers, but the publication also attracted the weirdos.

Eddie turned his house on Chicory Lane into a business. His mother still lived there, although her health declined rapidly in the eighties. Nevertheless, the house across from my childhood home became the *Godless Times* HQ. The newsletter made money, which attracted the attention of the local news. He was interviewed and soon became an infamous celebrity in Limite. What did he say on television? Eddie flaunted a belief in witchcraft and the devil. In a small town in Texas, something like that could end up with fatal consequences. His neighbors on the block almost rioted. Fortunately, I was far away and never got a sense of how hated he was until much later.

The neighbors tried to get the city to evict them—but Mrs. Newcott owned the house and paid the utilities. Technically, Eddie wasn't disturbing anyone with noise, or anything like that. No, he offended them with his words and ideas. He frightened them, and the natural response was to attack.

In 1983, some DA tried to charge Eddie with operating a business in a residential area, or something similarly ridiculous. Eddie went to court and won. He was a freelancer, and he simply operated a business out of his home—perfectly legal. The powers-that-be just didn't like his business.

It came to a head in the spring of '84. Why Eddie continued to visit the seedy oil field bars would always be a mystery to me, but that's where the fight occurred. You'd think he would have the sense to know that he was a controversial figure in town, and that maybe the rednecks and good ol' boys wouldn't take too kindly toward an atheist.

When recognized at the bar, Eddie practically had to fight for his life. The other man was seriously injured, since Eddie beat him to a pulp with the broken leg of a barstool. The same DA charged him this time with aggravated assault and battery. Eddie pled down to assault and was sentenced to two years in the penitentiary, which many thought was too harsh. In January of 1985, Eddie Newcott became a prisoner at Darrington Correctional Institution in Rosharon, Texas. He was paroled at the end of August '86 for good behavior. His mother had had a stroke that July, and the parole board must have felt sorry for him.

With Mrs. Newcott confined to a wheelchair and unable to speak, Eddie became a full-time caretaker. It would have been a difficult job for an experienced nurse, but Eddie rose to the task. Now he really did have a reason to stay in Limite. By all accounts Eddie did an admirable job caring for her, and I eventually saw the setup firsthand. He may have come to be called "Evil Eddie," but he certainly loved his mother.

He started up his business again once he was out of prison. *Godless Times* quickly rebuilt its subscriber base, and Eddie was once again Limite's most notorious Satanist; the only one, I imagine. He stayed out of legal trouble, but controversy clearly surrounded him. At one point, he painted the entire house black—that really freaked out the neighbors. Numerous visitors would stop by at night, and Eddie made sure they were quiet and didn't bother anyone. Rumors flew as to what went on in that black house. People actually believed Eddie was holding black masses and rituals in the neighborhood. Never mind that his mother still lived in the house.

The police paid visits to the home on several occasions. Turned out that the nuisance calls were never anything serious—Eddie diligently ensured he wasn't breaking any laws. Some phone-happy neighbors obviously hoped that he was.

For the rest of the eighties and early nineties, I didn't hear another word about Eddie or his mother. I visited my father in Limite three or four times at his new apartment, purposefully avoiding driving by the old neighborhood. Limite had become very different from the small town of the sixties where I'd grown up. It had increased in population by a hundred percent, and none of those vacant lots we used to play in were there anymore. Chicory Lane was no longer on the edge of town; the city had expanded a great deal with the addition of a second

mall, numerous shopping centers, fast food chains, and busi-
nesses. The sixties and seventies had been good to Limite, but in
the late eighties the oil business had a downturn and the town
experienced a recession. Hundreds of newly built homes went
into foreclosure, and people started leaving. It didn't affect my
father's business; he was about to retire anyway. The bank was
doing all right. Nevertheless, Limite had expanded too quickly
to support itself, and a lot of people were out of work.

I came home for the Christmas holidays in 1994 and planned
to stay at least a couple of weeks. Dad had an extra bedroom in
his apartment, which was where I always bunked whenever I visited. He looked older and more haggard, but he was in a much
better frame of mind, especially since leaving our old house. He
also had something of a girlfriend—Jane, a woman his age who
was a member of his church congregation. She was a widow, and
they had been seeing each other for a year or so. I liked her, and
I could see that she made Dad very happy.

Three days before Christmas, I found myself at the Limite
mall doing some last-minute shopping. It was a madhouse. The
stores were packed, and I wanted to get out as quickly as possible. The shortest way to the parking lot was though a wing
where several Limite artists traditionally set up kiosks to sell
their work—paintings, sketches, sculptures, and jewelry. It was
one thing about the Limite mall that I admired—year round,
they always allotted space to host a gallery and flea market for
local artists. There were table fees, of course, but it was still
a nice opportunity for craft makers and artists to display their
work. Being that time of year, almost all of the merchandise
was Christmas-themed—nativity scenes and velvet Jesuses
abounded. I was pleasantly surprised to see a fair-sized crowd of
customers gathered around these displays, so I decided to have
a look. A woman selling scarves had some pretty items, several
jewelers had beautiful pieces, and the paintings were remarkably

fine. But I'm not good at fighting a crowd; it makes me claustrophobic. Some young mothers had fussy children in strollers, the kids whining and crying with ever-increasing volume. It wasn't worth the ordeal. As I backed out of the throng, I noticed one table that seemed to be set apart from the others, as if it didn't belong. No one stood in front of it, for the work on exhibition there had nothing to do with Christmas. In fact, as I soon learned, everyone was offended that the artist could parade such "filth" next to religious art.

They were magnificently executed fantasy drawings and paintings of demonic and pagan imagery. Scenes depicted sinners falling into hell and being tormented by demons and monsters. Nude women were discreetly covered with masking tape for the public display. Another striking piece was a presentation of a war between angels and devils. The most controversial painting depicted a Nativity scene featuring demons and monsters instead of the usual cast of characters. It was truly breathtaking, but shocking, work.

Eddie Newcott sat behind the table, drawing in a sketch pad and paying no attention to his lack of business. Seeing him there took my breath away. All I could do was stare.

He was dressed entirely in black. His dark hair was long and stylish, almost like a Beatles haircut circa 1966. A goatee adorned his face, which gave him a Mephistophelean appearance. Despite the darkly sinister vibe, Eddie looked *marvelous*. I've said that he was a handsome man, but, my God, he was now more gorgeous than ever. Truly. There was a worldliness about him that exuded maturity, intelligence, and sensuality. Yes, he still displayed a bad boy image, but I'd put him in the same class as Elvis or Marlon Brando in the fifties or Johnny Depp in the nineties. Was it my imagination, or did an *aura* surround him? I didn't know. There was no question that he radiated charisma in spades, rock star stuff.

By my calculations, he was thirty-nine years old. I was forty at the time.

"Eddie." I must have blurted it, for his eyes jerked up. His irises had deepened to a darker brown, mesmerizing black holes into which, I dare say, any heterosexual woman could have fallen, never to return. Why wasn't there a crowd of females lingering around his table? Well, I knew the obvious answer to that. The subject matter of his art and the less enlightened attitudes of Limite's population were hardly a good match.

Those eyes widened when he recognized me. "Shelby! My God!"

I immediately went over to him; he stood, and we hugged each other. "I can't believe it," I said. "You look great. How are you?"

"I'm fine. You look terrific, too. Fame and fortune becomes you."

"Oh, hush. I'm still me."

"Yes, you are."

I nodded at his sketchpad. "And you're still you, I see."

"Oh, yeah. I can't understand why no one wants to buy any of my paintings for Christmas." He rolled his eyes and chuckled.

"Uh, maybe because it's not Halloween?"

"You think?" We both laughed. "Hell, I don't know why I bother. I should pack up and get out of here." He glanced over at a mother trying to shush her screaming toddler. Eddie winced and then asked, "What are you doing? You want to get a cup of coffee?"

That actually sounded lovely. I said yes. My desire to leave the mall in a hurry had dissipated. I desperately wanted to sit down with the man who, I suddenly realized then and there, still occupied a special place in my heart.

He started to pack up his things and I volunteered to help carry the stuff to his car. Most of it fit on a dolly that he'd hidden under his table, and it took us only one trip.

"Math was never my strong suit. How long has it been?" he asked as we stepped outside and crossed the crowded parking lot. West Texas wasn't Chicago, but Limite was still pretty cold in December. He wore a black leather jacket, naturally, and I bundled up in my down coat.

"Uh, seventeen years? Seventeen and a half, almost?"

"God." He shook his head. "How time flies when you're the most hated person in town."

"You must love it, though, if you've stayed all these years."

He laughed again. "You're right. I do love it. It gives me a purpose in life. Scandalize the neighborhood, provoke the Christians, and assert my rights according to the First Amendment."

His car was a small van that held his easel and paintings in the back. After packing it up and locking the doors, he said, "Shall we just go to the cafeteria in the mall, or do you want to go somewhere else?" This was before Starbucks had conquered America, although I believe stores were already starting to open in some of the bigger cities around the country.

"Let's go somewhere else, if you don't mind," I said. "Big crowds in a shopping frenzy make me nervous."

We ended up at Denny's. I followed him in my father's car, which I'd borrowed. Dad was off work and didn't mind hanging out at his apartment while I ran errands. At Denny's, a young waitress recognized Eddie and said hello in, what seemed to me, a provocative way. Eddie addressed her by name and returned the greeting. *Hmm*, I thought.

Our conversation over coffee was pleasant and informative. The bad feelings from our breakup in 1977 seemed to have been forgotten. He first asked about me and my life. There wasn't much to tell. I outlined the failure of my marriage and the fact that I couldn't have children. Intimate and personal details came flowing out; with anyone else that wouldn't have happened. Despite the years apart, it was as if Eddie and I were still best friends on

Chicory Lane, telling each other our innermost secrets. He asked about my writing career and admitted that he'd picked up a couple of my books. They weren't his "cup of tea." I laughed and acknowledged that my audience consisted of bored housewives who needed a little fantasy in their lives. Other than my authorial existence in Chicago, which wasn't as exciting as it sounded, recounting my biographical story didn't take up much time.

When it was his turn, Eddie didn't hold back. He told me all about the newsletter he produced at home. How it pushed buttons and asked hard questions and made people think—those who actually read it, that is. Its position was blatantly atheistic, spouting philosophies borrowed from real Satanists throughout history. It was very disturbing to me. Despite my loss of faith, my church upbringing prevented me from buying into such a thing. I asked him straight out if this was what he truly believed.

"Are you kidding? This is a way to make money," he answered. "I don't believe *any* of this shit. Really. It's all an act. You've heard of the Internet?" I nodded, since at that time the web was becoming the next big thing. I'd been advised by my publisher to create a website for myself, something that would happen in the near future. "Well, pretty soon my artwork and writings will be seen all over the world. If being successful means also being controversial, then so be it. I'll be the next Aleister Crowley or Anton LaVey. It's LaVey's work that really inspired me. You should read his *Satanic Bible*. Enlightening stuff."

He explained that he had cleaned up his act with regard to drugs. "I don't do them anymore. I'm under too much scrutiny by the police and the media. I can't give them a reason to arrest me. Alcohol—that's another thing. It's legal. I do still enjoy an alcoholic beverage or two. Or three or four. I've really gotten into wine."

I was glad to hear he had stopped his illegal drug use. I had, too, ever since I was married. The seventies was a long time ago.

Eddie told me about his stint in prison. "It was pretty horrible," he said, "but I managed to maintain a semblance of self-respect. I wasn't raped, and I didn't get involved in fights. There was a white supremacy skinhead gang that protected me, although I didn't join them. I'm no neo-Nazi, and I like my hair. I think most everyone else was afraid of me because of my reputation as a Satanist. The word got out that if I was harmed, the devil would exact revenge. They nicknamed me 'The Warlock.'" He smiled at that, almost as if he believed it himself.

How I managed to stay sitting at the table after hearing all this is a question I continue to ask myself. Red flags were flying. Of all the things to pretend to be, he had to pick a Satanist? It was shocking and strange. But I remained, because, I think, I was fascinated. I knew *nothing* about the things he was saying. As an author, I ate it up. Yes, I was disturbed by it all, but I was smart and curious enough to want to learn more. Perhaps it was material I could use in a novel.

He told me about his mother's stroke—something I hadn't known before seeing him. "Is that the real reason you haven't left Limite?" I asked.

"No, I like it here," was all he would say. He then suggested I come and "see the old neighborhood" and say hello to her. "She might remember you, but she can't say hello. I can tell if she's happy or sad by the expression in her eyes. She can nod and shake her head and grunt, but otherwise, I'm taking care of a living vegetable."

His terminology disturbed me, but I answered that I'd like to see her. After we finished the coffee—I offered to pay and Eddie accepted—I followed him to Chicory Lane. It was bizarre seeing that house I knew so well painted black. Talk about sticking out like a sore thumb. No wonder he was ostracized by the neighbors. Across the street, my former home looked the same.

When we got out of our cars, I gestured to it. "Who lives in our old place?"

"Oh, some young couple with a toddler," he said. "They're afraid of me." We went inside. Incongruously, the interior of Eddie's house appeared unchanged since I was last there. Some furnishings were different, but you'd never know the place was a "warlock's home" from the inside. It was further indication to me that what Eddie was doing was an act. He had converted one bedroom into an office where he produced the newsletter. He gave me some old issues "for my entertainment," as he called it. A young man with red shoulder-length hair was busy at a desk, stuffing newsletters into envelopes. Eddie introduced him as Wade and said that he was an employee and fellow Satanist. I wouldn't have thought it possible, but Eddie had found like-minded believers to help him. It was difficult to imagine more than one warlock residing in a town as small as Limite.

That was facetious. Eddie was no warlock. I knew that, even if no one else saw through his facade.

In the living room, Mrs. Newcott sat slumped in a wheel-chair in front of a television. Eddie brought me in and said, "Hey, Ma, look who's here. It's Shelby Truman! Remember her, from across the street?"

Her eyes darted to me and focused, but I didn't see any recognition in her gaze. I didn't see *anything* behind those irises. They say that the eyes are windows to the soul; if that's the case, then Mrs. Newcott's soul was dead. Poor woman. It probably hadn't helped that her son had become a "heathen" and was bringing strange people into the house to help out with his business. I told her it was nice to see her and I was glad Eddie was taking good care of her. No response.

Next, Eddie took me to the backyard to show me his "sanctuary," and I braced myself. There was a large padlock on the steel door. He fished a key chain out of his pocket, found the right key, and unlocked the device. I was hesitant to go down into the bomb shelter, but he said, "I still like to sleep here every once in a while, but it's not my 'room' anymore. Come on, you should see what I've done to the place." So I did. Curiosity got the better of me. Those Satanic masses that the media thought went on in his home? They were actually more likely to be conducted in the bomb shelter, which had been decked out in a pretty creepy fashion. The walls, floor, and ceiling had been painted black. The double bed was no longer there; instead six small pews sat on one end of the space, facing a large altar adorned with an upside-down pentagram. A pentagram had also been painted on the floor in front of the altar. An inverted cross hung on the back wall.

It was freaky, like something out of a horror movie. "Eddie, are you kidding? *This* is just an act?"

"Shelby it's a fucking *show*, oh, sorry, pardon my language."

"So, what, is this a Satanic church?"

He laughed. "Oh, I guess you could call it that. I think I might name it 'The Temple.' LaVey's Church of Satan is the model for everything I do. I steal it all from him. You know who he is, right?"

LaVey was still alive at the time. He was an occultist, writer, and musician in California who had become famous as the founder of a Satanic church. "I've heard of him. He's that devil worshipper in San Francisco, right?"

"Yeah. But he's not a devil worshipper. He doesn't believe in the devil. It's a common misconception."

"And does anyone come here?"

"Yep, I have congregants. Once a month we have about five to ten people come and 'worship.' I'm the high priest." Eddie continued to explain. "Listen, contrary to popular belief, this isn't 'devil worship.' In Satanism—at least the kind preached by LaVey—each individual is his or her own god. There is no room for any other god, and that includes Satan or Lucifer or whatever other name you might use. I don't believe in Satan as a deity. He's a symbol. In that regard, I guess I am a Satanist. I am my own god."

"But your, uh, congregants—don't they come to worship Satan?"

He shrugged. "Not really. We follow LaVey's Church of Satan philosophies. Like I said, Satan is more a symbol of a liberating figure. We're *atheists*, which means we don't believe in *any* deities, God or Satan. The word 'Satanism' is often used incorrectly, but it's generally utilized to describe the various movements that reject God and Christianity. We may use devil imagery, but it doesn't necessarily mean we believe in a devil."

Once we were back outside in the fresh air, Eddie asked if I'd like to get together again that night. Call me crazy—I still felt safe around him, I was still attracted to this mysterious and beautiful man, and I wanted to know more.

I made a date with a warlock.

18

The digital clock in the Livingston Best Western reads 2:35. In the morning. I lie there in bed, sleeping like a salad—constantly tossing. No matter what I do, I can't fall asleep. Of course, that's the problem; I am *trying* to go to sleep. That never works.

The motion picture in my brain keeps on running. The memories and flashbacks of my times with Eddie are nearing an end, so I figure it's best to simply let the movie play out. After all, the plan was to go over everything from the past that I can recall; I just didn't think it would take this long! The anxiety of facing him again is also a contributing factor to my sleeplessness. I wish there was an internal switch we could flip whenever we wanted to go to sleep. I'm often told I should learn to meditate, and I gave it a shot—several times in fact—but it never worked. My mind kept racing!

If Act One of my life with Eddie was the sixties, and Act Two the seventies and eighties, then Act Three is certainly what happened during the Christmas holidays of 1994. It's one of the few times in my life when I questioned my own sanity. The fact that I went out with Eddie again that Christmas season and slept with him and *almost* revitalized our relationship was truly not the act of a sensible woman. Looking back, I realize now that I was very lonely. Despite my newfound fame, success, and fortune, I was still alone. Oh, there were men in my life, that wasn't the problem. There was David, a cop, whom I often saw back in Chicago. That had been going on for a few months. His politics differed from mine, which was a bit of a sticking point, but otherwise he was kind and attentive. David was also good in bed, a major factor in his attractiveness. Nevertheless, there was a spark missing, that jolt of electricity I always experienced when I was with Eddie. To this day, I've never found another person who possesses that fire, someone who can bring out the fission in me. What can I say? David was good, but Eddie was the most intensely sensual lover I've ever known.

So I went with it. I was home for only two weeks, so I thought, *what the hell* . . . And who would know? I wasn't making any public appearances in Limite. No one knew I was there except my agent (this was before I employed an assistant). I figured that whatever happened, it would remain discreet—and it did. Still, it was a mistake. The consequences nearly pushed Eddie over the edge, and it forced me to seriously distance myself from him. The next time I saw Eddie after Christmas of '94 was at his trial in 2006, but we didn't speak. Tomorrow will be the first time we've spoken in twenty years. My God.

On that first date of Act Three, we went to dinner at the Red Shack. I suppose we did it for old times' sake because it reminded us of the Limite we'd known when we were younger. I was surprised it was still in operation. The Baker family, who has run it and other restaurants in Limite for generations, is a class act, and the Red Shack is still as popular today; I may just have to go for a steak this weekend when I'm in town. That night, the food, the wine, the atmosphere . . . I lost my inhibitions. Eddie still had that power of seduction. He charmed me, even though my inner Jiminy Cricket was pleading with me to recognize the warning signs and use my brain. The Satanist thing freaked me out, sure, but not enough to make me go running. In truth, I wasn't afraid of Eddie at all. I thought he was eccentric, bizarre, handsome, and brilliant; and despite his violent reputation, I knew he would never harm me.

I'm sorry I didn't recognize his depression earlier, and the fact that he suffered from severe emotional problems. Would anything have been different? Doubtful. He was on a predestined course of self-destruction and was oh so very good at hiding it in public.

That night at the Red Shack, he was the Eddie I remembered. Warm, dark, and mysterious, with a touch of ironic, black humor. He made me laugh, and we reminisced just as we had when he and I got together in 1976—a Christmas break event as well.

I went home with him after dinner. It felt strange parking Dad's car in front of Eddie's house. Looking across the street at our old place gave me the shivers. There were no lights on; the home was dark and soulless. The family with the young child had gone to bed. I wondered if they knew about the house's history.

We went inside so that Eddie could check on his mother. She was asleep in bed, so he led me through the back door. The near-full moon was bright in the sky. I followed him, unquestioningly, as he moved directly to the fallout shelter, unlocked the door, and opened it. Once we were underground, he lit some candles and covered the inverted cross with a black drape. Of all the devilish iconography in "The Temple," that cross creeped me out the most. Once it was hidden, it felt like we were back in the dungeon of lust. That's what the shelter was to me, a place you went to when you wanted to do something naughty. In 1994, it looked like a Halloween carnival haunted house. What could make it even more taboo?

Eddie pulled out another bottle of wine, and we drank the entire thing. By then, I was in no shape to drive, so I stayed. There was no bed in the shelter anymore, but there was the altar, which was long and wide enough for a couple of bodies. He placed a mattress and blankets on top, and that's where we did it, on his goddamned *altar*. In the moment, it slipped my mind that it was a place of sacrifice and worship that he used in his black masses.

Before we had sex, Eddie asked, "So there's no chance you can get pregnant?"

"No."

"That's good to know."

"Why?"

"I never want to have children."

I had no response to that. So we got on with it. The love-making was rougher than I remembered it, but intensely satisfying. I swear Eddie turned into a kind of beast; the next day, I found scratches from his fingernails on my forearms and back. He probably had marks on him as well. Later, when I reflected on what we'd done the night before, I was suddenly repulsed. And what was a mattress doing in "The Temple," anyway? Did he use it often? I didn't want to continue the thought.

I woke up in the bomb shelter with a hangover. Because we were underground with no windows, it was difficult to say whether it was day or night. A nightlight was always kept on whenever someone slept in the shelter, otherwise it would be pitch black. My eyes darted around the room and stopped on Eddie's wristwatch, still on his arm, a few inches away from my face. 9:35. Morning. Eddie was still asleep when I got up to pee in the toilet behind the partition. I was desperately thirsty after drinking so much wine only a few hours prior, and I couldn't find any water around. I slipped on my clothes, quietly opened the steel door—it still squeaked a little—and emerged from the lower depths. The morning air was chilly. The sliding back door to the house wasn't locked, so I went in and made my way through the living room to the kitchen. I found a glass, filled it from the tap, and drank up. I found some orange juice in the fridge and drank that as well.

A noise coming from the back of the house caught my attention. A moan? I put the glass down and gingerly stepped into the hallway that led to the bedrooms. Mrs. Newcott's door was open. Another moan. I moved forward and knocked. "Mrs. Newcott?" She sat on the edge of her bed, staring at me. "Good morning. Can I get you anything?"

She said something unintelligible, unable to move her mouth.

"How can I help you?"

I went to her, but the woman attempted to form more words. This time I understood her. "Go away." She gestured with her hand, waving me out of the room.

I left and went down the hall, and peeked in Eddie's office. Dark and quiet. My stomach lurched. The sudden intake of water and juice was a shock to my system, and I desperately needed to use the toilet again. There was a bathroom across the hall with a full-size commode, more comfortable than the one in the shelter. As I finished up, I noticed that the medicine cabinet above the sink was ajar. I peeked inside. Besides the usual grooming supplies and various toiletries, there stood some prescription pill bottles. Curiosity got the better of me, so I examined them.

One medication was Klonopin, or clonazepam, a tranquilizer my mother had taken. It was used for anxiety. The other bottle clued me in to the reality of Eddie's problems. Zoloft. That was the brand name for an antidepressant, an SSRI, used to treat not only depression but obsessive-compulsive disorders and anxiety.

If Eddie was taking that stuff, surely it wasn't good that he chased the medication with alcohol.

I put everything back, stepped out into the hallway, and listened for Mrs. Newcott. Silence. I made my way back through the living room, out to the backyard, and down into the dungeon of lust. Eddie was awake and staring at the ceiling.

"Good morning," I said.

"Hey there."

"You all right?"

"Sure. Are you? Where were you?"

I told him I'd gone up for water and said hello to his mother.

"Oh."

"Do you need to go inside and help her?"

"Nah, she doesn't like being bothered this early in the morning. She's able to get what she needs by herself. Come get back in bed."

I removed my clothes and snuggled next to his naked, warm body. He was still very fit, although he'd allowed some of those muscles he'd honed in the army to soften. As for me, my figure was darned fine for a forty-year-old, if I do say so myself. My weight could have been reduced a bit, but that's because I was a sedentary person by nature. My New Year's resolution was going to be the same as the previous year's and the one before that. Exercise more, damn it.

After Eddie got up to pee, too, we went at it again. An hour later, spent, we both decided that our stomachs could use some protein. First, he returned to the house to check on his mother. Thankfully she was able to go to the bathroom, get in and out of the wheelchair, and more or less dress by herself. Eddie simply had to prepare her meals and make sure she took certain medications. I helped him in the kitchen as we made a Mexican breakfast with eggs, tortilla chips, cheese, salsa, and peppers.

Mrs. Newcott joined us in her wheelchair, staring at me the whole time. I smiled at her and said things like, "I don't think it will be too cold today, do you, Mrs. Newcott?" She didn't respond—just shot daggers at me with her eyes. I suspected she didn't approve of me; maybe she was being protective of her son. Perhaps she knew how ill he was and didn't want me rocking the boat. Who knew.

I spent the rest of the day with my father, who didn't say a word until we went out to lunch. "So how's Eddie?" he asked.

"Geez, Dad, how did you know?"

"There aren't many other people in Limite you would spend the night with. Since I didn't get a call from the highway patrol about an accident, I figured you were with him."

"Sorry I didn't call you."

"Hey, you're a grown-up now. It was my car I was worried about." He smiled and I punched his arm.

I went about the rest of the day in a bit of a daze. Had I really done it? Slept with Eddie again after so many years? One thing was certain—he had rocked my world. It felt as if I had let go of years of stress and pressure from work, and I was totally relaxed. I was no longer Shelby Truman the famous author when I was with him, but simply Shelby the girl who once lived across the street.

That delusion would be overturned in less than twenty-four hours.

I hadn't admitted that it bothered me that Eddie was taking antidepressants. I suppose back then there was something of a stigma attached to the drugs. We know a lot more now about those kinds of mental illnesses than we did back then. However, my concern bubbled up that night when he and I got together again, this time at a new Mexican restaurant in town. A pretty hostess knew him by name and escorted us to the table. The waiter also knew who he was. At some point during the meal, I heard a woman tell her husband at another table, "Look, there's that devil worshipper!"

"See, I'm as famous as you are," he told me. "I think more people recognize me in Limite than they do you."

"Eddie, what's the Zoloft for?"

He ignored the question at first, talking instead about some of the items on the menu. I asked again. Finally, he said, "Shelby, I've been seeing a psychiatrist ever since I got out of prison. Right after I turned thirty-two."

"Okay."

He shrugged. "So I'm crazy. You knew that."

"Eddie. Stop. You're not crazy."

He shook his head. "Shelby, it actually started in the late seventies, but I did nothing about it. Panic attacks, mostly really scary ones. Compulsiveness. Depression. I started doing some crazy-ass stuff. I was still taking care of my mom, who had her stroke about a year before. I was having a hard time. I kind of freaked out one night when I was driving. I had an accident and smashed myself up. I was in the hospital for five days."

"I didn't know that! What happened?"

"Broken collarbone, two ribs broken, and a punctured lung."

"Jesus!"

"Nah, he had nothing to do with it. It was all my fault." Eddie laughed. "Anyway, I started seeing a shrink, and he recommended the medications." He shrugged again and looked away.

"Geez, Eddie. I'm so sorry."

"It's not your fault, either."

"Eddie, I didn't know. Does the . . . does the medicine help?"

"Yeah. It kind of makes me cloudy-headed at times. I laid off of it the past few days so I can be more myself with you."

"You shouldn't be drinking with it."

He waved me away. "They say that, but really, it doesn't hurt. Makes me feel better, actually." Eddie leaned closer and whispered. "I was mostly afraid the medicine would give me sexual problems, but that didn't happen."

"No, I guess it didn't."

A pitcher of frozen margaritas, which I hadn't realized he'd ordered, came to the table. I was about to refuse since I'd overdone it the night before, but Eddie had already poured two glasses. He held one up. "Hair of the dog," he said and clinked my glass. "It's the holidays, drink up."

"Jesus, Eddie, I don't think I can. My stomach and head still haven't recovered—"

"Then just have a few sips."

"You're not going to drink this entire pitcher by yourself."

"I will if you don't help me." He took a drink and sighed. "Ahhhh. Best margaritas in town."

Of course I ended up drinking with him. I could say it was because the beverage complemented the meal, but it wouldn't be the truth. While I attempted to take it easy, he didn't and got intoxicated very quickly. The mood at the table altered. At one point, Eddie placed his hand on top of mine. "Shelby, I've decided to make the big change."

"What do you mean?"

"I'll start packing. I'll come back to Chicago with you. It's obvious we're destined to be together, right? I mean, you felt it last night, too, didn't you?"

That threw me. "What?"

"Last night. Didn't you feel it? That bond between us? We're meant to be together, forever. I'm coming to Chicago. I'll find a place here where my mother can live and she can be taken care of properly. I'll move in with you and we'll get married. What do you say?"

"Eddie, I—"

"Oh, I know it'll be an adjustment. *Especially* for me. I've never lived anywhere else except Limite and Vietnam. It'll be a big change. I have to break that invisible umbilical cord that keeps me in that goddamned house. There are things . . . well, let's just say I've always felt I had to stay there because it was my destiny to turn the place into holy ground—or rather, unholy ground. Becoming a Satanist made everything clear to me. You see, I'm a god. Wouldn't you like to be married to a god? Then you would be a god, too!"

My stomach reeled. He started rambling and talking fast, saying bizarre, stream-of-consciousness things that sounded very unsettling. Things like how he and I were going to start our own Satanic church in Chicago and become famous like Anton LaVey. There were "relics of Hell" in the bomb shelter that had kept him in Limite, and now he wanted to break free of them.

"But you don't believe in Satan," I reminded him.

"No, no, I don't believe in the devil, but I know he's out there. He entered me when I was a little boy. I've lived with evil all my life, Shelby, and it's high time I get away from it. You will help me do that, won't you? We can run away from this evil place, and maybe I can turn my life around. No more black houses—we won't do any of that if you don't want me to. No more Satanic rituals. No more Davy Jones's Locker. No more—"

"Davy Jones's Locker?"

"Yeah, you remember that? Davy Jones's Locker. It's a source of pure evil. Everything that's wrong with me has come up from Hell through Davy Jones's Locker and enslaved me. The devil has touched me, Shelby, and I hear him talk to me at night."

I was beginning to get extremely disturbed. "Eddie, I think we should leave. When did you say you last took your medicine?"

He laughed. "I haven't taken it in a few days, actually."

"Eddie, you need to call your doctor."

"No way. I'm coming with you to Chicago, and we're going to get married. When do you want to leave?"

"Eddie, you're not coming with me to Chicago and we're not going to get married."

He wasn't listening. "I know you can't have babies, and that's good because I never want to bring a child of mine into the world. I don't want him or her to have my evil. Evil is hereditary, you know? I got it from my father . . ." He chugged another glass of margarita.

"Eddie, you're delirious. Stop drinking and listen to me."

"Whee, I feel so good! I'm finally going to be happy. *We'll* be happy, Shelby. I've seen it in my dreams. We'll live in your palace in Chicago. Maybe we can turn it into the biggest and best Satanic church in America. People will come from all around to—"

I stood. "Eddie! Stop it. Let's get out of here." I dug into my purse, pulled out a wad of bills that would more than cover the check, and pulled him to get up and come with me. He followed reluctantly, suddenly confused and disoriented. Once we were outside, I told him to take a breath of fresh air and calm down.

"I'm perfectly calm. I love you." He tried to embrace me, but I pulled away. I was frightened. I'd never seen him like this.

"What the hell's the matter?" he asked, abruptly turning from his euphoria to belligerence.

"Nothing. I'm going to drive you home. You can't get behind the wheel."

"Fuck you, of course I can."

"Eddie! Don't talk to me that way."

"Are you like all the others, too? You're scared of me? You're afraid of big, bad Evil Eddie? Mwahaha, the Devil Man is going to get you!"

He made like he was going to attack me, and I swear I screamed and backed away.

"Eddie! Let's just get in the car. I'll take you home and then drive to my dad's apartment. He can follow me back to your house and I'll leave your car."

"No. Spend the night."

"I'm not going to, Eddie. You're not well. You need to call your doctor."

"Fuck my doctor."

"Eddie!"

"And fuck you, too."

I slapped him. I couldn't help it. It was something I shouldn't have done, but the emotions and fear and confusion were too much. As soon as my skin struck his, his eyes grew wide with anger. I thought he was going to hit me. Instead, he leaned his head back and *howled* like a wolf. Loud and scary. He didn't stop. Just kept howling as people stopped and stared. I left him on the sidewalk in front of the restaurant, went back inside, and asked to use the phone. I called 911 and asked for an ambulance.

He was still outside, on his knees and howling at the sky, when the ambulance arrived. He got violent and struggled with the EMT personnel, but they finally subdued him and took him away.

The keys to his car were in his pocket. I was stranded. I didn't want to disturb my father, so I called a taxi and went home.

The evening left me with the shakes. I knew I couldn't stay in Limite. It wouldn't be wise to be near Eddie. The following day was Christmas Eve. I told Dad that I would be going back to Illinois the day after Christmas.

I never spoke to Eddie again.

19

My life went on, without too much drama, for the rest of the nineties and beyond the turn of the millennium. I thank my lucky stars for the success of my books; sales have remained steady and I don't believe I have to worry about retirement. There are no plans to stop writing any time soon, but someday I will want to simply relax and live off my nest egg.

Oh—there was that feature about me that appeared in *People* magazine in 2004, the year I turned fifty. I had been elected as one of those "50 and Still Hot" women, which was embarrassing and flattering at the same time. I would have been mortified, except that the article was a great one, covering my entire career and presenting me in a good light. I sat down for an interview with Alice, the woman who wrote the piece. She may have spent a little too much space on the fact that I was single and preferred to live that way, and there was an attempt to compare me to Patricia Harlow. Somehow, Alice had also managed to dig up information on what happened to our family in the summer of 1966. During the interview, Alice asked some uncomfortable questions about baby Michael, and I did my best to answer them truthfully. "It was a long time ago," I told her, "and I was only twelve at the time. The subject is very painful even still, so I'd prefer not to talk about it." To her credit, Alice replied that she understood and went on to other topics. The accompanying photographs were shot in Chicago on Michigan Avenue on a beautiful day—the sun was shining and fall was around the corner. I have to say I did look pretty good. Alice begged me to let her print a photo or two from my childhood, and I reluctantly relented. Warts and all, I now consider it to be perhaps the best piece of PR about me that I've ever seen. My book sales experienced a nice surge after the magazine hit the stands.

But what about Eddie? Upon my return to Illinois at the beginning of '95, I was still worried about his health. He had been hospitalized when I left Limite. I figured it was just a case of him not complying with his psychiatrist's orders and going off his meds. Some time passed, and I heard from my father that Eddie had been seen around town and that he still lived in the black house. I assumed that meant he was back on his meds and was doing all right.

Although we didn't speak, I received a letter from him in November 1996, written in the familiar printed block letters, with bad spelling and grammar, on what appeared to be Big Chief tablet ruled paper. The letter was sent to my publisher and forwarded to me. Eddie had written to say that his mother had died earlier in the year and that he was now all alone in the black house. That he missed me, but that I was right to have left him. That was it. I sent a sympathy card to his house, telling Eddie that I was sorry to hear about his mother and that I hoped he was feeling better. I didn't acknowledge anything else. He never sent a reply, and I was glad he didn't.

The next time I heard about Eddie was when my father sent me a newspaper clipping from the *Limite Observer*, dated April 30, 2000, which featured an interview with "Evil Eddie," the notorious Satanist living with a "witch" in a house in east Limite. A photo showed Eddie with a shaved head and a devilish goatee. He was obviously emulating Anton LaVey, who had died in 1997. That same year, Eddie officially founded The Temple, which was designated as a not-for-profit "religious" organization that funded various activities associated with his newsletter, website, and "church." A congregation of sorts gathered at the black house once a month. Eddie was known as the High Priest of The Temple. He had completely converted the Chicory Lane home to run his business—writing and publishing *Godless Times* and utilizing eBay to sell Satanic-themed jewelry (pentagram necklaces and the like), T-shirts, and other atheistic literature. Whether he still used the fallout shelter as a "sanctuary," the article didn't reveal.

Atheists, self-professed witches and magi, and other characters with dubious backgrounds came from all over Texas, Mexico, and sometimes from out of state. The largest assembly he ever hosted counted to seventeen. That didn't sound like a lot, but when one considered that Limite was a small town in Bible Belt Texas, it was remarkable. I was surprised he hadn't been run out of town and lynched.

"I'm the most hated man in Limite," he was quoted as saying. "My neighbors think I eat the corpses of babies and sacrifice virgins at the altar. That's what people think of when the word 'Satanist' comes up. That couldn't be further from the truth. A black mass is simply a parody of a Catholic mass. It doesn't involve blood or children or violence of any kind. It's an intellectual—and very funny—exercise."

He went on to add that he'd had plenty of trouble with law enforcement and complaints from the public, but the fact of the matter was he wasn't harming anyone. It was perfectly within his rights to practice his religion and operate his business. Was it offensive? Absolutely—at least it was to the population of Limite. But being offensive or having bad taste wasn't a crime.

A woman named Dora Walton was mentioned as being his "second-in-command" or High Priestess. The article wasn't clear whether or not Eddie was married to her or if she lived in the house. A "Magister Wade Jones," a CPA from California, was treasurer of the congregation. He had been a member of LaVey's Church of Satan in San Francisco.

When asked why he chose to establish his "church" in a small town like Limite, Eddie answered, "There's a sacred spot on the property where I grew up, the house on Chicory Lane. Call it a source, a vortex, or whatever—there is power emanating from it, the power of Satan. It's had a hold on me since I was a child. I can never leave it." Where on the property was this source? Was it in the house? "I'd better not say," Eddie replied. "For my own security."

Ha—I knew what that sacred spot was, and I had spent much time in it myself.

In closing, Eddie stated that all he wanted was to live and work and practice his beliefs in peace without harassment and discrimination.

I had to give credit to the *Observer* for presenting the piece without bias or judgment. The story made Eddie sound intelligent and well-spoken—albeit a little like a wacko freak who practiced Satanism in his backyard.

And who was Dora Walton, the High Priestess? What was all that about? Was she his lover? Maybe even his wife?

My curiosity was piqued, but not enough to warrant the trouble to find out anything. I didn't want to contact Eddie and wasn't about to ask my father to do any research.

I let it go and forgot about it.

That is, until Christmas of 2005, when Eddie made international news. He was a murderer. The headlines screamed the worst. EVIL EDDIE SLAYS LOVER. RITUAL KILLING SHOCKS NEIGHBORHOOD. DEVIL WORSHIPPERS IN BLOOD ORGY.

It occurred on Christmas Eve. Almost all of the houses on Chicory Lane in Limite were decorated in holiday lights, with front yard displays of Nativity scenes, Santa and his sled, and other common yuletide imagery. One house had no decorations—the black one, the home of Evil Eddie, devil worshipper and Satanist, the blight of the neighborhood.

Just after midnight—so in fact it was Christmas Day when the deed was discovered—Eddie decided to create his own holiday display in the front yard of his house. It was unclear when the actual murder had taken place—most likely just minutes prior—but he considered the final act to be the result of an "artist at work." Dora Walton was seven months pregnant. After her death, he performed an amateur Caesarean, removing the fetus. He then placed mother and child in the front yard, arranged as if they were a grotesque perversion of Madonna and child. Not only was it bloody and horrific, it was obscene. As the sun rose on the street, the calls flooded the police station.

As my assistant Billy had said, it was pretty creepy shit. Nothing says "Merry Christmas" better than an abattoir in a person's front yard.

Officers burst into the house. Over a hundred black candles illuminated Eddie's demonic artwork, which covered the walls. No one was there. The police searched the home and found no evidence of the crime. Then they went outside to the backyard. The bomb shelter door was closed, but they could hear music coming from down below. They opened the steel door, stormed the underground lair, and uncovered the scene of the crime. Eddie, naked, sat cross-legged on the floor in the center of the pentagram, lost in a meditational trance. He was drenched in gooey, coagulating blood. Two large knives lay next to the murderer. The music was Black Sabbath from the seventies.

The cops arrested Eddie, and he offered no resistance. He didn't say a word.

By noon of Christmas Day, the street was overflowing with news vans, police cars, ambulances, and dozens of curious onlookers. It was a circus.

I found out about it from my father, whom I had called midafternoon to wish a Merry Christmas. It was all over the news, he said, so I booted up my computer and found the stories online. I'm afraid I may have gone into shock. I don't remember crawling back into bed, but that's where I was when I opened my eyes at six p.m. that evening. Three or four hours had passed since I'd spoken to Dad. The news stories were still on my computer monitor. I must have been so repulsed that I'd turned away from the desk and stumbled back into my bedroom.

The tears flowed freely. "Why, Eddie?" I called out, to nobody in the house. "What happened? Why did you do it?"

The first thing I thought was that he would be found not guilty by reason of insanity. That was surely a no-brainer. After all, he was supposed to be on medication. Had he gone off of it? What had been the trigger for him to commit such a vile deed? The questions mounted, and I was determined to find out the answers. But what good could I do? I was stuck in Chicago. Eddie was in jail in Texas; he was fifty at the time. Would he be properly represented? Would he be able to afford a good lawyer? It was doubtful. He had no family or friends whom I knew of. Eddie was all alone.

On December 26, I attempted to phone the police station in Limite to find out information about Eddie's legal status, but I was unable to get through to anyone. All I learned was that he was being held in the county jail until after the holidays and that a public defender was representing him. A *public defender*. For Christ's sake, Eddie had no chance!

For a good part of the day, I debated with myself whether or not I should jump on a plane and fly down to assist him.

Eventually I dropped the idea. Aside from perhaps offering to help pay for legal services, what could I do? I also had my professional reputation to consider. The media would have a field day linking the famous romance author Shelby Truman with a "devil-worshipping" murderer who rivaled Jack the Ripper in his *modus operandi*. At the time, I didn't think it would be wise to insert myself into the investigation or judicial process. Later, though, I came to the conclusion that Eddie needed advocates.

News from Limite was sparse for the first few months of 2006. Eddie was held without bail. The trial was scheduled for September, so that meant the poor man would be stuck in a cell, possibly without medical attention. He needed a hospital, not jail. Through the media, I finally saw a photograph of the victim, Dora Walton. The woman with whom Eddie had been living—his "High Priestess"—was a brunette and beautiful in an "exotic" way; she may have had Mediterranean or Middle Eastern blood. She was forty-one years old at the time of her murder.

Things started looking up for Eddie in the summer. Robert Crane, a respected defense attorney in the state, volunteered his time *pro bono* to represent the defendant. I phoned Crane's office, explained who I was, and offered to help in any way I could. Crane explained that they were going for an insanity defense, but it was going to be a tough ride. The prosecution's psychiatric examinations were "inconclusive," and, apparently, Eddie was mostly lucid and rational and knew exactly what he had done. He'd even signed a confession outlining the steps he'd taken to drug, strangle, and eviscerate his victim. The fact that he had aborted a seven-month-old fetus was the clincher. Crane said the best he could hope for was to prevent Eddie from receiving the death penalty.

It was all so unbelievable. It made me physically ill for months to think that I had slept with—and loved—this beautiful but very sick man.

To make things worse, my father died at the end of August.

20

Limite was still hot in September. The arid climate could be stifling, especially when one was acclimated to an area of the country that usually had a short, moderate summer and seven months of winter. As soon as I stepped out of the airport to pick up a rental car, the "dry heat" hit me hard. The odor of petroleum in the air was something that residents became so accustomed to that they didn't smell it anymore. After being away for a long time, I'd forgotten about it, too. Boy, did Limite *stink*.

As I drove into town, familiar sights bombarded me; however, many spots were also overrun by new buildings and facelifts. The east side of town had expanded even farther, such that Chicory Lane was now fairly deep in the medium-sized city of a hundred thousand or so inhabitants. Limite had certainly grown, but had the people progressed with the times? When I drove into my father's apartment complex, I noticed a pickup truck in the parking lot with a rifle on the gun rack and a Confederate flag bumper sticker. No, sometimes social attitudes and trends never changed. I figured all smaller cities in rural areas were the same way. It'd take time for change to trickle down from the larger, cultural centers of the country—if they did at all.

My father had lived simply, so there wasn't a lot of stuff to get rid of from the apartment. Furniture and clothing would be donated, of course. Getting his personal affairs in order would take a bit of time, and I planned to stay as long as necessary to complete the task and put the apartment on the market. Billy was already on the payroll in Chicago, so I didn't have to worry about work.

The first thing I did after unpacking was drive to the funeral home where my father's body was being prepared. Some family friends from the church my parents had belonged to their entire lives had stepped up to the plate and graciously taken care of arranging a viewing and funeral for me. It was something I wasn't prepared to do myself; it was just too painful. The enormity of what happened didn't fully hit me until I saw him in the casket. I cried like a child.

A few days later, my father was buried in Limite Cemetery on the northeast side of town, right next to my mother. Dad had purchased the plots a long time ago, which was ironic since I could have paid for them with no sweat. Taking care of official death notices and Dad's estate was a slower process, so in the meantime I decided to look into what was going on with Eddie's trial. Coincidentally, it was due to begin in a couple of days.

I phoned Robert Crane to let him know I was in town. He offered to make sure I got a seat in the courtroom, but I wasn't sure I wanted to be there. "Your name will be on the list should you decide otherwise," he said.

"How's Eddie doing?"

"Well, he's fit to stand trial, and he can communicate when he wants to. Most of the time he stays silent. I fear being locked up is having a negative effect on his mental condition."

"Can't something be done? Can't you sue the county or something for inhumane treatment?"

"Unfortunately, no. Eddie was found to be mentally sound by the court-appointed psychiatrists. It didn't matter that the doctors I brought in said otherwise. They'll be testifying at the trial, though. We'll do what we can and hope for the best. Ms. Truman, there's no question that Eddie will be found guilty and will, at a minimum, get life in prison. The prosecutor's going for the death penalty, so the goal is to prevent that. Nobody 'wins' here, but perhaps we can save a life."

I decided to attend the opening of the trial. Luckily, no one from the press knew who I was. I went through the x-ray screener and checked in with the court officials so I could slip inside when they opened the doors. The courtroom held only so many seats; therefore, they were at a premium. Some news outlets weren't able to get in. No one showed up to support Eddie, but the victim was represented by family members and friends. Mr. Crane sat alone at the defense table. When he saw me, I gave him a subtle nod, and, recognizing me, he smiled back.

Interestingly, I saw an older man in the courtroom who I thought looked familiar. He was tall, had a head of white hair, and appeared to be in his late seventies. I'd seen him somewhere before. Who was he? It really bugged me. Was he someone from our church? One of my former teachers from high school or junior high?

A door on the side of the bench opened. A bailiff led out Eddie, who was dressed in an ill-fitting suit. He was bald and thin, with dark circles under his eyes. He didn't look well at all. He must have lost twenty pounds since I'd seen him last, almost twelve years ago. I'd aged, too. I was fifty-two and Eddie was fifty-one. He ignored the spectators behind the rail and sat at the table next to Mr. Crane. I was sitting in the back, so I doubted he could have spotted me had he attempted to look. I preferred that he not see me at all, but if he did, I planned to give him a smile. He probably needed it.

The trial began. Judge Fredrickson—a gruff-looking man with fat cheeks—took his place as we all rose. Then the jury entered and took their seats—twelve men and women and a couple of alternates. There was one black juror—a middle-aged man—and four white women of various ages. The rest were all clean-cut, white, all-American male citizens of Limite. The youngest appeared to be in his twenties, the oldest in his sixties.

The District Attorney, a man named Paul Shamrock, got things going with the opening statement. He was a slick good ol' boy type, perhaps fifty-something, and he spoke with a heavy West Texas accent. Shamrock was a charmer, used to putting on a show for the jury. He laid down the basics of the case. "Edward" Newcott had been living with a common-law wife, Dora Walton, at his house and place of business on Chicory Lane. When he started to refer to Eddie as a "known devil worshipper," Mr. Crane stood and objected; it was overruled. Besides, there was probably no way that anyone in Limite didn't already know about "Evil Eddie."

Eddie and Dora were friends with another unmarried couple who lived together in another part of town—Wade Jones and Catherine Carter. Jones, a former member of LaVey's Church of Satan, worked for Eddie, and Carter was a regular fixture at the "black house," as it was called. The quartet ran a Satanic church called The Temple—all stuff I already knew—and they were controversial figures in Limite. Crane didn't object to any of that. The DA promised that evidence would show the two couples had engaged in a drug-fueled "black mass" of Satanic rituals—objected to by Crane but overruled—and that afterward, according to the defendant's own written confession obtained by the police, "Mr. Newcott" drugged, strangled, and mutilated his victim in a frenzied state. Shamrock said the jurors would hear testimony about how Eddie had cut open Ms. Walton's abdomen, removed her unborn child, and then built a "demonic sculpture"—again the objection, again the overruling—in the front yard of the house for everyone to see "as a slap in the face to humanity," for this had occurred on Christmas Eve, a "sacred night for anyone living in Limite."

It sounded pretty bad.

The prosecution's opening statement was over in an hour. The judge didn't want to take a break, so Crane rose to outline what would become the defense's strategy—that the defendant was a mentally ill person who didn't realize what he was doing on Christmas Eve of 2005. Testimony from medical experts and psychiatrists would attest to Eddie's condition. After hearing all the facts, Crane promised, the jury would agree that Eddie should be found not guilty by reason of insanity.

I noticed one juror roll his eyes.

We broke for lunch. Eddie and Crane remained sitting at the defense table as the spectators got up to leave. It was then that Eddie turned his head around to look at the crowd that had come to see him. I noticed him nodding at the tall, white-haired man who looked familiar, and the old gentleman nodded back. Someone on Eddie's side? Who could it be?

Then Eddie's eyes found me. They grew wide with recognition. His jaw dropped slightly. I did what I'd planned—I smiled and gave him a thumbs-up. He was too shocked, I think, to respond. I went out with the throng and looked for a fast food joint in the area to get something to eat. As I walked, reflecting on the day's proceedings, I found it surprising that I wasn't as upset about the trial as I'd feared. It was terribly interesting, and as a writer, attending it could only help me in my work. But yes, it was also painful to see Eddie at the defense table. It hurt to see his shaved head and his decrepit body. For a man who was once spectacularly gorgeous, he appeared to be a completely different person. It was so very sad.

Outside in the street, a news crew spotted me and a young woman came over with a microphone, followed by a cameraman. "Pardon me," she said, "aren't you Shelby Truman?"

"Yes," I said, but I didn't want to be interviewed. "Please, no comment, I don't wish to talk, sorry." I started to walk away.

"But Ms. Truman, we understand you used to live across the street from Evil Eddie . . . Ms. Truman." She started following me in that irritating, obsessive way media people are so good at.

I turned and forcefully told her to stop following me. "I mean it," I said. Finally, she looked apologetic. "Very well, thank you," she said and pulled the cameraman away. He had been shooting anyway, so I figured I'd be on the ten o'clock news doing the get-out-of-my-face routine. It was interesting that she'd known about my connection with Eddie. But I didn't mind, as long as my romantic involvement with him over the years didn't come out. Even if it did, what the hell, it was the truth. My publicist would probably love the revelation.

A Wendy's burger joint provided refuge, and I spotted a few other folks who had been spectators that morning. Best to avoid them. However, as I sat with my salad and baked potato, I noticed the tall, white-haired man at a table by himself. He ate slowly, seemingly lost in thought. I built up the nerve to approach his table.

"Excuse me, sir?"

He looked up. "Yes?"

"I'm sorry, but I know you somehow, and I'm trying to remember how I do. My name is Shelby Truman, and I'm attending the Eddie Newcott—Edward Newcott—trial."

The man blinked, and I thought he would choke. "My word, little Shelby Truman."

"I beg your pardon?"

"My name is Jim Baxter. I used to be a police detective. You knew me as Detective Baxter, back in the sixties." He tried to stand up but I stopped him and sat across from him.

My God, it all came back to me. He was the nice policeman that had investigated the abduction of my little brother back in '66.

"You gave me gum," I said.

"Did I?"

"Yes, and you were nice to me. Gosh, I remember you, Detective. How nice to see you."

"Very nice to see you, too. I understand you're rich and famous."

I shook my head, embarrassed. "Well . . ."

"Don't look that way, you should be proud."

"Thank you, Detective."

"I'm not a detective any more. I'm retired. I'm seventy-eight years old."

"Well, you look great."

The man shrugged. "I golf sometimes, although I'm slowing down. I'm sorry to hear about your father. He and I saw each other around town once in a while. Terrific fellow."

"Thank you. Yeah, I'm here settling his affairs. Know anyone who needs a two-bedroom apartment on the east side?"

"No, but if I hear of anything . . ."

I gave him the realtor's information and went back to my table, but he gestured to me, asking me to join him.

"Mr. Baxter—"

"Call me Jim."

"Jim, why are you attending the trial?"

"I could ask you the same thing."

"Eddie and I lived across the street from each other, remember?"

"Yes, I do. He was a witness in what happened to your baby brother. Eddie was, what, eleven years old?"

"That's right."

The man shook his head. "That boy went through an awful time."

"Yeah, I guess he did. But you caught Mr. Alpine—the man who really did it."

"Yes, we did."

"Boy, I'd sure like to know more about your investigation. I don't think I really know much about it at all. I was only twelve then. A lot of those memories have been blocked out, you know what I mean?"

"Sure I do. Your family went through a terrible tragedy."

"So why are you here at the trial? It looked like you and Eddie know each other."

"We do. We got to know each other very well back in 1966. And I've had contact with him at various times throughout the years as he grew up and became an adult. Limite may be booming, but it's still a small town at heart."

"Eddie really did kill that woman, didn't he?"

"Yes, he did. But I agree with his defense attorney. Eddie Newcott is a sick man. Very sick, but his affliction is subtle. I'm supposed to testify."

"What are you going to say?"

"Ms. Truman—"

"Call me Shelby."

"Shelby, I can't tell you. In fact, I may not get to testify. The prosecution has filed a motion to keep Crane from calling me to the stand. They say it's irrelevant to the case. Mr. Crane and I don't agree. But the prosecution also wants to call a witness that the defense objects to. Maybe there will be an even trade. So if you're in the courtroom if and when I do testify, you'll hear it for yourself."

"When will that be?"

He estimated that the prosecution would take a week to present its evidence. Crane planned to call Baxter to the stand toward the end of the defense. It could be two weeks before his testimony was heard.

It didn't matter. I was hooked and had made up my mind to stay in Limite for the duration of the trial. Baxter gave me his card, and we traded contact details.

When I returned to the courthouse, it was time for the prosecution to begin presenting its case.

21

Over the next four days, the prosecution paraded several experts, witnesses, and policemen to testify against Eddie. During this phase, it all came out how Eddie had been to prison in the eighties for assault. His prior criminal record didn't look good. District Attorney Shamrock made a big point out of the supposition that Eddie was a time bomb of anger and hate. Next came the confession itself, read aloud for all to hear. Eddie had dictated and signed it in the presence of several officers, swearing that he was not under duress. A psychiatrist went on the record claiming that depression and an anxiety disorder was not a mental illness—*what?* The doctor believed Eddie knew what he was doing when the crime was committed.

One of the most compelling witnesses was Dora Walton's sister, whose testimony, I felt, might actually help the defense. She described how she and her sister came from a broken home in Hobbs, New Mexico. Dora had spent time with a motorcycle club—an "outlaw" gang similar to Hells Angels—in California for several years. In other words, she had been some biker's "old lady" for a while. She had been hooked on drugs and alcohol but managed to maintain her good looks. She'd had at least two abortions that her sister knew of. Dora eventually left the bikers in the mid-nineties and returned to New Mexico to admit herself to a drug rehabilitation center. It was there, her sister claimed, that Dora was diagnosed as bipolar. Right there, she had something in common with Eddie—they both suffered from mental illness. Dora began subscribing to *Godless Times* and felt that the words spoke to her. She began to correspond with Eddie and, in 1999, came to Limite to live with him, where Eddie made her "High Priestess." Together, the couple made news in the small town as "a warlock and his witch" with their goings-on. After that, Dora's sister never heard from her sibling again.

Mr. Crane made dozens of objections during the examination of the witness, almost all of which were overruled. What was left for the jurors to mull over was whether or not Eddie had "put some kind of spell" on Dora, taking advantage of her mental illness in order to bring her into his fold. On the other hand, Crane could perhaps use this testimony to show that Eddie was indeed sick, too, and therefore not responsible for his actions. That's what I hoped.

Next, a Limite patrolman named Sawyer, now a sergeant, testified about an incident that occurred in April of 2001. He and his partner were called to a disturbance at the black house on Chicory Lane around midnight. Several cars and trucks were parked on the street in front of Eddie's house. The 911 call, no doubt made by one of the neighbors, had been about the sight of "naked people" running around outside. When the police arrived, they heard death metal music coming from inside the house—but not loud enough to be a nuisance. No one answered the door, so they burst inside to find a houseful of revelers—all in the nude. When the prosecutor asked what the officer thought was going on, Sawyer replied, "It was one of them devil worship orgies."

Crane objected, of course, and this time it was sustained.

Sawyer confirmed that Eddie and Dora were among the participants. He counted twelve people in total, all couples. No arrests were made but a warning was issued—no one should be outside in a state of undress. Sawyer claimed that Eddie told him none of his guests had been outdoors.

Crane cross-examined and established that there were no signs of "devil worshipping" or anything Satanic that could be seen. No pentagrams, no incense, no inverted crosses, no men or women in hooded cloaks, and no creatures with horns or tails. That last bit got a laugh from the jury. "Couldn't it have been a gathering of swingers? You know, couples that engage in alternative sex practices?"

Sawyer blushed. "I guess so," he answered.

"Is there a law against that if all the participants are consenting adults?"

"I guess not."

Crane also managed to establish that if none of Eddie's guests went outside, then that might have meant that whoever called 911 must have been a peeping tom. The judge admonished the attorney for the remark, but it nevertheless scored points with the jury and made Sawyer look foolish.

Despite these minor "wins," as time went on, I began to realize that this was Limite, and the jury was made up of conservative Christians—good plain folks. They weren't going to find the concept of a swingers party acceptable, legal or not. They disapproved. I believe they went into the courtroom from the beginning ready to find Eddie guilty, thereby putting a final end to the black mark he had placed on their little town.

More testimony brought out how Eddie's neighbors had consistently tried to push him off their block. In 2003, everyone on the street staged a protest and marched up and down Chicory Lane with signs that read, "Evict Evil Eddie," "Evil Eddie

WILL GO TO HELL," "NO DEVIL WORSHIP IN LIMITE," and "EVIL EDDIE MUST GO!" The purpose of all this, it seemed, was to convince the jury that Eddie was a menace to the peace. He had purposefully antagonized his neighbors by not leaving. The way Shamrock couched everything made it sound as if Eddie was a blight on society, and that, in itself, was a good reason to be persecuted. Never mind that nothing Eddie was doing was criminal. Crane, in the cross-examination of several witnesses, brought out that just because you didn't like someone who lived on your block didn't mean you could force him to leave. Otherwise, he was unsuccessful in presenting Eddie as harmless. Every time someone testified that Eddie was performing Satanic rituals at his home, Crane shot it down during cross. Did they actually *see* the ritual? Did they *hear* it? What exactly *was* a Satanic ritual? How would they *know* it? Unfortunately, the judge appeared to be on the prosecution's side and limited Crane's ability to cast aspersions on the witnesses' statements.

Then came a witness who revealed a lot of Eddie's history I'd always wondered about—his time in Vietnam. It seemed this man was the witness the prosecution wanted but the defense didn't. It looked like the trade had been made. Did that mean Jim Baxter would get to testify?

"State your name for the record."

"Victor Blair."

"And how do you know the defendant?"

"I was his sergeant in the Second Battalion, First Infantry, Americal Division of the United States Armed Forces during the Vietnam War."

"Americal Division?"

"That was the unofficial name for our unit. The 196th Infantry Brigade of the army."

"And where were you stationed when you knew the defendant?"

"Da Nang, Vietnam."

"And when did you know him?

"From December 1971 to June 1972."

Blair was in his late fifties, had a buzz cut, and looked as if he had come from Central Casting as an ex-Army man. He was in fine shape and sported the appropriate ruggedness.

"Was the defendant in your battalion?"

"Yes, sir, he was a private."

Shamrock established that Blair was now retired and had been in the army for twenty years following the Vietnam War. He currently resided in California.

"How would you describe the defendant as a soldier?" Shamrock asked.

"He was a problem soldier, sir."

"What do you mean by that?"

"He had an attitude problem. He didn't want to follow rules, and he disregarded authority. But he was respected in many ways."

"Hold on. Go back to 'attitude problem.' What do you mean by that?"

"Private Newcott often went out in the shit—excuse me, Your Honor, I mean he often went out on his own to look for the enemy. It was very dangerous and against protocol."

"He went out on his own?"

"Yes, sir."

"I don't understand. Please explain it to the jury."

"Sometimes at night, Private Newcott would simply slip out of the base and go out on a patrol alone, without authorization, in search of enemy units."

"I see. Was he disciplined for these actions?"

"Many times."

"Why do you think he did that, Mr. Blair?"

"We all thought he was nuts. Brave, but nuts."

181

Crane didn't object. Shamrock continued, "Did he put the other men in his unit in jeopardy by disobeying orders?"

"I wouldn't say he disobeyed orders, he disobeyed *rules*. He wasn't supposed to go into the bush by himself. That was a crazy thing to do."

"Tell us, Mr. Blair, what kind of reputation did Private Newcott have among his fellow soldiers?"

"I'd say he was respected, in a way."

"How so?"

"Like I said, he was uncommonly brave. I mean, to go out into the jungle at night, *alone*, took some ba—er, some courage. And he got results."

"I beg your pardon?"

"Well, we all called him 'Snoop.'"

"Snoop?"

"He was good at reconnaissance. Private Newcott single-handedly brought back quite a bit of intelligence about the enemy—where they were hiding, how well they were armed. That sort of thing. He was sneaky."

"I see. Was there anything else about Private Newcott that bothered you besides his tendency to disobey the rules?"

"Yes. One day I accompanied Private Newcott's platoon on patrol. We came upon a village that we suspected of being a Viet Cong supply center. Our orders were to search the village for weapons and other evidence of enemy activity. It appeared that women, children, and elderly men were the only occupants. The kids were inside a hut that was apparently a small school. We stormed the village and rounded everyone up, including the children. The women became distressed, and the younger kids started crying. I put Private Newcott in charge of guarding the civilians while the rest of us commenced with the search. I was inside one of the huts when we heard gunfire outside. We ran out, ready to engage the enemy—but it turned out it was

Private Newcott. He had discharged his weapon at the civilians to 'scare' them. He shot up the ground where they were standing. I shouted at him to stop and demanded to know what he thought he was doing."

"And what did Private Newcott say?"

"He told me that we should just kill them all—especially the children—so that they wouldn't grow up to be enemy 'gooks.'"

"How did you respond?"

"I ordered him to stand down. I replaced him as guard and sent him to help search the village."

"What happened after that?"

"Nothing until that night. We didn't find weapons, so we left the village and went back to base. However, that night, the village burned down. There were civilian casualties. No one knew how it happened, but I found out the next day that Private Newcott had gone off on his own again the night it occurred. I confronted him about it, but he told me that he was nowhere near the village."

"Did you believe him?"

"Not really. I had no proof, none of us did. But we *all* thought he did it."

Serious objection! The spectators broke out in spontaneous murmuring. The judge banged the gavel and called for order. The attorneys were brought to the bench for a sidebar, and the jury was sent out of the courtroom. The judge continued to speak in hushed but earnest tones. Finally, counsel was released and the jury was brought back. The judge ordered that the witness's preceding testimony be struck from the record. But the damage had been done. The jury had heard it.

"Okay, Mr. Blair," Shamrock resumed. "Let's skip to June 1972. What happened with the battalion then?"

"We were deactivated and sent home."

"And was Private Newcott with you at that time?"

"No, sir, he was AWOL."

"AWOL?"

"Absent without leave. He had disappeared."

Shamrock put on an act of being very concerned. "Was that unusual?"

"Yes, sir."

"What do you know about the situation?"

"He simply vanished a few days before the unit was scheduled to depart Vietnam and return to the States."

"What was done to locate him?"

"Military police searched Da Nang from top to bottom. We finally learned that he had a Vietnamese girlfriend."

"What was her name?"

"Phan Mai. Mai. She lived In Country . . . er, out in the jungle, in a small village with her parents."

"And was Private Newcott found there?"

"Yes, he was."

"And was he ordered to leave Vietnam with his battalion?"

"Yes sir, but he refused. He planned to stay and live with her in Vietnam."

"I see. What happened after that?"

"We went home. Private Newcott didn't join us."

"And what do you know about the defendant's actions in Vietnam following the battalion's deactivation?"

"MPs were sent to arrest him for AWOL, but he and the girl had disappeared. Gone. Vanished. I received reports that no one knew where he was for an entire year. Then he suddenly showed up at the base in the summer of '73 in a state of dehydration, starvation, and delirium."

"What did he say had happened to him?"

Blair rolled his eyes. "He told investigators that he had acquired amnesia and was lost in the jungle for months."

"And you don't believe him?"

Crane objected before Blair could answer, saying that since the witness wasn't there at the time, he had no business testifying to what did or did not happen. The judge overruled, and Shamrock continued.

"I'll repeat the question—did you believe what you had heard about Private Newcott?"

"Not at all."

"Why not?"

"It's too far-fetched."

"What happened to his girlfriend?"

"We don't know. Private Newcott claimed that she had left him. Had gone off with another man. No one ever heard from her again."

More objections that the testimony was irrelevant. More overruling.

"So, Mr. Blair, knowing the defendant as you did, do you have an opinion on what might have happened to Private Newcott and his girlfriend?"

"Newcott was a good soldier, but he was rash and unpredictable. He had a rebellious streak. He bucked authority and thought he knew all the answers. I couldn't say what happened during that year he was missing. There were rumors that he had been captured and was a POW. At one point, he was suspected of working for the enemy. I know that when he returned, the army put him through the wringer with interrogations. In the end, there was no real evidence for or against him. They had to take him at his word. As for the girl, who knows? Maybe he killed her."

Objections. Pandemonium. Gavel banging. Once again, the jury was sent out of the courtroom and the lawyers were summoned to the bench. I wished I could hear what was said up there. Finally, things settled down and the jury returned. The testimony was struck from the record a second time.

When Shamrock handed over the witness for cross examination, Crane stood and asked, "Mr. Blair, you don't really know what was going on in Eddie's head during the several months the two of you worked together in the army, do you?"

"No, sir."

"And isn't it true that Vietnamese civilians disappeared all the time during the war? They were displaced and moved about?"

"That's true."

"Mr. Blair, you testified earlier that the defendant was 'crazy.'"

"Yes, sir."

"You are not a medical expert, are you?"

"No, sir."

"But you are trained to assess the mental states of your men, is that correct?"

"Yes, sir."

"Please tell the court why you thought the defendant was, as you say, 'crazy.'"

"Well, sir, he had a morbid outlook. All he talked about was death and the devil and how evil the enemy was. Everyone in his unit tended to ostracize him. That's not a good thing in the army. He was considered very weird, sir."

"Weird, how?"

"Just some of the things he'd say. He constantly tried to tell the men that there was no God. He once got into an argument with the chaplain at the base in Da Nang. It almost escalated into a fistfight, sir. I believe Private Newcott was a very violent person."

"Would you say he was 'disturbed'?"

"Absolutely."

"Thank you. No further questions."

We broke for lunch.

22

After lunch, Shamrock called Wade Jones to the stand. I realized he was the young man with the long red hair whom I had met in 1994 when Eddie had given me a tour of his home office. He was obviously over a decade older, but he still had his long locks. He, too, wore a goatee. Frankly, I thought he looked more sinister than Eddie.

Shamrock established that Jones was a member of The Temple and had known Eddie for seventeen years. His girlfriend of six years was Catherine Carter, who was also a member of the congregation.

"Were you paid by the defendant to work for him?"

"Yes, sir."

"What were your duties?"

"I was good with computers and stuff, so I handled the website and social media."

"Were you friends with the defendant?"

"Sure. We were friends." Jones appeared uncomfortable answering that.

"Did you ever have any conversations with the defendant regarding his girlfriend, Dora Walton?"

"Lots. I mean, we talked about all kinds of stuff. We talked about his relationship, we talked about my relationship with Catherine."

"And did the defendant ever say anything about Dora Walton that concerned you?"

"Yes. He had a hard time with her pregnancy. He didn't want kids. He told me that he begged her to get an abortion, but she wouldn't do it. As her belly grew bigger, his behavior became more erratic. He started doing drugs again."

"What kinds of drugs?"

"Pot, mostly, but usually he just drank. A lot. And he got very belligerent when he drank alcohol. Sometimes he got very scary."

"How so?"

"About a month before the, uh, crime, Dora came over to our house. I believe she was six months pregnant at the time. She had a black eye and a busted lip. She told us that Eddie—uh, the defendant—got drunk and became abusive. He threatened to 'cut out her baby.'"

"Those were his exact words?"

"According to Dora, yes."

I expected Crane to stand and object for hearsay reasons, but he didn't. He seemed to be allowing this testimony to play out.

"Mr. Jones, what happened on Christmas Eve of last year?"

"Catherine and I went over to Eddie's house for a party. It was just the four of us—me, Catherine, Eddie, and Dora. We had food, drank a lot of wine, and—well, Dora didn't drink because of her pregnancy. The rest of us got pretty intoxicated. And then we . . . well, we had sex, sir."

"All of you? Together."

"Yes. We practiced alternative lifestyles."

"By that, you mean you were swingers."

Jones turned red and averted his eyes. "I guess you can say that."

"Can you tell us what kind of mood the defendant was in?"

Jones shrugged. "Aside from being drunk, he was in a festive mood."

"Did you have any idea of what he was planning to do?"

"None."

"How did the evening end for you?"

"Around twelve thirty a.m., Catherine and I went home. We left Eddie and Dora in their living room."

Shamrock looked at Crane and said, "Your witness."

Eddie's lawyer stood and said, "I have no questions at this time, but the defense will be calling Mr. Jones to the stand at a later time."

Wade Jones walked out of the courtroom without looking at Eddie.

Next, Shamrock brought out the hard, physical evidence of the crime. Through his witnesses' testimonies, he had already set up Eddie as a devil worshiper who performed scandalous and immoral acts in his home, despite the will of his neighbors to take his "sins" elsewhere. The nitty-gritty facts of the crime were as horrific as expected, and the police officers, medical examiners, and forensics experts laid it all out in excruciating detail. Crime scene photos were shown to the jury—not to the spectators—and many of them turned their heads away in revulsion. At one point, the judge ordered a recess when one juror thought she might throw up. I didn't want to see the pictures. I'm pretty resilient, but that would have been too upsetting. Just the description of what went down that night was enough to put images in my head that would never go away.

Although no one can say for certain what the exact sequence of events was, investigators pieced together a scenario that made sense to them and acted as a frame for all the pieces of the puzzle.

The lead detective in the case, Lieutenant Seabolt, provided most of the testimony and his opinion of what happened.

On Christmas Eve, Eddie, Dora, Wade Jones, and Catherine Carter were together in Eddie's house. The place was decorated in Eddie's devilish artwork and lit entirely with black candles. It was evident that food and drink had been consumed. Evidence of sexual activity was present in the living room—pillows, sheets, and blankets strewn around the floor and furniture contained traces of bodily fluids. Seabolt figured that the party was a night of debauchery for the participants. The two couples had eaten and drunk and had sex.

The most damaging evidence was found in the kitchen. Traces of the drug flunitrazepam, otherwise known as Rohypnol or "roofies"—the "date-rape drug"—was found in a bowl. Investigators found an empty bottle of the prescription drug, which is illegal to possess in the United States. The pills had come from Mexico. Eddie had apparently crushed all the pills into a powder and spiked a glass of orange juice. An abundance of the drug was found in Dora's body.

After Jones and Carter left, Eddie and Dora moved from the house to the bomb shelter. There, death metal music played on the stereo system. It was unknown what took place prior to the killing. Seabolt suggested that the couple participated in a black mass, a ritual for their Satanic cult. Seeing that the date was Christmas Eve, it was to be a symbolic act of irreverence and blasphemy.

Crane objected, saying that Seabolt's statement was prejudicial and merely speculation. The judge, surprisingly, overruled it. The fact that the fallout shelter was painted black and contained a huge inverted pentagram on one wall and other iconography of the Satanist movement originally founded by Anton LaVey went a long way toward supporting Seabolt's contention.

Still, there was no proof that a "Satanic ritual" had taken place. I doubted that the jury would consider that.

If Dora had ingested the Rohypnol in the house, it would not have taken very long for her to pass out. Seabolt suggested that the couple had immediately moved to the fallout shelter after she had had her juice. Whether there had been a ritual or not, it was fairly clear what happened next. Dora fell unconscious. Autopsy reports were inconclusive on the matter, but the medical examiner testified that she had "most likely" been strangled to death before Eddie took the blades to her.

He used large butcher knives—very sharp, very strong. Bathrobes, presumably worn by the couple to traverse from the house to the shelter, lay on the floor in a lake of blood. Seabolt suggested that Eddie had removed the robe from the dead victim and then proceeded with the evisceration. Bloody tracks and trails led from the bomb shelter door across the lawn to the side of the house, through the gate, and into the front lawn. Eddie had carried or dragged Dora's body and the aborted fetus and then used an easel to prop them up, assembling the parts into a Madonna-and-child tableau.

Once the deed was done, Eddie apparently went back to the bomb shelter, sat cross-legged on the floor, and waited for the police to arrive. Seabolt testified that Eddie never resisted arrest and didn't say a word.

When the prosecution rested, I was so shaken and disturbed that I had to go back to my father's apartment with a bottle of tequila. I had a whole weekend to drown my shock and horror before the defense began its case on Monday.

23

The Best Western hotel clock reads 4:22 in the morning. I actually attempt to stop the documentary film that is playing in my brain and at least *pretend* to get some sleep, but it's useless. After getting out of bed, going to the bathroom, and staring at the bags under my eyes in the mirror, I curse aloud. I really don't want to face Eddie at the prison without a night's sleep, but now it's unavoidable. I'll just have to arm myself with a shitload of coffee beforehand. I will certainly crash afterward. I just hope it's not on the drive back to George Bush International for my flight to Limite, where I'll attend the park dedication. But I will catch an hour on the plane, I imagine, and surely sleep well tomorrow night. It might have been a better idea to spend another night in Livingston, but I pictured wanting to get out of town as quickly as possible after seeing Eddie. I'll be all right. It won't be the first time I've pulled an all-nighter, though it's not a lot of fun at my age.

Nevertheless, I crawl back in bed and let the images, recordings, and memories float across the screening room in my mind. The end of the movie is almost at hand, so I figure I might as well finish it.

Mr. Crane launched his defense after the weekend, and I dutifully sat in the courtroom to observe. The demand for seats hadn't diminished; in fact, it seemed as if even more journalists and curiosity seekers had crowded the halls in an attempt to get inside. They'd come from all over the country. More than one news outlet reported my presence at the trial. There were a couple more interview requests, but I declined all of them.

Throughout the trial, Eddie never looked at me again. He wouldn't turn his head to see who might be in the room. He sat at the table, practically comatose, staring straight ahead. Rarely would he lean over and whisper anything to his lawyer; usually, it was Crane who, every now and then, imparted something into Eddie's ear. Eddie would nod or not respond at all. I wondered if he'd been given a sedative; he seemed to be drugged. At any rate, he appeared very calm throughout the proceedings.

Mr. Crane's first witness was Wade Jones, making a repeat appearance.

After preliminary refresher questions to remind the jury of the man's relationship to Eddie, Crane quickly got to the point. "Mr. Jones, is it true you attended the monthly 'services' at my client's home, is that correct?"

"Yes, sir. They were in The Temple."

"You are referring to the bomb shelter in the backyard?"

"That's right."

"Please tell the jury about those services. What was the content? What went on there?"

Jones provided a detailed description of Eddie's beliefs regarding atheism and Satanism. The Temple was, of course, inspired by Anton LaVey, and Eddie structured his black masses along the same lines as those of the Church of Satan in San Francisco. The mention of LaVey reminded me of the man's death in 1997, which I had read about in the news, recalling to my mind

Eddie's fascination with the Satanist and his tenets. Jones went on to describe every blasphemous step of the black mass, which was indeed a wicked parody of a Catholic mass. The jury was beyond shocked.

"Did you really worship the devil in these services, Mr. Jones?"

"Not really," the witness answered. "The devil—Satan—is a symbol. We don't believe he's a real entity or deity. For Satanists, the devil merely means liberation."

"Liberation from what?"

"The confines of Christian society. We believe that man should embrace his carnal and animalistic instincts. It's natural. It's human. We believe religion was foisted upon us to keep us in line."

"So there were no animal sacrifices, no blood rites, no conjuring up demons from the underworld?"

Jones laughed. "No. That's just what everyone thinks Satanism is. They're wrong."

Shamrock objected, saying the witness wasn't qualified to define what "everyone thinks." The judge sustained.

Crane went on. "Very well. Mr. Jones, you testified the other day that you worked for my client. Would you please repeat what you told the jury?

"I was the IT guy, I guess you could say. I made sure all the technical stuff behind running the business worked. I maintained the website and handled our presence on social networking media."

"Social networking media?"

Back in 2006, *social media* was a brand-new term. We had MySpace, Twitter had just launched, and Facebook existed only for students—although in a month it would open to the public. Jones gave a thumbnail description of what is now common knowledge for nearly everyone on the planet.

Crane handed Jones some sheets of paper. "Do you recognize these?"

The witness nodded. "These are copies of emails that were going around."

"Could you please identify the first email?"

"Yeah, it's from me to Dora."

"What is the date of the email?"

"December 18, 2005."

"That's about a week prior to the date of the murder, is that correct?"

"I guess so."

"Could you please read the email?"

"Sure. Uh, 'Dear Dora. Eddie seems to be getting worse with the anxiety. Today he became unusually belligerent. Is he off his medication? Sorry I have to ask. Signed, Wade.'"

"Fine," Crane said. "So you knew my client was on medication for an anxiety disorder and depression?"

"Yes, sir. The whole inner circle knew."

"When you say, 'inner circle,' what do you mean?"

"The core group of The Temple. Eddie, Dora, Catherine, me . . ." He named a couple of other people as well.

Crane thanked Jones, took the paper, and submitted it to the court as evidence. "Now, Mr. Jones, please do the same for the second email in your hands."

"Uh, it's dated December 19. It's from Dora to me. 'Wade—Eddie and I decided that the drugs the doctors give us are evil. If he doesn't want to take the medicine, it's his right not to. I support his decision. However, I agree with you that he is becoming more unstable. He keeps saying my baby is going to be evil. I will try to reason with him.'"

Crane submitted that missive as evidence and went on. I was starting to get what he was doing—establish that Eddie was mentally off balance at the time of the crime.

"Mr. Jones, when you and Ms. Carter went to my client's home on Christmas Eve last year, were you planning to worship the devil?"

"No, sir."

"It was just a party?"

"Yes, sir."

Crane paused to consult his notes. "Now, Mr. Jones. What was the defendant like, in general?"

Jones shrugged. "Most of the time he was fine. Very smart. Very charismatic. He was fun to be around."

"Were there other times when he was 'off his meds,' as you put it?"

"Yeah. There was a period a couple of years ago, about a month long, I think it was in the summer of 2004. He went a little nuts and was in that babbling state. Nervous as he—heck. I could see it was torture for him. Eddie did keep his sense of humor, though. He'd say that demons were tormenting him for his past sins."

"He thought that was funny?"

Jones raised his eyebrows. "Yeah."

"Did he say what these past sins were?"

"No. Just that he'd done horrible things. He was in Vietnam, you know. I really don't know a lot about Eddie's past."

"So, it's your opinion that the defendant was disturbed by events that took place when he was in the armed services?"

Shamrock objected, saying that the witness was no expert in psychiatry and also had no knowledge of Eddie's actions in Vietnam. The judge sustained.

Crane studied his notes for a moment and then asked, "Mr. Jones, back to Christmas Eve last year, how was the defendant during the party?"

"He was all right. At least he acted like he was. There was a moment when the two of us were in the kitchen while the two ladies were in the other room. I noticed his hand shaking when he poured some wine. I asked him if he was all right. He said, 'I'm never all right.' But after that he seemed fine."

"Thank you. No more questions."

Shamrock then got up for cross-examination. "Mr. Jones, when you and Ms. Carter went to the party on Christmas Eve, did you notice if the defendant had set up the house in preparation for a party that night?"

"Uh, yeah. He had put up his artwork, and placed candles all over the house. I'm sure Dora helped him."

"What was the food, refreshments, and that sort of thing?"

"There were a couple of new bottles of tequila and vodka he'd bought. He always kept wine in the house. Food, let's see, we had turkey and stuffing, broccoli, and squash. We brought the vegetables. Eddie cooked the turkey."

"So he had the presence of mind to decorate and prepare a meal for the festivities that night?"

"I guess so."

"No further questions."

Uh oh. That plainly obliterated Crane's contention that Eddie wasn't of sound mind.

The defense's battery of medical experts took the stand next. In opposition to the prosecution's doctors, three generic psychiatrists spent an entire day testifying. The first psychiatrist spoke about anxiety disorder and depression, claiming that Eddie was definitely suffering from both. Another doctor testified about how Zoloft and clonazepam work and what would happen to a patient if medications were to suddenly cease. Symptoms of withdrawal could cause emotional instability, and he might be a danger to himself or others.

The third psychiatrist talked about phobias. It was his opinion that Eddie suffered from something called *pedophobia* and *tokophobia*. The former referred to an irrational fear of children, especially infants. Someone with pedophobia would become agitated and anxious when around babies, although the phobia is not limited to that age group. The latter referred to a fear of pregnancy and childbirth. People with tokophobia were usually women, but men have also been known to be repulsed by the reproductive process.

"And you believe Mr. Newcott suffers from these phobias?" Crane asked the doctor.

"Yes, I do."

"What causes phobias like these?"

"It's usually due to something that occurred during an individual's childhood." The psychiatrist went on to spout a bunch of medical and psychological terms and theories that I'm sure went right over the jury's heads. I'm not sure I understood it all. But the idea of pedophobia struck me as significant.

"So you believe that my client's act of cutting his own child out of the body of the baby's mother is a result of pedophobia?"

"I do."

There wasn't much Shamrock could do in his cross-examinations to shake the doctors' testimonies. It was up to the jury to decide which physicians to believe—the prosecution's or the defense's.

It had taken two whole days to present Eddie's defense, and I was afraid it was inadequate. Of course, Eddie didn't take the stand. But what else could Crane have done? He trotted in the doctors and let them have their say. He established there was no devil worshipping component to the crime. It was clear that Eddie had indeed committed it, but what person in his right mind would do what he had done? Was Eddie "crazy" or not? It seemed pretty obvious to me.

Then, just when I thought the defense was about to rest, Crane called his last witness—none other than former police detective Jim Baxter.

24

"State your name for the record."

"James Baxter."

"You go by 'Jim'?"

"That's correct."

"Please tell the court what your profession is."

"I'm retired. But I was a law enforcement officer in Limite for forty-two years."

"And what rank did you hold when you retired?"

"I was a captain. Prior to that I was a lieutenant, and before that I was a homicide detective. I started out in 1952 as an officer."

Crane paused to let that sink in. "Very impressive, Mr. Baxter. Please tell the jury, do you know the defendant, Edward Newcott?"

"I do."

"When did you first meet him?"

"It was July of 1966. He was eleven years old."

"And you have kept in touch with him since then?"

"Not in quite a while, but I kept tabs on him through the 1980s. After I retired, we never spoke."

"Could you please tell the court how you came to meet him?"

I prepared myself for some painful memories. To be frank, I wasn't sure I could handle it. It was something I'd managed to block out of my life for years, with the help of the therapy I had gone through in the eighties. But of course, no amount of therapy could cause it to totally go away. Now, here was a reminder of that horrible summer unfolding in front of me. What was going to be the point of Baxter's testimony? Why was Crane bringing this up?

"There was a case of a child abduction," Baxter said. "We questioned Mr. Newcott at the time. He was a neighbor of the victim."

"This was here in Limite?"

"That's correct. It was the Truman Baby Abduction, as it was called in the newspaper at the time."

"It was an infamous case in the history of the city, is that correct?"

"I suppose so."

"Please give us the details."

At this point, Shamrock stood and objected. "Your Honor, what is the purpose of this? This has no relevance to today's case."

Crane replied, "Your Honor, I'm attempting to establish that a traumatic event in the defendant's childhood has bearing on who he is today."

The judge pursed his mouth and then said, "I'll allow it. Please continue."

Baxter proceeded to tell the story. "On the night of July 4, 1966, my partner, the late Detective Blake Donner—he was my superior officer at the time—and I were called to the home of the Truman family. They were a couple in their late thirties with a daughter about to enter her teens. They'd recently brought a baby boy into the family. He was two months old in July. Unfortunately, he disappeared from his crib while the family was in the backyard watching fireworks. In the course of the investigation, we interviewed everyone on the street, including Eddie—uh, Mr. Newcott. He lived directly across the street and was known to the Truman family. He was never a suspect, of course, but we felt he was an important witness. As I said, he was eleven at the time."

"I see. And was the crime solved?"

"Yes, an arrest was made."

"Please tell us about that, Mr. Baxter."

The former detective sighed and continued. "His name was Gordon Alpine, a man who lived a few doors down from the Truman family on the same block. Some of you may remember he was the brother of Limite's mayor at the time. We got . . . we, uh, we received a tip that he might be a person of interest. Based on the serious nature of the crime, we were able to get a search warrant for Mr. Alpine's property."

"And what did you find?"

"Evidence that Mr. Alpine was responsible for the abduction."

"You recovered the body of the child?"

"Uh, no. The body was never found. However, we uncovered physical evidence in Mr. Alpine's home that the child had been there."

"But that's not all you found."

"No. We found some other very disturbing material."

"Can you please tell the jury what that was?"

Baxter sighed again. "Mr. Alpine possessed photographic equipment and a cache of child pornography." There was an audible gasp from some of the jurors. I may have emitted one as well. This was news to me.

Crane shook his head. "Are you talking about photographs? Movies?"

"Both. Back then, we didn't have computers, you know, so that kind of stuff was all tangible, physical material. Photographs, homemade movies. Mr. Alpine apparently belonged to a ring of pedophiles that traded this material through the mail."

Shamrock stood again. "Your Honor, this is all very shocking and salacious, but what does it have to do with the defendant?"

Crane replied, "I'm getting to that, Your Honor."

The judge nodded, intrigued. "Proceed."

"Please continue, Mr. Baxter."

"Well, we arrested Mr. Alpine and locked him in the county jail. The next day, he confessed to abducting the child. He refused to say where the body was hidden, and that maybe he'd tell us next time we talked. But two nights later he managed to hang himself in his cell. He never went to trial. However, over the next few days we were able to examine all of his material and trace some of the other members of the ring. They were scattered all over the country, so the FBI stepped in. Arrests were made, contraband was confiscated, and the ring was successfully closed."

"Well, that's good news. But tell us, how does this involve the defendant?"

Baxter shook his head. "Among the hundreds of photographs and reels of film footage we found of children in Mr. Alpine's collection—and in the collections held by other members of the ring—were images of young Mr. Newcott."

I felt a spear penetrate my heart. *Oh my God*, I thought. I wanted to scream. My heart began to palpitate.

"Can you be more specific about what the pictures portrayed?"

"The boy was photographed solo and also with Mr. Alpine performing sexual acts."

Crane paused to let this news hover over the courtroom. Dead silence. Finally he asked, "And did you determine how long young Mr. Newcott had been abused in this way?"

"Yes, we did. It had been going on for three years, since the boy was eight years old." Another pause and more shocked stillness. I wanted to bolt from my seat, run from the courtroom, and scream in the hallway, but I remained frozen in my seat, riveted by the revelations unfolding in front of me.

Crane: "Can you tell us what happened to the defendant next?"

"Well," Baxter said, "as I said, we had questioned the boy during the investigation. We took him to the police station and questioned him all day. About Mr. Alpine and his relationship with him. Eddie was very frightened. But I believe he was more afraid of his father than of us."

"His father? Could you elaborate?"

"It was my personal opinion that his father was possibly guilty of domestic violence. To his son—and to his wife."

"How would you know this?"

"It was only a perception. I had no proof. I was still a fairly young man then, but I had seen enough domestic violence in the previous decade to be able to recognize certain signs. I believed that Mr. Newcott's father was physically and emotionally abusive to his son. I reported my thoughts to Social Services."

"And what happened?"

"Nothing. After we revealed what we found to the defendant's parents, Mr. Newcott's father sent the boy away to a psychiatric hospital for a year."

"A psychiatric hospital? Why?"

"The elder Mr. Newcott thought that his son was a 'pervert,' a homosexual, or that he would grow up to be one. That, of course, wasn't true—he was a victim. What happened to him wasn't going to 'make him gay,' but his father didn't believe that. So Eddie was sent to an institution in Wichita Falls where the poor boy underwent shock therapy and other inhumane treatments. He continued his school work as a patient. I believe he was more of a prisoner. The elder Mr. Newcott had some extreme views about the situation. In those days, homosexuality wasn't understood like it is today. It was thought that homosexuality could be 'cured' or 'prevented.' Eddie—young Mr. Newcott—went through a nightmare at the behest of his father."

It was all coming to light. So that's where Eddie had been when he vanished for a year—he'd spent his sixth grade being a lab rat for sadistic doctors. No wonder he hated his father. No wonder Eddie had killed him. Christ, I didn't blame him. I didn't blame him at all.

"Mr. Baxter, in your professional opinion, how do you think young Eddie became a victim of this Mr. Alpine?"

"It was the opinion of Social Services—and me, too—that Eddie had such an abusive and unloving situation at his own home that he was vulnerable and primed to be a victim. Mr. Alpine was kind to him. The man gave the boy presents. The man showed him affection. Before Eddie was old enough to know better, he probably thought that the kind of attention he got from Mr. Alpine was better than what he received at home."

The courtroom remained hushed.

"Mr. Baxter, it was well known at the time that Mr. Alpine confessed to abducting the Truman child and committed suicide in his cell. Why were the revelations about the child pornography kept from the public?"

"That part of the case was suppressed. People with higher pay grades than mine made the decisions. Let's just say that the late Mayor Alpine did some negotiating with the Chief of Police and Detective Donner. The mayor's brother was already going down for kidnapping and murder. He didn't want his brother's name tarnished any more than it was. We were sworn to secrecy. They're all dead now, so I figured it was time to tell it."

Everyone in the courtroom started murmuring. Some of the reporters ran out of the room to make the scoop with their media outlet. I sat there, dumbfounded, my stomach in knots.

The judge banged the gavel and called for order. After the room quieted down, Crane continued. "Mr. Baxter, you stated earlier that you kept in touch with the defendant through the eighties. Why?"

"I felt sorry for him. I hoped he might look up to me as a kinder male authority figure than what he was used to, so I checked in on him every now and then to see how he was doing. He was responsive to me, for a while, anyway."

"Then what?"

"Once he grew up, went into the army, and returned, he was a changed man. He avoided talking to me. But we saw each other in town every once in a while. It was friendly, a 'Hello, how are you' kind of thing."

"Isn't it true that the defendant witnessed the death of his own father?"

"That's correct. The elder Mr. Newcott was in a drilling accident and fell from the top of an oil rig. This was after the defendant had returned from Vietnam and was working for his father in the oil fields."

"And are you aware of the activities the defendant became involved with in the last decade?"

"Yes."

"And may I ask your opinion of the way the defendant has become something of a public figure in Limite? The Satanism. The black house."

Baxter shook his head. "He's a very disturbed individual."

"Mr. Baxter, do you believe the sexual abuse and physical abuse the defendant suffered as a child had an impact on his emotional and mental growth?"

"How could it not?"

Shamrock stood and objected, stating that the witness was not an expert in psychiatry. The judge rubbed his chin and, shockingly, sustained. But the jury had heard the opinion, and I couldn't see how any reasonable person in the courtroom could argue with it.

"Thank you, Mr. Baxter," Crane said, and then nodded to Shamrock. "Your witness."

"No questions."

The former detective stepped down and left the courtroom. The judge called for a recess. I remained in my seat, stunned. As other spectators left the room, I watched Eddie. For the first time since the trial began, he turned and looked at me.

The sadness—the damage—in his eyes was heartbreaking.

25

Crane did the best he could with his closing argument. He said the defense wasn't denying that Eddie had killed Dora Walton and her unborn child. The issue was whether or not the defendant knew what he was doing—whether he was "insane" or not. The jury had heard testimony that Eddie was diagnosed with depression and a severe anxiety disorder, and that he had gone off his meds. They heard how he had been abused as a child, not only by his sadistic father but by a pedophilic neighbor. Was it any wonder that Eddie would grow up to have "unusual" views about the world, hence, his interest in Satanism? All of this contributed to the commitment of the crime. Crane asked the jury to "do the right thing" and find the defendant not guilty by reason of insanity.

Prosecutor Shamrock went into his closing argument with guns blazing. He reiterated the grotesque and salacious physical description of the crime itself. He hammered home how Eddie was a "devil-worshipping Satanist" who performed blasphemous rituals in his home located in the otherwise "clean, respectable neighborhood" of Limite. Shamrock refuted the defense's claims of insanity by illustrating how Eddie had planned the murder in advance—the procurement of Rohypnol, the grinding of the pills, and the spiking of the drink. It was "willful and premeditated with malice aforethought," and thus first degree murder. The word "heinous" was used a lot.

"Don't let the blank look on the defendant's face fool you," Shamrock said. "The defendant knew very well what he was doing that night. He committed murder in the name of the devil. It is your duty to find him guilty."

But was it capital murder—deserving of the death penalty? Technically, the crime didn't meet the conditions of capital murder. "Crimes of passion"—usually domestic-oriented violence—were not considered capital murder. However, Eddie's offense lay in a gray area because he had taken the life of an unborn child along with his conjugal partner.

When I left the courtroom to wait for the verdict, I already knew the outcome. You could feel it in the air. The presence of the Rohypnol at the crime scene sealed Eddie's fate.

It was very depressing, and I didn't want to stay. I felt as if I'd done my duty and supported Eddie throughout the trial, but I had no desire to sit there and watch him be found guilty. I went back to my father's apartment, called the attorney handling his estate, and left all the loose ends in his capable hands. He would sell the car and the apartment, and settle outstanding issues without my presence. I returned to Chicago.

The flight home was uneventful, but my townhouse in the city seemed very foreign to me when I walked in the door. I was a bit shell-shocked. It was good to see Billy, who had dutifully held down the fort in my absence.

"Are you all right, Shelby?" he asked.

"Yeah. I guess so."

"You've heard, then?"

"Heard what?"

"The verdict?"

"Oh. No, I haven't."

"It was just announced on the news. The jury must have come back while you were in the air."

"And?"

"Guilty on all counts."

I nodded. "I thought that would be the case."

"He stood and cursed the jury."

"What?"

"He pointed at them and told them that Satan would take them all to hell. Caused quite a furor. The bailiffs had to drag him out. He went nuts in the courtroom."

"Oh my God. Really?"

"Yeah."

"Christ."

"I'm sorry."

"I am too."

That was all we could say. I went on with my life and work and did my best to forget about Eddie. The penalty phase came a little later; I couldn't help but pay attention. I offered to be a character witness, but Mr. Crane told me that Eddie rejected my offer. Admittedly, I was surprised he received the death penalty. I thought that surely the judge would have a little sense and compassion to see that Eddie was a sick man. But it wasn't to be. I phoned Mr. Crane's office, and we spoke for a short time. He said there would be appeals and that nothing was set in stone. It would be a long process.

That was 2006, and it is now 2015. Eddie has given up and told his lawyer to stop the appeal process and let him die. Crane didn't stop, though. He filed the appeals on his client's behalf anyway. Several advocacy groups got into the act to protest the death penalty and, specifically, Eddie's case. I donated money to the National Coalition to Abolish the Death Penalty—NCADP.

When they figured out who I was, the organization asked if I would officially endorse them with my name. Two years ago, I did so.

Nothing worked. And now the appeals have run their course. Unless the governor steps in at the last minute—and there is no reason to think he will—Eddie will receive the lethal injection in a little over forty-eight hours.

The sun is rising on Livingston, Texas. I didn't sleep a wink in my little room at the Best Western hotel. What the hell. I get up, shower, dress in a conservative blue pantsuit, and go downstairs for the free continental breakfast. And coffee, loads of coffee.

I hop in my rental car and follow the directions Crane gave me—onto Highway 190, and then, shortly after leaving Livingston city limits, a left turn onto Route 350 to the prison. I'd read a little about the Polunsky Unit before traveling to Texas. It sits on the eastern shore of Lake Livingston, which happens to be a man-made body of water. On the other side of the lake, a little bit inland, is Huntsville, the location of another maximum security prison where the actual execution takes place, from what I understand. Death row, however, is located only at Polunsky. The prisoner remains there, alone and isolated, until the day of his execution, when he is transported to Huntsville. Normally, an inmate at Polunsky can have one regular or special visit each week, unless they are a "level one" prisoner—someone who is in trouble for some infraction of the rules. At each visit, up to two adults (children are an exception) can visit, providing they are on the inmate's approved visitor list. A regular visit lasts two hours, while a "special visit" consists of up to four hours and can be on contiguous days. These are reserved for visitors traveling more than 250 miles to the prison, like me. Death row inmates are allowed only one special visit per month. During the week the execution is scheduled, the inmate is allowed two full days of visits, then four hours on the morning of it. Up to ten people on the approved list can visit then, but that is a moot point in Eddie's case. I'm the only person, other than Mr. Crane, on his approved list.

I come to the turnoff into the prison grounds, pull in, and approach a checkpoint gate. A corrections officer asks me what my business is. He asks to see my ID and tells me to step out of the car. Crane had warned me that the guard might want to look in the trunk or under the hood, but all he does is glance at the inside of the car.

"It's a rental," I tell him.

He nods and asks me for the name and number of the prisoner. I sign his form, get back in the car, and drive to the visitor parking lot. On Crane's advice, I've brought along a baggie full of quarters. I leave my cell phone in the car, along with my purse, and carry only the car keys, change, and my ID into the facility.

The butterflies in my stomach are going berserk. I am *scared*. The foreboding appearance of the buildings that make up Polunsky would send shivers down anyone's spine. I have no doubt that I am about to glimpse into hell. The place emanates a powerfully cold, oppressive vibe. It's a world of pain, fear, and despair. I can almost hear the voices warning me: *Stay away. Do not enter. Abandon all hope.*

Inside the entrance, I walk through an x-ray metal detector, like the one at the airport. I have to place my belongings in a tray on the belt and also receive a pat down by a female corrections officer. She asks if I have a cell phone, dollar bills, or weapons, and I'm glad I anticipated that.

Mr. Crane is sitting in the reception area when I walk in. He stands and shakes my hand. "Hi, Shelby. How are you this morning?"

"Awful. I didn't sleep at all last night."

"I'm sorry. Yeah, the prospect of a visit here can do that to people."

"I'm okay, though."

"Good. You ready to do this?"

"As ready as I'll ever be."

He accompanies me to the desk, where I hand over my ID. The officer checks that my name is on the approved visitor list and hands me a blue slip with all the details of my visit, as well as a plastic badge to wear around my neck. It's red, with the word VISITOR and initials DR—for death row—on it. Crane leads me to a waiting area where visitors can find vending machines, restrooms, and benches. Attached to the wall are what appear to be post office boxes—Crane explains that these are safes where law enforcement officers can store and lock up their weapons. The most bizarre thing in the room is a sign by the door to the rest of the prison that reads "NO HOSTAGES BEYOND THIS POINT." That makes no sense to me, but I don't ask what it means.

I opt to visit the ladies room before proceeding. My hands shake as I wash them. I feel like crying. This is going to be very difficult.

Back outside, I see that an escort has arrived to take us deeper into the unit. We have to go through several doors—buzzed open by officers—and then we are outside in a yard. A sidewalk is enclosed and bordered by a cyclone wire fence on either side, topped with barbed wire. The path leads to one of the main buildings, maybe fifty yards long. As we walk along this open air corridor, Crane points to the "pod" at our left. "That's death row," he says. Featureless and gray, all the buildings look the same to me. Big, awful block boxes.

I lose count of how many barred doors we're buzzed through. Passes are checked and double-checked, and finally we are in the visitation room for death row. It's a dreary, plain place. Along one wall are cubicles that are essentially phone booths. Each cubicle has a chair in front of it, a counter, and bullet-proof plexiglass separating the visitor from the inmate. And a phone.

Crane suggests buying a Snickers out of a vending machine for Eddie, so I do. "Wouldn't he want something more substantial?" I ask.

"It's always a waste of money. He never eats it."

The guard takes the candy bar out of the slot and informs us that the prisoner is being brought from his cell to the visitation cubicle on his side. He tells me to wait at the numbered cubicle that was assigned to me.

"I'll give you some privacy and sit over here," Crane says and takes a seat at a table on the other side of the room. I sit in front of the glass window and wait. By now, the butterflies are drilling holes in the sides of my stomach; they want to make sure all the acid and bile spreads through my body so that I am thoroughly queasy. My nerves scream with anxiety. I suddenly want to bolt from the room and never look back. But I don't.

After a few eternal minutes, I notice movement on the other side. And there is Eddie, sitting in front of me.

26

He is almost unrecognizable.

Eddie's scalp is still shaved bald, and there's an inverted cross tattooed on his forehead. The goatee has become a full beard that hasn't been trimmed in some time. He is extremely gaunt; he probably weighs thirty or forty pounds less than he did when I last saw him. Worst of all, his eyes reveal a wild contempt that reminds me of a fierce animal in a zoo. The way a tiger or a lion looks at you from behind the bars in its cage.

This is not the boy across the street I knew and loved. The powerful charisma he once possessed is long gone.

"Hello, Eddie." He stares at me as if he doesn't know who I am. "It's me. Shelby." His eyes continue to bore holes through me. His silence is unnerving. "I . . . I came a long way to see you. Aren't you going to say hello?"

He starts to laugh. It begins quietly, but it grows until he is practically belly-laughing on the other side of the glass. I don't know what to do.

"Eddie. Do you want me to leave?"

With unnatural abruptness, he ceases the laughter and then says, "Shelby, Shelby, Shelby, Shelby, Shelby, Shelby. Shelby Truman, Shelby Truman, Shelby Truman, Shelby Truman."

"Eddie, are you all right?"

Back to the silence. Then he picks up the Snickers I'd bought him, tears off the wrapper, and starts eating it. Chewing. Not saying a word.

"Eddie? I know that's a stupid question. I'm sorry. But . . . have they treated you well? Are you *all right?*"

"I'm fine." It's the first thing he says that sounds normal. "I'm just fine. Thank you for coming. And thanks for the candy bar."

I breathe a sigh of relief. Perhaps our conversation will be coherent after all.

"You're welcome. Mr. Crane—your lawyer—he says you wanted to see me. That you made a special request for me to come and visit. You have something you want to tell me."

He continues chewing. I watch him eat the entire Snickers before he answers my question.

"Tell you? No, no, no, no, no, no, no, no, I can't tell you, I could never tell you, how could I tell you? I mean, you know, I couldn't, because, well, you know—I mean, that's just the way it is, the way it is, the way it's always been, the way it'll always be."

Maybe I am wrong about the conversation. I want to run. I can't take the torment. But I remember that Crane had said Eddie often rambles and babbles, speaking nonsense, and then suddenly he's lucid. I force myself to remain and see how it plays out.

"I don't know what you're trying to say, Eddie," I say, and he starts to laugh again. "Eddie. Please. I know . . . I know you're ill. I'm so sorry. I'm so sorry you have to go through this."

The laughing stops abruptly again. "Don't be sorry. I'm the one who should be sorry. Am I sorry? For some things. Yes, I'm sorry for many things. Sorry, sorry, sorry. But not for all. Not for *him.* Or for *him.*"

"Are you talking about your father?"

215

"Him, him, him, him."

"Or Mr. Alpine?"

He shakes his head violently. "Evil, evil, evil. It was all so evil, evil, evil."

"Yes, I know. Be careful what you say, Eddie. Although I suppose it doesn't matter now."

"Evil, evil, evil, evil. The evil came to our street. Our *street*! It got inside me. Inside me, inside me. Then I was inside you, inside you. Are you evil, too? Are you, Shelby? Are you?"

"I don't think so, Eddie. And I don't think you're evil either."

"Oh, oh, oh, yes I am. Don't kid yourself, don't kid yourself. Evil, evil, evil, evil. It came to our street and got inside me. Got inside me. Me. Me. Me."

"Eddie . . ."

"Hey!" His eyes grow wide with excitement.

"What?"

"Remember our game?"

I have to think again. "What game?"

"Our game, our game, our *game*! Davy Jones's Locker, Davy Jones's Locker, Davy Jones's Locker!"

At first I don't make the connection. Even though I'd gone over that period of our lives over the past twenty-four hours, I don't understand what he means. "What?" I say.

"The *hiding place*! The hiding place, hiding place. Davy Jones's Locker!"

Ah, right. "Of course, Eddie. I remember. In the bomb shelter."

"The shelter, the shelter, my sanctuary, my church, my sanctuary, The Temple, my private self, my evil."

"What about Davy Jones's Locker, Eddie?"

"It all started there, don't you see? It all *started* there. The evil is inside the hiding place. The evil came up through the ground and got inside me through Davy Jones's Locker!"

The poor man. He is so far gone. I feel tears welling in my eyes. Not wanting him to see me cry, I turn away, grab a tissue from my pocket, and wipe my face.

Eddie keeps on babbling nonsensical phrases and words about evil and the hiding place and other things I know nothing about. He speaks some words in a language that sounds like Vietnamese. He laughs. And then he jabbers on, blathering about the devil. Satan visiting our street in Limite and getting inside his body.

I can't take it anymore. "Eddie, stop. Please. I need to go. Please."

"All the answers, all the answers, all the answers are *there*. Davy Jones's Locker. It all started there. The evil, evil, evil, evil, evil. Didn't you get the letter?"

"Letter? What letter?"

"The police didn't find it first?"

"What are you talking about, Eddie?"

"Davy Jones's Locker! Davy Jones's Locker!"

He's not making any sense. I stand, and he suddenly shuts up. Our eyes meet each other, and I see there are tears in his as well. "Don't go," he whispers.

"Eddie, this is so hard. I can't talk to you. We can't have a real conversation." Nevertheless, I continue to hold the phone to my ear. I hear him breathe rapidly. He is quite agitated. It scares me.

Crane calls to me. "Shelby? Everything all right?"

I turn and answer, "We'll be finished in a minute." Back to Eddie. "I came to see you, Eddie, what was it you wanted to tell me? Was it anything at all?" I sit again.

Then it strikes me. The expression on his face. Aside from the scalp with no hair, he once again reminds me of that doomed soul going to hell in the old painting, the tormented man in Michelangelo's *Last Judgment*. Eddie *is* that creature. Silence.

217

"Well, if that's it, then I'd better go. Eddie, I'm sorry this happened to you. I love you. Try to remember that."

Eddie slaps the palm of his hand on the window and holds it there flat. I slowly reach up and place my own hand on my side of the glass. We stay like that for nearly a minute, and then he unexpectedly rises and disappears from view. I call into the phone, "Eddie? Eddie?" I think I hear shuffling and knocking on the other side. Is that it? Did he leave? Could he terminate the visit, just like that?

I hang up the phone and sit there for a few seconds. The guard appears, looks at me, and shrugs. I nod in acknowledgment. I stand, my legs weak, and walk back to Mr. Crane.

"I take it that didn't go very well?"

I shake my head. "I didn't understand anything he said to me. Oh, Mr. Crane, he is so very sick. How can they execute him? He has no concept of reality!"

He stands and gives me a hug, and I start to cry in heaving sobs. Crane pats me on the back, saying, "I know, I know."

We separate. "Don't they give him his meds?"

"They do. But he might not actually swallow the pills. Sometimes he does, sometimes he doesn't. Like I told you, he can be very coherent. Just the other day, we had a very reasonable conversation."

"Is . . . is it an *act*? I mean, he seems much more mentally ill than just having anxiety and depression."

"No one knows but him, Shelby."

I turn to look at the cubicle, just in case Eddie had decided to resume the visit. No one is there.

"I have no idea what it was he wanted to tell me."

"I'm sorry you came all this way."

I shake my head. "I'm not sorry."

"Okay."

"But let's get out of here now."

And that is it. We retrace our path through the many secured doors and hallways and checkpoints. I retrieve my ID, and Mr. Crane and I walk outside to the parking lot together. The bright sunlight is an immensely welcome sensation.

"Are you going to be all right?" he asks.

"Yeah. I have to fly to Limite now, of all places."

"You're getting a park named after you, right?"

"I'm not sure I'm up to it now."

"You'll feel better on Friday."

"The dedication is at six o'clock—exactly when Eddie will be getting the lethal injection."

"Try not to think about that."

"How can I not?" I look pointedly at Crane and ask, "What's it like?"

"What?"

"Being put to death? I mean, you've witnessed executions before, haven't you?"

"Yes."

"What's it like? Do they feel pain? Are they usually scared? Do they scream and cry for their mothers? What?"

"I've seen all sorts of responses. The inmate is given a chance to say something into a microphone so that the witnesses can hear him. Sometimes they confess their crimes and ask for forgiveness, sometimes they simply say goodbye to their loved ones, other times they don't say anything at all. The drug used is pentobarbital. It acts pretty quickly. They go to sleep first and don't feel a thing. Sometimes, in a Caucasian man, their skin turns color, maybe a little pink, sometimes even purple."

I'm sure the disgust registers in my face. "Really?"

"It takes about ten minutes, and then a doctor checks all the vital signs. Then he makes the announcement that so-and-so died at whatever the exact time is."

"It's so cold and calculated."

Crane holds out his hands. "It is what it is. I suppose there's still a chance the governor will come through, but I wouldn't hold my breath."

"No. I've resigned myself to what's going to happen." We reach my car, and I unlock it. "You'll be at the execution?"

"Uh huh."

"I think the NCADP will be out on the road protesting."

"They always are."

"They wanted me to join them, but . . . well, you know."

"I understand."

"Thank you, Mr. Crane."

"Robert, please."

"Thank you, Robert, for everything you've done."

"You're welcome." We shake hands, and I get into the car.

The nearly two-hour drive to George W. Bush Intercontinental Airport is a blur. Part of it is spent crying. For the other part, closer to the city, I have to concentrate hard to combat my fatigue and not cause an accident. It's a small miracle that I make it on no sleep.

Once I am on the plane and in my seat, I immediately nod out. My dreams are vivid and fitful—about Chicory Lane.

27

Limite is flat, hot, and barren. The odor of petroleum permeates the air. It's just as it always was; nothing has changed. West Texas will forever be the desert, populated by pumpjacks and oil derricks, football stadiums, and churches. As I grew older, my connection with my hometown became more tenuous. The last time I was here, I buried my father in the cemetery next to my mother and attended Eddie's trial—not pleasant memories. Now, here I am again, staying in a Holiday Inn on the outskirts of town on a Wednesday night and wondering what the hell I'm going to do before the park dedication on Friday evening. Originally, I had planned to arrive on Thursday, but the side trip to Livingston changed that.

At least I brought my laptop, and I hope to do some work. There is no one to see—no friends from high school—and no favorite restaurants to visit. Perhaps the hotel room is the best environment in which to begin the next Patricia novel. I still haven't found the premise for this one; I haven't a clue what I'm going to do. But something will pop up; it always does. The only trouble is that I'm emotionally drained and exhausted. The nap on the plane gave me enough of an energy boost to rent a car and drive it safely from the airport to the hotel. I take comfort in knowing that I will sleep well tonight. So this evening, all I want to do is have some dinner—truthfully, I could go for more Tex-Mex; I can't get enough when I'm in my home state—watch a little television, read my Sandra Brown until my eyelids become heavy, and then hit the sack.

And I sleep very well until dawn, when something wakes me up earlier than I wanted. I'm not sure if it was a dream, but I bolt upright and gasp for breath. My heart is pounding. Am I having a heart attack? I don't think so, there's no pain. Just anxiety. There is an overwhelming feeling that I've *missed something*. Eddie had been trying to tell me something. Crane had originally said that Eddie had wanted to talk to me, and I assumed it was about something specific. But since my visit to the prison, I assumed he had requested my presence for no other reason than to, perhaps, see my face; after all, all he did was speak gibberish. I went away disappointed, upset, and confused.

The morning light streams through the window. I glance at the digital clock on the night stand next to the bed. 6:35. It's a bit earlier than I prefer to get up, but I do so and go to the bathroom. When I'm done, I cross the room to the window and peer outside. The glow of the new day nestles over the hotel parking lot and the highway alongside.

I have to speak with Jim Baxter. If he's still alive. How old was he at Eddie's trial, seventy-eight? My God, he'll be eighty-seven or thereabouts if he's still with us. Chances are he isn't around. Damn. I grab my cell phone, which was charging overnight, and switch it on. Somewhere back in my office at home, I have his business card. Billy won't be there, so I have to find Baxter's number the old-fashioned way. I dial directory assistance.

There are several James Baxters in Limite. Double damn.

I decide to shower, dress, and get some breakfast, just to let a little time go by. Then I'll call Billy and ask him to head over to my house pronto and find the former detective's card.

Around eight o'clock, I figure it's late enough that Billy won't kill me for phoning. He answers sleepily. I apologize profusely and make my request.

"All right, but you better remember me generously when it comes to Christmas bonuses," he says.

"When have I ever given you a Christmas bonus?"

"Exactly my point."

"Okay, I'll be sure to tell Santa. Could you get over there as quick as you can, please?"

"All right. Geez. How was your visit to the prison yesterday?"

"Oh, Lord. Very creepy and disturbing. I'll have to tell you about it later, all right?" By nine thirty, I have Jim Baxter's phone number in hand, and I make the call. The former lawman answers.

"Jim Baxter."

"Mr. Baxter, this is Shelby Truman, the writer."

"Ms. Truman. How are you?"

"Fine, and you?"

"Still kicking, if you can believe that."

"Let me guess, you're eighty-seven?"

"Good guess."

"My, my. And your health? Everything okay?"

"*Okay* is about the best I can say for it. Had a hip replacement four years ago, and every time it rains my whole body feels like I've been sawed in half. Luckily it don't rain much in Limite. But guess what—I can still drive! Knock on wood. I may get around like an old codger, but I get around. So what can I do you for? And call me Jim, please."

I take a breath and say, "Jim, I went to see Eddie Newcott yesterday in prison. Death row."

"Lord have mercy. His execution's coming up, isn't it?"

"Tomorrow."

"Right, right. I remember. There was something in the paper on Sunday. Did you see that?"

"No."

"It was one of those retrospective pieces about the crime. Evil Eddie and his Satanic church and all that. It said all his appeals had run out."

"That's correct. It looks like he will die at six o'clock tomorrow evening."

"Well, that's too bad. I never thought he should have been found guilty. That man was very disturbed. Very disturbed."

"I agree with you. Listen, I have a question for you."

"Shoot."

"Jim, you investigated the abduction of my baby brother and arrested Gordon Alpine."

"That's correct."

"Whatever made you go back to Alpine after interviewing him the first time?"

"Excuse me?"

"Well, as I remember it, it was a few days after the abduction, and you and your team had talked to everyone on our street. Then, one morning, the police showed up at Mr. Alpine's house with a search warrant. What was it that led you to suspect him and get a search warrant?"

"Oh, it was a phone tip. Someone called the police station and said Alpine had done it. Not only that, the caller said Alpine had been making 'naughty movies' of children. Those were the words he used, 'naughty movies.' Back in 1966, we took that kind of thing seriously, just like we do today. Then there was another thing. We had interviewed young Eddie Newcott as a witness, you know. We talked to him again at length a couple of days after the abduction."

"I remember that. Boy, do I. You took him to the station and questioned him all day."

"That we did. And *he* said that Alpine was probably the one who had done it. When I asked him how he would know something like that, Eddie told me that he'd been in Alpine's house the day after the Fourth and heard a baby crying in a back room. When I asked what he was doing over at Alpine's house, he told me how Alpine always gave him presents and candy and stuff. Had been doing so for three years. Eddie's father was in the room with us, and he went ballistic. He started yelling, 'I told you never to go back over there,' that sort of thing. I calmed down Mr. Newcott and questioned Eddie some more. After a while, Eddie lost it. He started crying and said Alpine had 'touched' him. That was enough for us to go to a judge. Mind you, we didn't have any real evidence except the phone tip and what Eddie had said, but I went to the judge anyway. It was a tricky situation since his brother was the goddamned mayor. But since we were getting nowhere in the search for your little brother, and we'd had *two* accusations against Gordon Alpine, we got our search warrant."

"But all you found was my brother's rattle."

"That's right, but it was with the portrait Alpine had taken of your brother. Why would he remove the picture from the wall and stash it with the rattle in the drawer if they weren't 'souvenirs' of the crime? And *then* we found all the child pornography."

"And Eddie was a part of it."

"I'm afraid so. That man Alpine had been abusing Eddie for three years."

"I remember your testimony at the trial."

"Another thing," he tells me. "After Alpine had hung himself, we talked to Eddie and his family again, and the boy admitted that he was the one who had called in the tip."

With those words, my heart freezes. Eddie *was* trying to tell me something yesterday. A letter I hadn't gotten. *Davy Jones's Locker.* He wanted to play our old game again.

"Jim, what happened to Eddie's house?"

"It's still there."

"Does anyone live in it?"

"Lord, no. No one would touch it after the murders. A real estate company owns the property, and they've rented it out a few times in the last ten years, but nobody stays very long. It got repainted and all that."

"Is the bomb shelter still in the backyard?"

"It is. Padlocked so no curiosity seekers will get inside."

"Jim, do you own any bolt cutters?"

He pauses for a second. "Why do you want to know that?"

"I need to get inside the bomb shelter. Will you help me? Can you meet me over there?"

"Why do you want to do that?"

"I . . . I can't explain right now. I just need to follow through on something Eddie said yesterday."

He is quiet for a moment. Then he asks, "What time do you want to meet?"

28

The house is painted white, probably to contrast what had been there before. It appears to be an abandoned property, certainly unkempt, but it hasn't been vandalized. Its condition isn't as bad as I thought it might be. A rusty, years-old FOR SALE sign stands in the front yard.

I park in the driveway and wait for Baxter to arrive. In the meantime, I get out of the car and gaze at my old home across the street. A couple of teenagers are shooting hoops; a basketball hoop has been erected next to the drive since I'd last seen the place. Flowers decorate the beds in front, and the lawn is neatly manicured. It's pretty. I don't believe the house ever looked so nice when we'd lived there.

Since I'm a few minutes early, I stroll down the sidewalk until I come to a spot across from Gordon Alpine's old abode. It, too, appears to be occupied by happy people. The lawn, flower beds, and windows display life and joy.

Perhaps the darkness that once permeated Chicory Lane in the sixties has finally been evicted.

I return to the Newcott house and go around to the side to examine the old gate in the fence. It's still there. A sign warns, NO TRESPASSING. That doesn't stop me from opening it—no locks on the gate—and scanning the backyard. The steel door to the bomb shelter is rusty and somehow sunken deeper amidst tall grass and weeds. At that point, I hear a vehicle in front of the house. A blue pickup truck has pulled up to the curb. Jim Baxter steps out and, with the help of a cane, walks slowly around the back end to greet me.

"Hello, Jim," I say, shaking his hand. "You don't look a day over seventy."

"Liar. But I appreciate it. You, on the other hand, don't look a day over forty, and that's the truth."

"Hardly, but thank you."

"May I ask how old you are?"

"Sixty-one."

He shakes his head. "No way."

"Way. I appreciate you coming to meet me."

He shrugs. "It's a bit unorthodox, and it's officially trespassing, but what the hell. The bolt cutters are in the back of the truck." He grabs the tool out of the cargo bed and points. "Lead on." Baxter follows me to the side of the house, through the open gate, and into the yard.

"I believe Eddie wanted me to look in Davy Jones's Locker. At least I think he did."

"Look in *what*?"

"A secret hiding place in the shelter that we used when we were kids. I bet you didn't know it was there."

"I don't have a clue what you're talking about."

"I didn't think so."

The steel door has a serious padlock on it. I take the bolt cutters from Baxter and work the magic myself. The thing snaps off easily enough. I drop the cutters in the grass and open the squeaky, heavy door.

"Is there still electricity here?" I ask.

"Don't know."

I glance at Baxter's cane and legs. "I don't expect you to navigate the steps. I'll go down myself." I find the old light switch, but nothing happens when I flip it. Unfortunately, the shelter is dark and dank, and it smells of mildew and who knows what else. The walls are still black. It will be impossible to see anything in here.

"No lights!" I call up the stairs.

"I have a flashlight in the truck. Be back in a sec."

The sunlight streaming in from the open door illuminates the immediate area around me. Cobwebs cover much of the space. The partition separating the shelter from the toilet is still behind the stairs. I'm dying to peer behind it, but I figure I won't be seeing anything without the flashlight.

"Here you go!" His head appears above. We make eye contact and he drops the torch. I catch it—it's the heavy-duty kind that police use. I flick it on and shine it over the main room. It has been completely cleared of any furniture and wall decorations. Eddie's artwork is gone. The pentagram on the floor, however, is still there, albeit worn and faint. It's a creepy, haunted place now, even in the daytime.

I move around the partition. The toilet has been damaged. The seat is missing and the cracked top looks as if someone had smashed it with a sledgehammer. The floor is dusty, and cobwebs cover the space behind the commode. I grimace as I use the flashlight to sweep away enough of the webs so that I can kneel and touch the concrete floor. I don't see any giant spiders or cockroaches, thank goodness.

Holding the light in my lap, I feel around where I remember the sides of the slab are located. The grime is thick and it takes some doing. I wish I'd brought some gloves. Eventually, I discern the demarcations in the surface and recall that it was often difficult for me to lift the cover.

"You all right down there?"

"Yes! I found the spot. Now, if I can just get it open!"

"Do you need help?"

"I'll let you know!"

I tug, push, press, and scratch, getting nowhere. Will I need a chisel? A lever of some kind? Another minute ticks by as I work at it.

"Shelby?"

"I'm still trying!" I hear his footsteps on the stairs. "You don't need to come down, Jim."

"It's all right, I won't break my neck. What the heck are you doing?" He peeks around the partition and finds me on my knees.

"I've almost got it—" And then, it gives. I manage to lift a side high enough for me to use the friction of my fingertips. Once I get it to where I can grasp it from underneath, it's cake.

I lift the slab and shove it to the side, revealing the square hole in the ground.

A faded envelope sits atop a dark cloth. Written on it, in Eddie's familiar block-letter printing, in pencil, are the words To Shelby Truman.

"Oh my God."

"Don't touch it!" Baxter says. "Wait." He pulls out a cell phone and takes a photo. "Okay, go ahead."

I lift the envelope. It's sealed.

"Should I open it?"

"Go ahead." He takes another photo as I do so.

It's a letter, again scribbled in block, printed letters. I start to read it, but my eyes jump to the cloth. It's dark blue. *Blue*. It's a bundle. The cloth is wrapped around something.

"Oh shit. Oh Christ."

It's Michael's baby blanket.

I carefully lift the thing out of the hole. Light as a feather.

"What is it?" Baxter asks.

"My baby brother's blanket."

He snaps another photo.

I slowly unwrap it.

My scream echoes off the walls of that dank, dark portal to hell.

Inside the blanket are the skeletal remains of an infant.

29

AUGUST 14, 1966

DEAR SHELBY—

I AM GONE AWAY. MY DAD IS SENDING ME TO A
PRISON HOSPITL PLACE. I DONT KNOW IF I WILL
SEE YOU AGAIN. IN CASE HE FINDS THIS OR IF
POLICE FIND THIS, I HOPE YOU GET THIS LETTER.
IT WILL BE HERE TIL SOMEBODY FINDS IT.

I CAME OVER YOUR HOUSE ON JULY 4 TO SEE IF YOU
WANT TO WATCH FIREWORKS WITH ME IN THE
PARK. YOU WERE IN YOUR BAKYARD WITH YUR
MOM AND DAD. I HEARD BABY CRY. I WENT TO HIS
ROOM AND PICKED HIM UP. I TRYED THAT BOUNCE
YOU SHOWD ME. I THINK I DID IT TOO HARD. HE
STOPED CRYING. I DIDNT MEAN TO HURT HIM. I
GOT SCARED. REAL SCARED. I THOUGHT I HAD TO
HIDE HIM. I PUT HIM IN DAVY JONES LOCKER. I

DIDNT KNOW WHAT TO DO. YOUR MOM WOULD KILL ME. MY DAD WOULD KILL ME.

SO I BLAMED MR. ALPINE. I PUT YUR BROTHERS RATL AND PICTUR IN MR. ALPINES BEDROOM. I DID IT BECAUSE HE DID BAD THINGS TO ME. AT FIRST I DIDNT KNOW THEY WERE BAD. MAYBE SOMEDAY YOU WILL FIND OUT WHAT HE DID. IM SORRY. SO FAR NO ONE KNOWS ABOUT YUR BROTHER. IT WAS A ACSIDENT. IM NO GOOD. I LOVE YOU BUT NOW I AM A BAD PERSON. DAD SAYS IM CORUPTED. I HOPE YOU CAN FORGIV ME.

EDDIE

30

It's ten minutes to six on Friday, and the ceremony is about to begin. At the very same time, on the other side of the state, Eddie Newcott is about to be put to death.

I was at the scene yesterday longer than I wanted. It was a very difficult couple of hours for me, but Jim Baxter smoothed the way with the authorities—he knew everyone there. He had me report the crime with my cell phone, and then he waited with me until the officers arrived.

While we sat inside my car, Baxter told me he was sorry. "I should have been smarter," he said. "I should have realized that Donner and Mayor Alpine and the chief had made a deal."

"What do you mean?"

"That Gordon Alpine would confess to the kidnapping and murder of your brother in exchange for no charges or mention of the child pornography crimes. That's surely what happened. I wasn't in on it. I wish I could have stopped it. Then maybe we would have learned the truth."

I didn't know what to say.

In a half hour, Chicory Lane had become a circus for the third time in five decades. Medical examiners, forensics teams, and the media crowded the street. Luckily, I sat in the back of a patrol car and avoided the frenzy without the press being aware of my presence. I called Billy, got hold of my attorney, phoned Mr. Crane, and felt a little more secure by the time a detective by the name of Hodgkins interviewed me. I told him what I knew, holding it together long enough to talk rationally about the history of the case and my knowledge of what had happened. With the understanding that we would talk in more detail before I returned to Chicago, he let me go back to my hotel so I could have a breakdown in peace and quiet.

It now made perfect sense—Eddie's pedophobia. His own guilt for accidentally killing Michael had given him a lifelong fear of babies. He never wanted to have any children of his own. I recall the times he always made sure I was using contraception. I remember his reactions when we were around babies in public. And it was why he killed Dora Walton and their unborn child. And it's why he believed evil emanated from the hiding place in the bomb shelter—it was the place where he had buried the source of his guilt.

The tears flowed from anger, certainly, and a little from the painful feeling of betrayal. Mostly it was the guilt. My own. It was irrational, perhaps, but real. What was my role in this horrible tragedy? Not locking the goddamned front door? Or was it more than that? I had been intimate with the boy who had done this, as well as with the man he grew up to be. Throughout my entire life, there had been a fatal connection between Eddie and me. Could I forgive him? Could I forgive *myself*? That was something I didn't think I could answer until some time had passed.

Of immediate concern was how I was going to stand at the dedication ceremony. It didn't seem right that they were naming a park after *me*. There had to be a change of plan. With my hands still shaking, I dialed Mr. Bennett, my contact for the parks commission. I made my request, and he said he'd reach out by phone to the board members and other folks in charge. Bennett promised to call back, which he did today in the early afternoon. It was a unanimous decision to back my wishes, which I suppose is a little compensation for what I'd been through for the past two days.

I had also spoken to Robert Crane earlier today. He had told Eddie that I'd discovered the contents of the shelter hiding place. There was little response, only a nod and what Crane perceived to be an "acceptance." "I think a great burden was lifted from Eddie's shoulders," Crane told me.

"Well, I think he could have removed that burden a long time ago," I said. "His deathbed confession didn't do me any favors."

"No, I suppose not. I'm sorry, Shelby. Of course, you know these new revelations are not going to help his cause to avoid the death penalty. I'm sure the governor won't step in at all at the last minute."

"No, I wouldn't expect he would."

Before we hung up, Crane promised to let me know if Eddie had any last words before the administering of the lethal drugs.

Now, at five minutes until six, I envision Eddie strapped down on the table, the IV already connected to his arm. Witnesses, if any, besides his attorney, are seated in the observation room, watching him through a window. The warden is present and ready to give the go-ahead.

I try to focus my attention on the crowd of people at the park that holds so many memories for me. Of course, it looks completely different today than it did in the sixties. Receiving a new name is a good thing. It will help mark a delineation between the past and the future. And then, once the ceremony is over, I plan to go back to Chicago and never return to Limite. My parents are buried here, but would it matter if I traveled to West Texas just to stand at their gravesides? Will they know or care? I don't need to stand beside a mound of dirt and read their names on tombstones to remember them.

But perhaps I'll feel differently once some time has passed.

The gathering at the park consists of maybe a hundred people. More than expected, but the news yesterday probably attracted the curious. Jim Baxter is here, as well as Detective Hodgkins. I don't recognize anyone else. There are several fans holding books, hoping that they will perchance receive a signature. I'm not in the mood to give out autographs, but I suppose it's my duty at such an occasion. I'll grin and bear it, and then take my heavy heart with me and quietly disappear.

Mr. Bennett steps up to a portable podium promptly at six. He says a few words about the park and then introduces me. "Please join me in welcoming one of Limite's distinguished former residents, internationally bestselling author, Shelby Truman."

Applause. Cheers. I join Bennett at the podium; he shakes my hand and moves away to give me room.

"Good evening," I begin. "When I was growing up on Chicory Lane, this park was a sanctuary for me and my friends. Some of you older folks might remember there was the hulk of an old World War II–era airplane sitting right over there that we could play on top and inside of. Ultimately, I guess the powers that be decided it wasn't the safest contraption to have in the park. There were some jagged edges here and there, and of course we didn't have the kinds of safety rules in place back then. And right in the spot where we're standing, there used to be an old yacht sitting in the grass. I think the authorities took that one away because the teenagers used it as a place to neck." A little laughter from the crowd. "At any rate, it's been fifty years since those days, and the park has changed a lot. The surrounding neighborhoods have changed, too. When I was a young girl, everything beyond the eastern edge was still desert land. Development happened pretty quickly in the seventies, and now Limite extends several miles in that direction. But for me, this park will always be the unnamed haven where I would go to escape. I suppose I didn't really know what I was escaping from until much later. I'm sure you know to what I am referring.

"But enough of that. Let's do this, all right? I am very pleased that the Limite Parks Commission allowed me to make a change in the dedication at such short notice. It means a lot to me. It brings closure to a very painful period of my life, and hopefully also to a dark mark in the history of Limite.

"I hereby dedicate this park to the memory of my little brother, who died in July 1966. Hereafter, this plot of land shall be known as Michael Truman Memorial Park."

There is applause.

Refreshments are served under a small canopy. I sit at a table and sign books and greet everyone who showed up. It isn't as bad as I'd feared. It's all over in thirty minutes.

And by then, Eddie Newcott is dead.

31

I'm back in Chicago on Saturday. Mr. Crane phones me to say that the execution went "smoothly," as if it had been a routine medical procedure. Eddie had offered no final words and went peacefully. I thank him, hang up, and set about catching up on correspondence and business that had accrued in my absence. Billy has been on top of everything, so there isn't much to do. Surprisingly, I had a very good sleep Saturday night, and I awake on Sunday morning with a clear head and a renewed sense of purpose.

It's time to get back to starting that next Patricia Harlow novel, but somehow it doesn't feel right. How can I possibly get back into the swing of churning out fantasy romance fluff after the revelations I've uncovered? There's nothing wrong with romance fiction—it's been good to me—but perhaps now it's time to try something different. My publisher will give me hell, but so what? I'll convince them.

But one of the most frightening and challenging things a human being can do the first thing in the morning—and by that I mean *after* you get out of bed, pee, put on something warm, and have some breakfast and coffee (that last part is essential)— is to sit down at a computer and begin to write a new novel.

My instinct is that this one is going to be about the nature of Evil. Evil with a capital "E." After all, I have some experience with that creature. "Write what you know." Ha. I've looked Evil in the face, touched it, and bared my heart to it. It insinuated itself into my existence. It paid a visit to the street where I grew up and changed many lives. It destroyed two families. I'm now an expert on Evil. I know now that Evil can visit anyone, anywhere, anytime. It is a powerful energy within nature that resides where you least expect it. I've also come to believe that it is the dominant force when compared to Good. That's why human beings have to work extra hard to fight it and be Good.

It's tragically easy to be Evil.

The new work won't be about a heroine in a tight bustier. Whatever the book turns out to be, it will become my catharsis, an exorcism of the demons that have plagued me since the summer of 1966. And it will be a tribute to the love of my life and the burden of my soul.

A story of absolution for the boy across the street.

ABOUT THE AUTHOR

Raymond Benson is the author of over thirty-five books and pre-viously penned *The Black Stiletto* (2011), *The Black Stiletto: Black & White* (2012), *The Black Stiletto: Stars & Stripes* (2013), *The Black Stiletto: Secrets & Lies* (2014), and *The Black Stiletto: Endings & Beginnings* (2014). The ebook anthology, *The Black Stiletto: The Complete Saga*, has been a digital #1 bestseller.

Between 1996 and 2002, he was commissioned by the James Bond literary copyright holders to take over writing the 007 novels. In total, he penned and published worldwide six original Bond novels, three film novelizations, and three short stories. His book *The James Bond Bedside Companion*, an encyclopedic work on the 007 phenomenon, was first published in 1984 and was nominated for an Edgar Allan Poe Award by Mystery Writers of America for Best Biographical/Critical Work.

Raymond recently co-edited with Jeffery Deaver the anthology *Ice Cold—Tales of Intrigue from the Cold War*. His original suspense novels include *Evil Hours*, *Face Blind*, *Sweetie's Diamonds*, *Torment*, and *Artifact of Evil*. The "rock 'n' roll thrillers," *A Hard Day's Death* and the Shamus Award–nominated *Dark Side of the Morgue*, appeared in 2008 and 2009, respectively. A prolific tie-in writer, Raymond has also penned original and adapted works based on various video game franchises such as *Tom Clancy's Splinter Cell* (using the pseudonym "David Michaels"), *Metal Gear Solid*, *Homefront* (co-written with John Milius), and *Hitman*.

The author has taught courses in film genres and history at New York's New School for Social Research; Harper College in Palatine, Illinois; College of DuPage in Glen Ellyn, Illinois, and currently presents Film Studies lectures with *Daily Herald* movie critic Dann Gire. Raymond has been honored in Naoshima, Japan, with the erection of a museum dedicated to one of his 007 novels, and he is also an Ambassador for Japan's Kagawa Prefecture. Raymond is an active member of International Thriller Writers Inc., Mystery Writers of America, the International Association of Media Tie-In Writers, and ASCAP, and served on the Board of Directors of the Ian Fleming Foundation for sixteen years. He is based in the Chicago area.

www.raymondbenson.com
www.theblackstiletto.net